ORCHIDS AND LIES

ALSO BY FIONA GARTLAND

In the Court's Hands
Now That You've Gone

Published by Poolbeg

ORCHIDS AND LIES

FIONA GARTLAND

POOLBEG
CRIMS☉N

This book is a work of fiction. References to real people, events, establishments, organisations, or locales are intended only to provide a sense of authenticity, and are used fictitiously. All other characters, and all incidents and dialogue, are drawn from the author's imagination and are not to be construed as real.

Published 2020 by Crimson
an imprint of Poolbeg Press Ltd
123 Grange Hill, Baldoyle,
Dublin 13, Ireland
Email: poolbeg@poolbeg.com

© Fiona Gartland 2020

The moral right of the author has been asserted.

© Poolbeg Press Ltd. 2020, copyright for editing, typesetting, layout, design, ebook.

A catalogue record for this book is available from the British Library.

ISBN 978178199-394-1

All rights reserved. No part of this publication may be reproduced or transmitted in any form or by any means, electronic or mechanical, including photography, recording, or any information storage or retrieval system, without permission in writing from the publisher. The book is sold subject to the condition that it shall not, by way of trade or otherwise, be lent, resold or otherwise circulated without the publisher's prior consent in any form of binding or cover other than that in which it is published and without a similar condition, including this condition, being imposed on the subsequent purchaser.

www.poolbeg.com

ABOUT THE AUTHOR

Fiona Gartland has been a journalist with *The Irish Times* for fifteen years and currently works as assistant news editor. She has been shortlisted for the Francis McManus short story competition on half a dozen occasions. Her debut novel *In the Court's Hands* was published in 2018, followed by *Now That You've Gone* in 2019.

Fiona lives in Dublin with her husband and four adult children.

For Paul

Chapter One

Monday, February 20th, 2017

When a high-pitched scream perforated my peace at the Botanic Gardens in Dublin it seemed that it was not only audible but almost visible. It was as though the sound had made the light there vibrate – as though the plants and trees were altered by it. I had always found the gardens tranquil at this time of year and not just because of the particular quality of light there. Its calmness came from a combination of things – the faint smell of winter jasmine, the relative emptiness compared to summertime and, of course, its proximity to Glasnevin Cemetery. I imagined that burial place's eternal hush seeping between railing posts and over stone walls, spreading like a fine mist through the gardens.

On Monday, under a cool, grey sky with the promise of rain in it, I was sitting on a bench close to the herbaceous border, admiring the spring bulbs beginning to show colour through their thinning buds and the magnolia tree about to burst into blossom. I had arrived just as the gates opened, nine o'clock, my preferred time, before visitors begin to trickle around the garden's winding paths – the mothers with children too young for school, the retired people out for a walk or in search of cuttings and coffees and cream cakes.

I can sit at that time of day and let silence, interrupted only by the calls of winter birds, envelop me. And I can let my mind wander. But there was my problem. On this Monday morning, when a sharp mind would have been of most benefit, mine was drifting. And though I now know how valuable my observation could have been, of the person moving on the right at the edge of my vision, flickering through the Cactus House and away at an irregular speed for such a place, I barely registered it then.

It was only the scream that roused me a few minutes later, that unnatural piercing of air. I got to my feet and moved to my right in the direction I believed the sound had come from. I walked quickly and then, with a growing sense of urgency, ran along the path that outlined the Palm House and led to its back door. I was not alone. A man in dark-green gardener's clothes was running too.

Round the back of the Palm House, we came to a cream, wooden double door, set into a grey stone building, which made a grand entrance lobby for the garden's largest glasshouse complex. One side of the double-door was open and a woman came through it running toward us, panicked and shaking.

"*I think he's dead!*"

She gestured behind her into the empty lobby building in the direction of another double door, which opened into the main glasshouse, then she turned back towards it and we followed her. We went through the main door, the gardener ahead of me and the woman ahead of him, and then turned to the left. Just past the Panama Hat Palm we saw him, lying face down on the flagstone path, arms outstretched, lengths of vine entangled in his fingers and a pool of crimson growing like a halo around his head.

"*Paddy! Jesus! Paddy!*" the gardener said, rushing forward. He made a movement as though searching for a pulse at the man's neck, a pointless gesture. "*Call an ambulance, will you!*"

The woman who had found him, who looked like a visitor to the gardens, took out her phone and walked back toward the entrance. I could hear her voice shaking as she spoke.

"There's been an accident," she said.

The warm, moist air of the glasshouse was heavy around us, its equatorial-forest odour infiltrated by the metallic tang of blood. I felt nauseous. The gardener was on his knees now, for some reason, stroking the man's back as though comforting a hurt child.

"What should we do?" he said.

I shook my head. "Nothing, there's nothing we can do for him now."

I looked at the walkway high above us inside the glasshouse. It was about forty feet up and a section of it passed over the flagstones where the body lay. I could see Trumpet Vine growing close to it, its tendrils partly entwined in the walkway and partly hanging free. Some of it had been torn away. The gardener followed my gaze.

"He must've fallen . . ." He looked puzzled when he said it, as though he couldn't imagine how anyone would.

The wrought-iron walkway had a railing that looked to me to be about four feet high, up to the chest of an average man. Here and there giant leaves tipped against it and bougainvillea twisted around it, softening the hard, cream-painted metal.

"What was he doing up there?" I asked.

"I don't know – maybe checking the irrigation lines." He shook his head then. "He needn't have, I only checked them yesterday."

Just then the irrigation system, which ran on the underside of the walkway, switched on above our heads, hissing fine water droplets and creating mist around us. The gardener stood up and there were red stains spreading on the knees of his trousers. He took off his jacket – under which he had a green, collared T-shirt and strong, sinewy arms – and laid it over the body. He was shaking but not, I thought, from any chill. I thought I should keep him talking in the hope it might prevent him, prevent us both, from going into shock.

"Had he been working here long?" I asked.

"What? About five years – came in not long before his father died – Jackie Hogan – he was head gardener here."

The sound of sirens could be heard now and I pictured for a moment the man at the security desk coming out and opening the tall, black, iron entrance gates, creaking them outward on their great hinges attached to granite pillars so that the ambulance could pass through and on between the great trunks of the 60-foot twin lime trees, planted gate-width apart. Were the paths wide enough for it to drive on?

There would be gardaí too and we would have to talk to them. There would be statements to give. I was already running through in my head the order in which everything had happened.

A small group of people had gathered just inside the

entrance to the Palm House. It was as though they had got that far but some instinct had prevented them from coming any closer. One or two, though, had their phones out and seemed to be filming the scene. The gardener noticed.

"*Stop that, you pricks!*" he said and the people around them made them put their phones away. Then he turned to me, his jaw tight. "Bastards." He twisted the gold band on his left ring finger. "What's wrong with people? Have they no humanity anymore?"

"I don't know," I said and then, in an effort to ease him, asked, "Are you here long yourself?"

"Fifteen years – long enough."

I could see the outdoors beginning to show in the year-round tan of his face and in the fine lines either side of his hazel eyes. I put him in his late 30s though I knew I might be wrong.

"*Mind yourself! Excuse me!*"

There were shouts from behind the group as paramedics pushed through them, carrying a stretcher and other equipment. A young woman, in a uniform of green trousers and luminous lime-green jacket with **Ambulance Service** written across it, approached us.

"If you wouldn't mind just standing back," she said. She took the gardener's jacket off the body. "Yours?" she asked him.

"Yeah." He took it and put it back on though it was stained with his colleague's blood.

We walked outside as all four paramedics crowded round the body. Close to the entrance we'd run through an ambulance was parked. Its back doors were open, showing off its interior – its oxygen tank and blankets and defibrillator and drip stand.

We stood together under the nearby Strawberry Tree – myself, the gardener and the woman who had come screaming out of the glasshouse. There was a cool breeze on my skin that made me aware that I'd been sweating.

The gardener was hugging himself, then turned and retched onto the grass. Someone gave him a bottle of water. He rinsed his mouth and spat, then swallowed a few gulps. Then he reached into his pocket, took out cigarettes and a lighter and lit up.

The woman leaned against the red tree trunk, its glossy bark peeling in places. She looked to be in her sixties and was short and barrel-shaped with a stiff grey bob. Her eyes were closed and she was holding her hand over her mouth as though trying to stifle another scream. A Garda car pulled up and three officers got out and began talking to the people who were standing around.

A young garda approached the three of us. "Who found the man?"

I looked at the woman beside me. "You did, didn't you? That was you screaming?"

"Yes," she said, breathing rapidly as though she might have a panic attack.

"Give her a minute," the gardener said. "We went in when she ran out."

"Right." The garda reached into his pocket and took out a notebook. "Can I have your names?"

I told him mine and gave him my address on Clontarf Road.

"Beatrice Barrington?" the garda said. "Why does that sound familiar?"

"I've no idea."

He looked me up and down, taking in my trainers and jeans, my padded navy jacket, the blue scarf wound round my neck. He squinted at my freckled face, the deepening lines around my eyes, the red hair pinned in a chignon. I felt a knot forming in my stomach as though I had done something wrong. How did gardaí manage to have that effect on me?

"I can't place you," he said then shrugged and turned his attention to the gardener.

"George Delaney. I work here."

The garda wrote slowly, blinking repeatedly as though he had dust in his eyes.

We both described what we'd heard and seen – my version and the gardener's roughly concurring. The garda thanked us and then turned to the woman.

"Are you able to talk to me now?" he asked.

She nodded and told him her name was Constance Anderson. She gave a landline number to him instead of a mobile and said her address was St Mobhi Road. "So I'm in and out of the gardens all the time," she said, putting a piece of stray hair behind her ear as she spoke. She said she had been in the Orchid House, which was attached to the Palm House, and was admiring the *Phalaenopsis* before walking on. "I walked down and went through the door – the one that brings you from the Orchid House into the Palm House – and I turned and there he was, just lying there." She shuddered. "That's when I screamed."

"When you were in the Orchid House, did you hear anything at all?" the garda asked her.

She shook her head. "No, it was very quiet."

I mentioned I thought I'd seen someone earlier, before

Constance screamed, on the periphery of my vision, running, but I could give no description.

"Dark clothes," was all I could tell the garda.

He didn't write it down.

"Jogger maybe," he suggested.

"Through the Cactus House?" I couldn't imagine why anyone would want to run indoors.

"We don't allow joggers here," George Delaney said.

The garda took our phone numbers and said he'd be in touch and that we'd have to make formal statements at the station. He didn't say which station.

The paramedics emerged then, heads down. They put their equipment into the ambulance and drove away slowly down the path. Another garda unfurled a roll of blue-and-white tape and stretched it across the entrance to the Palm House. It flapped a little in the breeze.

"They didn't bring him out," Constance said.

"No. They'll be waiting for the pathologist," I told her.

She made a noise of revulsion, as though she too might be sick. But she wasn't.

"They don't need us anymore, do they?" she asked.

George said he supposed they were finished with us for now. She didn't move. We all stared at the entrance to the Palm House and at a garda who was standing now with his back to it, hands clasped behind him, rocking slightly on the balls of his feet. I turned away and walked slowly and a little shakily in the direction of the exit, past the yew trees and the Orchid House and an ancient fenced-in fir. There were gardeners approaching visitors – telling them they would have to leave. I passed hydrangeas and the lovely home of the garden's director, and then another house next to the main entrance.

At the wrought-iron gates there was a small queue to exit. The central gates, through which I'd imagined the ambulance had passed, had been closed again though not locked. And visitors were being funnelled through two of the six pedestrian gates, to the left and right of the central gates. There were turnstiles on some of these gates and for the first time I wondered if visitors to the gardens, when it first opened in 1800, were required to pay in.

Gardaí were in position at each exit and were asking people if they'd seen or heard anything unusual. I recognised one of them, a woman with a heart-shaped face – Francine Something. What was it? I remembered her sitting at a kitchen table in south Dublin last year, the glint of her pink nail polish as she took notes while Detective Inspector Matt McCann questioned my friend, Georgina O'Donnell. Francine Gibson – that was it.

"Hello," I said to her when my turn came.

She looked hard at me, her brown eyes scrutinising.

"Beatrice Barrington, isn't it?"

"Yes."

"What are you doing here?"

I wanted to say I wasn't doing anything. I was out for a walk and a bit of peace, and why shouldn't I be? "Just visiting. And what about you? You're a bit far from Store Street."

"I got a transfer to Ballymun."

So that was the station taking charge of this. "I'd say that's different to the city centre."

"New boss." She looked over my shoulder at the increasing queue. "I'd better get on."

"I gave a statement already to one of the other guards."

"Good." She wrote my name down anyway.

Outside the gates, photographers and reporters had gathered. There was a broadcast unit from RTÉ and the station's reporter was wielding a microphone, waylaying people as they left. I could hear other reporters garnering opinions, quantifying the extent of shock with their words, speculating on whether the death was accidental, whether he had jumped or if it was something else. There were plenty of people happy to describe how horrified they were and what a terrible thing to happen in such a lovely place.

I kept walking in the direction of where I'd parked my car on St Mobhi Drive, head down, no eye contact, the best strategy to avoid any approach.

Did I believe even then as I walked away that it wasn't just an accident? I think perhaps I did. And I was resolved too and absolutely sure that I would not involve myself in it.

Chapter Two

St Mobhi Drive had a row of 1920s houses on a height on one side of the road. Their long front gardens, with driveways, ran down to the footpath. On the opposite side of the road, where I had parked, there were no houses – just a grass bank and then the River Tolka. On the far side of the river, the pyramidal Our Lady of Dolours church stands on Botanic Avenue, which, like its parallel St Mobhi Drive, meets Botanic Road at a T-junction. From there it is a few yards to the gates of the Botanic Gardens.

As I reached my car, I stood still for a moment, bewildered by an uncharacteristic urge to walk back the way I'd come and go into the church and light a candle for Paddy Hogan. But it began to rain then, large, sullen drops, and I shrugged off the sensation and sat into my car. I sometimes liked to park on the avenue instead of using the car park attached to the gardens, which was accessed through a lane at the side of the main entrance. It was so I could enjoy entering the gardens through those elegant, old gates as intended by those who designed them more than 200 years earlier. The price I paid for that, though, was a tight parking spot and it took a few manoeuvres to get out and turn my car back in the direction I needed to go.

Before I pulled away, I saw Constance Anderson going in the driveway of one of the houses in the middle of the row. I'd thought she'd told the garda that she lived on St Mobhi Road, not St Mobhi Drive. I must have misheard. She was talking to a tall young man dressed in black jeans and a black leather jacket. She paused and turned to look in the direction of the Botanic Gardens. He bent and kissed her on the cheek. She patted his arm in a satisfied way and turned back then and continued up to the house. The young man walked down the drive and away in the direction of Washerwoman's Hill.

In my own house, on Clontarf Road, I sat on the couch in the living room and looked out the picture window at the waters of Dublin Bay. A ripple of wind was passing over them, making furrows in the surface and distorting the reflection of the grey sky. I thought about the man still lying in the Palm House. Had he known in those seconds as he fell that he would die? How terrified he must have been. I closed my eyes and I could see him, splayed on the flagstones. I could see his hands, entwined with Trumpet Vine. He must have hoped it would break his fall but it couldn't possibly hold his weight. Would a man who was jumping have grasped like that? Perhaps he might if he'd changed his mind at that last moment when he felt himself about to leave the world. What else could I recall? The knuckles on his right hand were grazed. What could have caused that? Had he been fighting with someone on the walkway?

I picked up the mobile phone I'd left on the coffee table

before me and turned it over, weighing it in my hand. Should I call Gabriel Ingram? The last time I'd spoken to the retired detective was two weeks earlier, but we hadn't seen each other in how long? Five months, was it? He'd been staying with his sister in Donegal since he'd taken ill last November. He'd had a heart attack and needed surgery to have stents put in. For a short while I'd thought he might come to live with me in Clontarf. I had been prepared to compromise my independence so that I could look after him. But then his sister had arrived and taken him away to recuperate.

What was it he said to me in the hospital when he was leaving with her? That he would only stay in Glenties for a few weeks. But "a few weeks" had elongated and December, and then Christmas passed, and he said he would stay where he was until the end of January. Now, it was almost the end of February and he still hadn't come back to Dublin. I wondered if perhaps he'd found himself somewhere else to live up there. He might have moved out of his sister's without telling me. He would know that once he'd told me I would recognise that as a decision to stay. Of course, he'd invited me up for a visit once or twice before Christmas but it didn't feel right to intrude on him when he was with his family. And it felt now as though the village of Glenties, his childhood home northwest of the Blue Stack Mountains, might as well have been in Australia.

I put the phone down. It would be unfair to call him now while I was still brimming with intensity from the morning. What could he do anyway, so far away? And I knew he would worry about me and that would only cause him stress. I didn't want to do that, not when he had made such a good recovery. I didn't ever want to cause him stress again.

I went into the kitchen at the back of the house, made some soup, took it back to the living room and switched on the TV in time for the one o'clock bulletin. Paddy Hogan's death was the lead story.

"*It's understood that the deceased was a gardener employed at the National Botanic Gardens,*" the newsreader said. "*Our reporter is at the scene.*"

A man appeared on screen, the gates of the gardens behind him firmly closed to visitors. I could see a cardboard sign hanging from one of the gate's golden curlicues, no doubt giving notice of the closure.

"*The National Botanic Gardens is a popular visitor attraction here on Dublin's north side. I'm told there were a good many people in the gardens shortly before nine-thirty when the tragedy occurred.*"

A clip of footage showed the gardens earlier when people were leaving. Another clip was of a man speaking to the reporter and detailing the intensity of his shock. A second, older man said he'd thought he would "never see the day". He shook his head mournfully and wondered what the world was coming to.

Then a familiar face appeared – it was Constance Anderson. She told the reporter how she had seen the body and called for an ambulance. She looked directly into camera and spoke slowly, giving details of where the body was and how it looked. I thought she seemed to be enjoying herself in the same way as a neighbourhood gossip might when imparting fresh information about a local scandal. And though I knew it was unkind of me, I felt she was pleased to be the focus of such attention.

"It looked as though he'd jumped from a height," she said.

I wondered why she would say that – "jumped" and not "fell"?

I found it hard to watch then. I was sad and a bit weary. I had seen enough tragic deaths in the last couple of years. As a stenographer at the Criminal Courts of Justice a part of me had been glad when stenography work had all but dried up once they introduced their digital audio-recording system. It meant I didn't have to listen to any more horrific murder or manslaughter cases. Though at the time I didn't consider it, I felt now that it had worn away some element of faith in humanity only damaged by acquaintance with the nuances of evil. I told myself firmly that I'd do my utmost not to become too involved in Paddy Hogan's death. I'd do what I had to do – make a statement to gardaí when they asked for it – but that would be all.

The reporter signed off from outside the gardens and the screen returned to studio and a story about backstops and borders.

My phone rang then and Gabriel's name flashed. A kind of relief tingled through me before I answered it.

"I seen you on the telly," he said by way of greeting.

I picked up the TV remote control with my left hand and turned down the volume.

"Did you?"

"Wasn't that you walking out of the Bots behind a reporter?"

"You have some eye." I was amazed because I hadn't spotted myself. I supposed I'd been too focused on what the reporter was saying.

"I knew it." He laughed, pleased with himself.

"How are you keeping?" I asked, enjoying the sound of his laughter.

"Grand, sure, lovely and peaceful up here, and Bernadette's looking after me well."

So she was still managing to hold on to him. I had a vision of him sitting at her table eating platefuls of homemade stew and apple tarts. He'd often said she made lovely apple tarts.

"There must be lots you can do around the house for her, and lots of nice walks?" I wanted to ask him how much longer he would be away or whether he was planning on staying up there permanently.

"Oh plenty, plenty to be getting on with . . ." His voice trailed away.

"And the children must be great company?" He had three nephews, in their teens now, I supposed.

"They're good boys. A bit noisy sometimes but sure isn't that how they're meant to be? But never mind me – what happened in the Bots?"

"I found him, Gabriel – that man who died."

I told him all about it then, though I'd promised myself I wouldn't, and as I described the scene in the Palm House my voice wobbled.

"You must have got a terrible fright," he said in that quiet, solid way of his that made me suddenly want to cry.

"But I'm angry with myself," I said instead. I told him how, if I'd been a bit more attentive, I might have been able to describe the person who'd been running just before I heard the scream. "I can't remember anything but a dark shape."

"You can't expect yourself to notice everything all the time, Bea."

"I know, but sometimes . . . I feel like I fail people." I hadn't thought that before but as soon as the words were out I believed it was true.

"Ah now. Don't be so hard on yourself."

"I feel like there's a cloud that follows me around, Gabriel. I think I've felt like that since Laurence died." The words almost stuck in my throat. Why did it always come back to losing my brother? After all that had happened since 1981 and all the people who had died, why was his loss the one that stung most?

"Ah now, Bea!"

He didn't know what to say and I felt ashamed, then, of my own self-indulgence. Why was I talking to him like this when I had promised myself I wouldn't burden him?

"Don't mind me – it's probably just shock," I said.

"That'll be it all right." He cleared his throat with a short dry cough. "Have the lads been in touch yet?" He meant the gardaí, his former co-workers.

"Only briefly – after it happened. They said they'd get back to me for a formal statement." I'd known the young garda who'd questioned us had only scribbled down a few words. They would have to come back if they wanted any real detail. "There was a young guard. I don't think he was paying all that much attention to what I was saying or to the other two."

"Doesn't matter – it's only the names and numbers he had to be sure of getting."

I considered that. I would have thought that what was in the mind of a witness at the time of an event would not necessarily be there later. But perhaps it worked both ways – things could be recalled with time that might not be remembered initially.

"Would you like me to give Matt a call – see if he's involved?"

He was talking about Matt McCann, a detective friend of his who'd helped us when we, or rather I, was in trouble on more than one occasion. I felt instantly better at the thought that he might be looking after the case.

"Would you mind? I think someone in Ballymun is taking the lead but it would be good to know who."

"Not at all. I'll ring you when I find out."

"Thanks, Gabriel."

"No bother."

He hung up then and I put the phone aside, pulled my legs up under me and leaned back into the corner of the couch. What was that feeling now? Loneliness? Longing? Loss? I was familiar with those. They had been my companions since my early twenties. As a young woman, alone in London after Laurence took his own life, I had found other ways to smother those feelings. After work in a typing pool, I'd drink in the bars around Camden Square with other young Irish people, mostly men, adrift in the English capital, in search of oblivion. But my appetite for that had waned and I'd stopped drinking and let work fill the gaps that alcohol had left behind.

When I came home to Dublin, my stenography business was successful and fully occupied me. But contracts were fewer now and, I supposed, I was not fighting hard enough for the ones that were available. I felt I had lost some intrinsic hunger that had driven me before. But what was there for me if not work?

I admonished myself again for maudlin self-indulgence. That would have to stop, I told myself, and stood up and went in search of my laptop. I had no office now, unlike in the past, and the machine was where I had left it, in its slim bag in the hall. I brought it into the kitchen and set it up on my round, wooden-slatted table. When I'd bought the table in 1995 and the white-painted cabinets with blue door handles, and the driftwood fruit bowl on the countertop, it had been because of my delight at being so close to the sea. I'd moved in after selling my London city-centre flat. The market was just taking off there and property in Dublin was still relatively cheap. I knew how lucky I was to have what I had – to be able to open a window and breathe in salt air in a home of my own with the mortgage long since paid off.

Once the laptop had warmed up, I checked my emails, scanning down through the spam, deleting without opening, until I came to a message from O'Connell Brophy Solicitors. It was an offer of work covering an unfair dismissals hearing at the Labour Court, beginning on Wednesday the 22nd and it would take at least three days. I hadn't been asked to cover too many of those. They weren't usually high level enough to need a stenographer. I wondered what might be so important about this one that my services were required. I responded to it saying I'd be happy to attend, left my laptop plugged in to ensure it was fully charged and went in search of my stenograph.

It would be good to be occupied, good to be distracted from what was, having talked it over with Gabriel, surely a murder.

Chapter Three

Wednesday, February 22nd

I left my car at Clontarf train station and took the DART to Lansdowne Road, carrying my stenograph in one bag and my laptop in another. I'd got good at packing the contents of my handbag into the outer pocket of the laptop bag and I felt like an office on legs striding along through the dry and bright morning in my winter navy work suit and navy wool coat.

The Labour Court, at the Workplace Relations Commission in Lansdowne House, was a five-minute walk from the station, which was next to the gleaming doughnut that is the Aviva Stadium. It still looked to me like an alien spaceship that had landed in the centre of leafy Dublin 4. I admired Lansdowne Road as I walked along, with its elegant redbrick, three-storey homes and its footpaths lined with trees that were beginning to waken after winter. It reminded me of the less genteel and shabbier North Circular Road close to the Phoenix Park.

It was sad, I thought, that this dignified highway had been allowed to end in a series of concrete carbuncles, the ugliest of which was Lansdowne House. It was nine storeys of grey and glass and no doubt it had swallowed many Victorian houses when it was constructed in the 1960s. I went in through its glass double doors to the lifts, as instructed by O'Connell Brophy Solicitors, and up to the fifth floor where the hearing was to be held.

There were two tables in the long room, at right angles to each other, making a T-shape. I assumed the Labour Court committee would sit at the top and the employer and employee teams would sit facing each other at the longer table, which ran down the centre of the room. I couldn't see a place to put myself and I had to ask the court secretary for a chair and a separate, small table to place the machine on. Acoustics in the room seemed poor too and I feared I might not catch every word. I had found that acoustics were rarely considered by people choosing or even designing venues for such hearings. This bothered me more now than when I was a younger woman. Still, I would have to make do and, though I was apprehensive, I reminded myself that if nothing else I was a professional.

I took off my coat, hung it from a stand in the corner and settled myself to one side of where the committee members would sit. Shortly afterwards, a woman approached me in the black suit of a legal professional and extended her hand.

"I'm Caroline Brophy of O'Connell Brophy – we commissioned you." Her voice had uplift at the end making what was a fact into a question. She was in her late thirties with brown, shoulder-length hair that parted in the centre and was pulled back into a ponytail, accentuating an equine face.

"Oh, yes. Nice to meet you," I said.

"You come highly recommended . . . by . . ." She put her hand up to her mouth and spoke behind it, namedropping a prominent member of the judiciary.

"Nice to know I'm not forgotten," I said. And it was nice.

She gave me a sheet of paper with details of the case on it.

"We're working with Joe Waldron on behalf of Marina Fernandez. If you need anything else, let me know," she said. "Next-day transcript all right with you?"

"That's fine. Thanks."

"And just to be clear, both parties will be paying for your services."

"Right."

"I'm only saying it because we don't often use stenographers here. But I imagine as the case goes on you'll appreciate why you're needed."

She went back to her place on one side of the long table near the front of the room and I busied myself typing the details on the sheet of paper she'd given me into the stenograph. I would include it on the second page of the transcript. The first page would read "**Marina Fernandez v Chapels Nursing Home**". The sheet said she was bringing a case of unfair dismissal against her former employer. I inputted the details – the where and when and how. The case would be decided by a three-member committee, a division of the Labour Court, which included, according to the information, a chairwoman, a representative of employers and a representative of workers. It would be for the nursing home to prove that the dismissal was not unfair. I could see from the note that a Workplace Relations Commission adjudication officer had already ruled that Marina Fernandez was not unfairly dismissed and this hearing was an appeal of that decision.

A woman, in her thirties with black, shoulder-length hair, wearing a green dress and navy jacket walked into the room then and, when directed by her companion, sat next to Caroline Brophy. I took her to be Marina Fernandez. She looked woebegone, and though she was wearing make-up on her clear olive complexion it was insufficient to disguise the dark circles under her eyes. Her barrister, a man in a creased navy suit with unruly grey curls, black eyebrows and a nose that pointed off-centre, sat down beside her and whispered in her ear. She nodded repeatedly but said nothing back. Her large brown eyes were shiny as though they might spill over with tears at any second. I thought there was a softness about her and wondered what she possibly could have done to find herself dismissed. But then, I knew, no one could be sure what anyone else was capable of. If I had learnt nothing else in the last few years, I had at least learnt that.

My thoughts were pulled to Paddy Hogan and I could see him lying face down on the slabs of the Palm House floor. He would be on another slab now, I supposed, under the pathologist's knife in the state morgue on Griffith Avenue. Cause of death would hardly be a mystery but toxicology would ascertain whether he'd taken anything before his drop. I felt sure, though, that what brought him to the morgue in the first place wouldn't be answered there.

The committee, made up of two men and one woman, walked in then and just as they did the employer's team arrived, taking their places opposite Marina Fernandez and her people.

I brought my mind back to focus on the work.

"Good morning. My name is Miriam Lynch. I am chairwoman of this division of the Labour Court. Before this hearing begins, I want to emphasise that the onus is on the employer to prove the dismissal of Ms Fernandez was fair and not the other way around." She had brown wavy hair to her shoulders, pinned back firmly on both sides, and the air of a purposeful and disciplined civil servant.

I was relieved that she spoke clearly as she introduced the other members, a Mr Higgins and a Mr O'Toole.

Joe Waldron introduced himself as Marina Fernandez' barrister.

"Caroline Brophy is here to my right. Ms Fernandez is next to her, and then her union rep, Fred Byrne."

The nursing-home team's barrister gave his name as Reginald Taylor.

"Senior counsel," he said. "To my right is junior counsel Ann Fahey, solicitor Belinda Regan and nursing-home manager Olive Madden."

Though he didn't stand up, he was, I guessed, about six foot, and willow-thin, with side-parted, coarse brown hair.

He began his opening statement.

"Nurse Marina Fernandez registered to work in Ireland as a general nurse in 2012, having trained in Brazil. She was an agency nurse with Medics Ireland, working at various hospitals and care settings, before taking up a position at the Chapels Nursing Home on October 21st, 2015. Following her arrival, a series of incidents occurred involving thefts, the details of which I will expand on in due course, and which culminated in Ms Fernandez' suspension pending an internal investigation on December 18th." He paused to turn over his notes. "The investigation led to her dismissal on January 25th, 2016. Ms Fernandez then filed a complaint at the Workplace Relations Commission and, after a hearing there, its adjudication officer found she had *not* been unfairly dismissed. At this stage I wish to make it clear that Dr Adrian Dunboyne did feel a degree of sympathy toward Ms Fernandez and decided he would not seek the help of An Garda Síochána in this matter, though it is still open to him at this stage to do so."

When he paused again to take a breath, I glanced in Marina's direction. She no longer looked tearful – her face was a mixture of embarrassment and anger. She leaned toward her barrister and muttered something. He nodded.

Once the session started, all extraneous thoughts were pushed aside. The acoustics were not as challenging as I'd feared. Mr Taylor went through each allegation of theft and detailed how Marina Fernandez was the only nurse on night duty looking after 20 residents. Two care assistants worked on nights at the home, but one had recently resigned and hadn't been replaced. Each time there was a theft, the other care assistant had been assigned to sit at the bedside of a man with late-phase dementia who had been disruptive, unsettled and at times violent.

"Nurse Fernandez was in effect the only staff member looking after the remaining 19 residents," Mr Taylor told the committee.

I thought I heard one member of the committee tutting, but I didn't include that sound in my transcript.

By one o'clock, the case had been outlined and the committee was ready for lunch. As the three members left, Mr Taylor walked to the back of the room and shook hands with a man in a grey herringbone overcoat who had just arrived. I passed them on my way out to find some lunch of my own and heard Mr Taylor say, "You'll be called at two, Dr Dunboyne".

When I left the building I was momentarily dazzled by February sunlight on the white granite slabs at its entrance. I blinked and looked in both directions before deciding to turn right. I walked to Ballsbridge to Paddy Cullen's pub where I ordered vegetable soup, a chicken sandwich and a pot of tea. My head was filled with Marina Fernandez and the picture being drawn of a devious woman who requested night duty so that she would have access to the lockers of vulnerable residents while there were few staff around to see her. There was something about the case that made me uneasy though I couldn't say right at that moment what it was. I wondered why criminal charges hadn't been brought by the owner.

When Dr Adrian Dunboyne began to give his evidence that afternoon, having taken a seat close to the committee, the sense of uneasiness grew in me. I couldn't say what it was about him that I didn't trust except that perhaps he smiled too often and in that smile there was a superciliousness I had learnt to associate, through years of working in criminal courts, with those who had a strong sense of entitlement and who trod the borderline between moral and amoral behaviour. He was taken through his qualifications in detail and was happy to expand on his eminence at length. I liked him less and less the more he boasted.

"Moving on to events in late 2015 . . ." Mr Taylor said.
"Yes?"
"In your written statement to the court you say that on the evening of November 5th, 2015, you saw Ms Fernandez beside the locker of a patient, Mr Roy Patterson. These are the steel lockers with keys, on the corridor outside of each

ward, as opposed to the lockers next to patients' beds, is that correct?"

"Yes."

"And when you asked her what she was doing she said the patient had requested her to fetch a book for him. You said, however, that Ms Fernandez did not have a book in her hand and when she opened the locker, there was no book inside, is that correct?"

Dr Dunboyne nodded. "That is correct, and when I walked back with her to the ward the book she claimed to have been looking for was on the patient's bedside locker and the patient was asleep." He nodded his head again at the end of his sentence as if to emphasise the definitive nature of his version of events.

"Did you point that out, Dr Dunboyne?"

"I did, and Ms Fernandez said she hadn't noticed the book there and the patient must have forgotten he already had it."

"And did you respond to that?"

The witness scratched his chin. "No, but I thought it odd, so much so that I made a note about it in my desk diary."

Mr Taylor turned to the committee. "We believe this was the occasion on which one hundred euro was stolen from Mr Patterson's locker. Now, Dr Dunboyne, there are two other occasions when you expressed concern about Ms Fernandez. If you turn to page five in your booklet you'll see a diary entry you made dated November 12th, 2015."

Papers rustled as the doctor, the committee and the legal teams all sought out the correct page.

"Can you tell us what that says, Dr Dunboyne?"

He squinted for a moment. "It's hard to read my own

writing. It says – '*Nurse F at it again, careless, Mrs O'Connor's locker left open*'."

"And by 'Nurse F' did you mean Ms Fernandez?"

"I did. I was making a note of what I thought was her carelessness rather than anything else. It was only a few days later that I heard things had been stolen from the locker."

"Yes, a watch and twenty euro were stolen from Audrey O'Connor." Mr Taylor turned to the committee again. "That is the second accusation. I won't keep you much longer, Dr Dunboyne. If you turn now to the last entry in your diary related to Ms Fernandez, dated December 1st, 2015."

The pages were turned again and I had a moment to stretch my fingers. I had noticed a stiffness in them and attributed it to lack of practice.

"Shall I read it?" Dr Dunboyne asked.

"Please."

"It says '*Saw Nurse F arguing with patient – patient had asked for money from her purse and F refused to get the purse*'."

"Yes – was Lillie Brennan the patient you refer to here?"

"It was."

Mr Taylor made what I thought was a slightly theatrical shift of his gaze from Dr Dunboyne to the committee. "According to Mrs Brennan's family, that purse contained €150 to be used the following day to pay the visiting hairdresser and to buy items from the visiting bookshop. There was no money in the purse when Ms Brennan sought it the following morning. There was also a silver charm bracelet missing, a Pandora brand I believe, with numerous charms and worth close to €1,100. It was also of great sentimental value. Mrs Brennan's late husband gave it to her the year before he died and her children bought her the charms for birthdays and Christmas. One charm in particular, a ruby heart on a silver loop, was bespoke, uniquely made for her."

"That's correct," the doctor said.

Mr Taylor nodded a 'thank you' at him and Dr Dunboyne began to move from his seat.

"If you'd remain there my colleague has some questions," the barrister said.

"Good afternoon, Dr Dunboyne," said the opposing barrister. "My name is Joe Waldron and I'm acting for Ms Fernandez, or 'Nurse F' as you seem to prefer calling her." He raised his bushy black eyebrows up to meet his grey curls.

Dr Dunboyne bristled. "It's just shorthand."

"I understand – you're a very busy man. At any time, did you see Ms Fernandez take money or other items from patients' lockers?"

"No."

"And these entries, were they contemporaneous?"

"More or less . . . I may have made them the following day, but no later."

"Are you sure?"

"Definite."

"If you'll just turn to page ten of the blue booklet in front of you with the blue cover – yes, that's the one."

There was a pause while the page was found.

"This is a report from an expert in forensic document examination." He turned to Mr Taylor for a moment. "If necessary, the specialist will take the stand." Then he turned back to Dr Dunboyne. "I'm going to just summarise the findings of this report. The expert concluded that each one of the entries referring to Ms Fernandez was added to your diary at a different time to other entries on the same dates and, in fact, all entries related to Ms Fernandez were made at the same time, with the same pen, at some point after December 1st, 2015."

"That's ridiculous!" the doctor laughed. "Pseudo-scientific nonsense."

"I can assure you, Dr Dunboyne, this is not pseudoscience. The techniques described in this report are scientifically validated and documented. If necessary, I can read them into the record?"

He turned to the chairwoman of the committee, Miriam Lynch, who addressed Mr Taylor.

"Do you intend to challenge the veracity of this report?"

"Certainly, but I'll be reserving my position on that for the moment."

"In that case, there's no need to read the document into the record at present. You can take it that the committee will read it thoroughly."

I was pleased at that, having had too much experience of reports being read verbatim into the record, usually at high speed.

"You are denying that the entries were added retrospectively?" Mr Waldron asked.

"I most definitely am."

"I'll move on from that for the moment. I *will* be addressing each of the allegations you have made in turn but first tell me – how well do you know Ms Fernandez?"

"Not well – hardly at all. She wasn't long with the Chapels when these incidents happened."

"Did you like her? Before the incidents, I mean."

The doctor puzzled over the question for a moment as

though it was something he had never considered. "I neither liked nor disliked her. I didn't know her."

"I see, but did you want to get to know her?"

"What exactly are you implying? I'm a married man."

Mr Waldron nodded. "Yes, twenty-three years married, I believe. Let me put this to you, Dr Dunboyne. Ms Fernandez says you did want to get to know her. In fact, you asked her to come for a drink with you on two occasions."

"Why would I?"

"Ms Fernandez also says that on the night of December 14th, 2015, you had called in to attend to a patient who had pneumonia. Do you recall that?"

"I . . . I'd have to check my records." He was obviously unsettled by the direction the questions were taking.

"After you'd seen the patient, you followed Ms Fernandez into the nurses' station. She will say that when she was organising the medicines trolley you reached over and grasped her right breast."

The doctor let out an indignant gasp. "I did nothing of the sort!"

"I believe you did, Dr Dunboyne. And when Ms Fernandez said she would complain about you to the manager, you concocted a story that she was the person stealing from lockers and you retrospectively made those entries in your diary to implicate her."

The doctor was puce and could barely control his temper.

"She stole from my nursing home and now –" he wagged his finger in the direction of Ms Fernandez, "she tries this!"

The chairwoman looked at Mr Taylor and Dr Dunboyne and then at her watch.

"I think perhaps we've heard enough for today," she said. "Dr Dunboyne, would you mind checking your records for the 14th of December before our next hearing? We are sitting again on?" She turned the pages of a diary in front of her. "Friday?"

Both sides agreed they were.

"Fine, see you all then."

I stayed behind, with permission from the court secretary, so that I could transfer the day's work to my laptop and make use of the facilities there to produce the transcript. I emailed it to both sides, as agreed, and then sent them both text messages at the numbers they'd supplied.

Only Caroline Brophy responded. **Great to get it so quickly**, she said.

On the DART on the way home, with the city lights a shimmer of orange beads around the bay, I thought about my day's work and the rhythm of all the court cases I had worked at over the years, the flow of evidence, how stories were constructed around what had happened, and the search for truth – or at least an acceptable version of it. I wasn't sure if the whole truth ever came out in any court case, whether it was criminal or civil. I felt, too, that I was as good as anyone else at spotting the more likely version of events. And in Marina Fernandez' case, I was beginning to feel that the story built up around why she had been sacked, though compelling, was a version created by strong authority against someone who was powerless.

Chapter Four

Thursday, February 23rd

I woke late, sweating and exhausted on Thursday morning and relieved that I didn't need to go to work. The night had been windy with intermittent rain that hammered my seaward bedroom window and interrupted dreams of Paddy Hogan. In one he was suspended in mid-air, halfway between the Palm House roof and the cold slabs, by vines that were wrapped around his body too tightly, squeezing life from him as I stood below with others waiting for him to fall. In another, he was already on the ground and the hard rain was shattering the glass of the Palm House roof, sending shards of crystal down on him that were penetrating his skin. The visions were fresh in my mind still when I dragged myself downstairs and I felt that if I turned around quickly enough I would see him lying on my own floor.

Over tea and toast, swaddled in a blue, fleece dressing gown, I worried that my nights might go on being disturbed and that the gardens might become the landscape to my nightmares for a long time. The best thing I could do, I thought, was go back to where I had seen Paddy Hogan. Seeing the place again on a normal day, with people enjoying the plants and space might dispel the intensity of the experience I'd had there, dilute the potency of my dreams and exorcise his ghost from my subconscious. I remembered then that there'd been someone else in my dreams too – Janine Gracefield, a friend who'd worked with me until 2014. She'd left the country after the Stephen O'Farrell trial and I'd lost track of her, yet there she'd been glowing through the darkness, as kind and gentle as I remember her, smiling at me. It seemed like another lifetime when we'd worked together and I supposed it was. I hadn't talked to her in so long. How strange of my subconscious to send me her for comfort in my dreams.

I parked on St Mobhi Drive and walked round the corner to the gardens. It was ten-thirty and the day was cool but dry so there were plenty of visitors. Though I'd intended going straight to the Palm House I couldn't quite bring myself to walk in its direction. Some instinctive mechanism overtook me – my hands were sweating, my heart beating too quickly. Instead I went to the small coffee shop at the back of the visitor centre. It is reached by passing through a stone archway and crossing a courtyard containing tables and chairs for those who want to sit outside in warm weather. Though it was too early for that, one table was occupied by George Delaney who was drinking coffee from a takeaway cup, smoking a cigarette and intermittently scrolling through his mobile phone.

"Hello," I said to him and he squinted up at me as if the sun was in his eyes though it was cloudy. "It's Beatrice Barrington. I was with you, remember, when Paddy died?"

"Oh yeah," he said, looking me up and down.

He didn't ask me to sit and so I rested my hand on the back of a vacant chair.

"Sit down if you like," he said then.

I did. "How are things? Any . . . news?"

He gave me what I thought was a hostile look but which he softened quickly with a shrug. "Not really, no. People here are just trying to get on with it. And everyone misses Paddy – he was a good fella."

"It must be hard to lose a workmate like that. Do you know when the funeral is? I'd like to go."

"Next Monday across the road." He nodded in the direction of Our Lady of Dolours church.

"He was local then?" I said.

"A lot of us are." He took a drag from his cigarette.

"Have you heard anything about what happened to him?" I asked tentatively.

"I would have thought that was obvious." There was that hostility again. He took another drag. "Look, I know you were there an' all but you shouldn't be . . . have you no respect?"

I stood up. "Sorry. I didn't mean to upset you. I just wanted to talk." I realised then that I had needed to speak to someone who would understand, who had seen what I'd seen.

He gave me a grudging nod. "Yeah . . . I suppose it's a shocking thing for anyone."

"Can I get you another one of those?" I indicated his coffee cup.

"No, thanks. I need to get back to it." He stubbed out the remains of his cigarette on an empty foil cake-holder, finished his coffee and left.

I crossed to the glass door and went into the little coffee shop.

It was a simple room with a counter to the left of the entrance, an array of cakes and sandwiches, and perhaps a dozen tables to the right, a couple of which were occupied by a group of young people, with A4 notebooks and biros. I took them to be horticultural students.

There was a young girl behind the counter from whom I bought tea and a pastry and took them to a table against the back wall. I thought I would sit a while and then, if I felt like it, walk over to the Palm House. What I wanted was to feel that sense of calm again that the gardens usually engendered, though that desire, I knew, was unrealistic given what had happened.

The door swung open and a man in a grey suit walked in. The students' chatter dropped to a low murmur. He waved in their direction as he walked to the counter.

"Hi, guys," he said.

From where I sat, I could get a good look at him – a tall, triangular man in his early forties with black hair in a floppy sort of cut that reminded me of a 1980s pop singer. He was tanned and had facial bones that might have been sculpted. Some of the students were gazing at him with more than a touch of admiration and little was said until he'd got his coffee and left again. When the door swung shut behind him the chatter resumed.

"He's a fine thing," one young woman said.

"Too old though," said another.

"Too old for what?" the first woman said, triggering a bout of raucous laughter.

"Forget about it," a third young woman said. "He's married with kids."

"Aren't they in America, though?" the first woman said.

"True."

Her friends laughed again.

I finished my tea and pastry and left with the intention of walking to the Palm House. I thought I would go in through the Orchid House, the single-storey wing attached to the Palm House that was the mirror of the Cactus House on the opposite side. But when I reached the Orchid House there was a sign on the door "**Greenhouse complex closed February 22nd to 24th for repairs**". I would be lying if I didn't admit a feeling of relief. Though the purpose of my visit had been thwarted, I wasn't sorry. I walked a hundred yards away from the complex and looked back. There were two smashed panes of glass – one in the Orchid House and one high up in the Palm House itself. What would have caused that, I wondered. Or perhaps, *who* would have caused it was a better question.

I didn't go home after my visit to the gardens but instead drove into the city centre. I parked on Hill Street and walked over to Henry Street to visit Arnotts department store. It was, after all, February and time for me to consider choosing a new work suit for the season. It was only when I walked through that emporium and took in the scent of fresh make-up and perfume that I realised there was probably no reason to buy a new suit. I wasn't getting enough work now to justify the cost and my purchase this time last year, a classic nude two-piece, would suffice. Still I wandered from floor to floor from department to department until I felt almost normal again. I had a mid-afternoon meal in the store's restaurant before half-heartedly buying a lipstick too pink for my complexion but which the sales assistant assured me would do wonders to lift my pallor.

Then I drifted home. And that was how it felt – like I was drifting.

Though I had done little shopping and little of anything, I was surprisingly tired when I got back to Clontarf. I kicked off my shoes and lay down on the couch in the living room. It was dusk but I didn't switch on a lamp or close the curtains, and as it got darker the headlights from passing cars cast intermittent spotlights across the ceiling. I could see that it was in need of paint and there were lines here and there where the plasterboard had cracked and would benefit from filler – much like myself, I thought. I checked my watch – it was too late now at six fifteen to call the painter and decorator. He was a family man and I knew he switched his phone to silent after five-thirty. I resolved to ring him in the morning or at least over the next few days and ask him to look at it for me.

I wanted to call Gabriel then to talk about my day and the dreams I'd had. I wanted simply to hear him tell me that everything would be fine, was fine. I stretched my arms above my head, yawned, and reached down for my bag which I had dropped beside me. I took out my phone and dialled his number. I let it ring six times before cutting it off, disappointed. Had he heard it and decided not to answer? Or maybe he'd gone out somewhere and left it behind him. I tried to picture him in a pub in Glenties – I imagined it would be small and dark perhaps but with a turf fire and good company. Maybe he was sitting there with some old friends talking about life in Dublin and how much better off he was in Donegal.

I got off the couch and drew the curtains. I picked my shoes up off the floor. I would change and then eat and then read and then sleep. And I would try not to dream of Paddy Hogan. My phone beeped then with a message from Gabriel.

Will call you in the morning.

Chapter Five

Friday, February 24th

Gabriel phoned on Friday morning. I was getting ready to travel to the Labour Court, which, I had been told in an email, would not sit until eleven-thirty but would run through lunch until it was finished for the day. I was tempted to ignore him. But I couldn't resist.

"I'm coming home," he said, after the briefest of enquiries about how I was.

"Home?" I had been wondering if he still considered Stoneybatter his home. "How did Bernadette take it?"

He coughed. "I haven't told her yet. It's not easy. She's been so . . . so kind."

"Well, you can't just sneak away."

"I wouldn't do that." He sounded insulted and I was sorry.

"I know you wouldn't, what I mean is . . . I'm glad, Gabriel." Was I babbling? "When?"

"I'm getting the one o'clock to Letterkenny, so I should be in Busáras about seven-thirty."

"Today?"

"No point in hanging around when I've made my mind up, Bea."

He was defensive though I wasn't accusing him of any wrongdoing.

"No, of course not. I'll come in and give you a lift home."

"I don't want to put you to any trouble."

"It's no trouble, Gabriel. I'm really looking forward to seeing you." I said it quietly because it had just occurred to me how true it was. What was it my mother used to say about absence and the heart? Was that what was happening to me?

"Well, thanks so. I'll see you later."

"Yes."

I hung up and pictured him then, getting on a bus with his hold-all, finding himself a window seat. He had left his car in Dublin, being too unwell at the time to drive himself to Donegal. Would he use the earphones I gave him when he was in hospital so that he could listen to music or the radio on his phone to pass the time? It warmed me to think that he might. There'd be two buses of course. The first from Glenties, meandering its way to Letterkenny, time for a sandwich in the town and then the second bus from there to Dublin. He could fly to New York in less time.

I organised my work things, drove to Clontarf train station and took the DART to Lansdowne Road, all the time thinking about Gabriel. There was a longing in me that I hardly recognised and a combination of excitement and uneasiness about how we would be together. Would we slip back into the pattern of our comfortable-uncomfortable friendship? Did I really want more from him now than I'd been willing to give him in the past? Would he care anymore if I did?

I was preoccupied too with the aftermath of another dream about Paddy Hogan. He had turned and shown me the crushed side of his face and when he spoke his voice was hoarse and painful to listen to, and he called me by my name. I had woken up shivering. But I was at least grateful that it was morning and I had slept through the night undisturbed.

On the DART I tried to shake myself free of all feeling and focus my thoughts on Marina Fernandez. I thought she was lucky to have a strong legal team behind her. Apart from Caroline Brophy and Joe Waldron, her union representative, Fred Byrne, sat close to her and whispered to her often, words of comfort, I supposed, or encouragement. Once in a while he had written something on a notebook in front of him and pushed it up the table to the barrister who read it and nodded. But though the team was strong, it was outranked by the nursing home's representatives. Joe Waldron was a junior counsel while Reginald Taylor, for the nursing home, was a senior and had a junior working with him. At the Labour Court, both sides must pay for their own costs regardless of whether they're successful or not and I supposed that senior counsel would have been too great an expense for the union, which was probably funding Marina Fernandez' case. Perhaps that was why Caroline had said they needed a stenographer – they would have to work twice as hard as their opposition and a daily transcript would help with that.

As the DART pulled into Lansdowne Road station I was thinking of Dr Adrian Dunboyne. Was he capable of doing what they claimed he had done – of molesting Marina and then making false allegations against her after she complained? He certainly carried himself like a man who thought he could do whatever he liked but that was not the same as actually doing whatever he liked.

When I arrived in the hearing room, the doctor was already there, standing in a corner, in conversation with Reginald Taylor. Both men had removed their overcoats and thrown them across the backs of chairs. Dr Dunboyne was in a light grey suit with a blue shirt and tie. His gold tiepin glinted at me as I crossed the room and I saw that it matched a set of cufflinks he was wearing. They lowered their voices when they saw me.

I set myself up at my desk, smoothing out as I sat the skirt of the navy fitted suit I'd matched with a pale-pink blouse.

Shortly afterwards, Marina Fernandez' team arrived followed by the committee.

"Good morning," Chairwoman Miriam Lynch said when everyone was seated. "Dr Dunboyne will be continuing, yes?"

The doctor moved to a chair close to the committee and waited for his cross-examination to begin again. He had adopted a look of piety and suffering that I had last seen on the face of a character from my mother's *Lives of the Saints*. And predictably, Mr Taylor reminded the committee that the doctor had a very busy schedule, had been very cooperative and was now in attendance longer than anticipated. Caroline Brophy caught my eye for the briefest second when that was said and I saw a hint of mockery in her gaze.

"Thank you, doctor, we do appreciate your time," Ms Lynch said, "but, equally, I'm sure you appreciate Ms Fernandez is entitled to test your evidence." She turned then to Joe Waldron. "Before you begin, Mr Waldron, may

I ask whether your client made a complaint about this allegation of sexual assault on," she looked at her notes, "December the 14th?"

"She did, and if I may I'll expand on that at a later stage," Mr Waldron said.

"That's fine."

He turned his attention to the doctor. "Dr Dunboyne, yesterday we were discussing an incident on December the 14th – were you able to check your records overnight?"

"Yes. I can confirm I was on call that evening and my records show I *did* come in to attend to a resident who was recovering from pneumonia."

"And do you remember Ms Fernandez being on duty that night?"

"Not specifically, but the roster shows she was, so she must have been."

"Do you recall talking to her at all?"

"Again, not specifically but I imagine I would have needed to talk to her to discuss the progress of the resident with pneumonia, a Mrs Briscoe."

"And after seeing Mrs Briscoe, do you remember following Ms Fernandez into the nurses' station?"

"I have no memory of it though it's possible. I may have needed to advise her about medication or give her some other instruction." His tone was supercilious.

"Do you remember that Ms Fernandez was checking the medicines trolley?"

"I don't."

"It's a tight space, the nurses' station, and when the trolley is being examined it's quite limited. You would have had to be quite close to her?"

The doctor shrugged. "The space is more than adequate."

"Is it possible that in that restricted space, so close to Ms Fernandez, so late at night, and relatively alone, that you felt you could safely sexually assault her?"

"*Certainly not!*" He was indignant.

The barrister lifted his shoulders and then dropped them as though he was talking to dishonest child.

"Is it possible that it was an accident – that you were reaching for one of the medicines on the trolley?"

"There is absolutely no way that would happen."

"Ms Fernandez has a clear recollection of the event. She says you groped her."

"I definitely did not!"

"For a man who can't remember what he did do on that night, you seem to have a strong memory about what you didn't do. Are you sure of it, Dr Dunboyne?"

Dr Dunboyne, fists clenched, appeared to be forcing himself to stay in control. "Of course I'm sure."

The chairwoman intervened then.

"I think the doctor has been clear, Mr Waldron, thank you."

"Let me ask you one last question then, doctor – you had concerns about Ms Fernandez' behaviour. And money had gone missing on three occasions from patients' lockers . . ."

"Yes."

"The last occasion was on December 1st and you made a note of it in your diary."

"Yes."

"You are not only the nursing-home physician but also the owner?"

"Yes, yes. This is all well-known." He looked at his watch.

"Why did you wait until December the 18th to have her suspended – more than two weeks after the third time you recorded a concern?"

The doctor sighed and shook his head.

"You have no idea how busy and pressurised my role is. I attended to that matter as soon as I had the opportunity."

"I suggest you were told about Ms Fernandez' complaint against you for sexual assault and you concocted your concerns retrospectively."

"Certainly not." Though he didn't lose his temper, his cheeks were like two plums beginning to ripen.

"Your retrospective diary entries prove that, Dr Dunboyne. So does your delay in making a complaint."

"*No.*" He spoke firmly and loudly.

"Thank you, doctor," Mr Waldron said.

There was a brief pause during which I found myself rubbing my hands. My fingers had been stiff earlier but now the knuckles were sore.

Mr Taylor coughed. "Now, Dr Dunboyne . . ." He reiterated questions that he'd already asked and drew from the doctor the answers that he wanted emphasised. It was a tool I'd seen used many times by barristers. Its aim was to mitigate any damage done to the case during cross-examination.

By the time Mr Taylor was finished with him, Dr Dunboyne was calm and entirely in control again.

"Thank you for your time, doctor," Ms Lynch said.

The doctor nodded to his legal team and left the room.

Mr Taylor told the committee then that his next witness would not be available until March the 2nd. "We've agreed under the circumstances that Mr Waldron's only witness, his document-examination person, will give evidence in advance of that on the afternoon of February the 27th."

He said "document-examination person" as though he thought it were ridiculous.

"That's disappointing. I had hoped we could have made progress more quickly," the chairwoman said. "Very well, but I would ask both parties to try to remember this is the Labour Court and not the Criminal Court of Justice."

She stood and left, the rest of the committee following her.

Caroline Brophy approached me when the committee had left.

"Thanks for the quick transcripts," she said. "It means we're super-prepared."

"You're welcome."

Then she dropped her voice. "Can you believe this Dunboyne character?"

I wasn't sure how to respond. I was unaccustomed to lawyers on either side of any case making comments to me about witnesses. It seemed unprofessional to me and I wondered what her motivation was, though perhaps she was only being friendly.

"I'll get this to you as soon as I can," I said, and put my head down to finish my work.

I was on the DART shortly before four and grateful for the early finish. I googled the Dublin to Letterkenny bus on my phone to check on Gabriel's arrival time. Then I searched for "**sore knuckles**" and recoiled at what I read. I supposed I'd better speak to my doctor.

Chapter Six

I picked up the car at Clontarf and drove directly to Oxmantown Road. Before leaving for Donegal, Gabriel had given me his key and I'd agreed to look in on Number 9. I'd been dropping around now and then, checking the little house was secure, picking up any post and sending it on to him.

When I arrived at the redbrick mid-terrace and opened the hall door it was as I had left it, tidy enough, but the air was stale and there was a layer of dust over the surfaces. The living room and dining area were just inside the door – a brown sofa of creased and faded leather was opposite the empty fireplace, with an armchair to one side and a small TV set to the other. There were bookshelves too, crammed with paperbacks, sports autobiographies and history books, and a low coffee table in the centre of the living area. The dining area had a dark wooden table and four chairs and, as far as I knew, was never used by Gabriel for eating. He preferred to sit on the couch, his feet on the coffee table, with his plate held close to his chin. A kitchen extension had been shoehorned into the yard by previous owners and there was a downstairs bathroom.

I started by opening all of the windows. Then I vacuumed and dusted and set a fire, ready for Gabriel to put a match to when he arrived. I found some fresh bedclothes in his hot press, went to his room and changed the bedding. It had been a long time since I'd been under those bedclothes with him and changing them now seemed almost too intimate an act. I did it quickly and closed the bedroom door behind me. I called into the corner shop and bought bread, milk, rashers and eggs and a few other essentials. When I'd finished, it was after seven. I was sorry I hadn't time to make myself a sandwich before going to pick him up, but food would have to wait.

I felt hopeful as I drove back into town, though I wasn't quite sure what to hope for. I was afraid to put a name to it.

I parked my car in the Talbot Mall and walked the five minutes to Busáras, arriving shortly before seven-thirty.

Gabriel was already there, outside the wave-roofed building where the bus had disgorged its passengers, standing tall and straight. He had a holdall in one hand and a suitcase in the other, his donkey jacket turned up at the collar against a cool evening breeze that swirled and funnelled around the buses. His grey hair was neat and a five o'clock shadow was barely visible on his chin.

He looked healthy to me, a little leaner and more relaxed, and I wanted to say 'You're a sight for sore eyes' but I thought better of it.

"There you are," he said when I was a few feet from him.

"Hello, Gabriel." I leaned in and kissed his cheek and he half-hugged me with the arm that was carrying the holdall.

I stood back from him for a moment. "You look well anyway."

I smiled, he nodded.

"The car is this way." I moved to take his suitcase but he wouldn't let me.

"I'm grand," he said.

We began walking. I felt simultaneously elated at seeing him and disappointed, as though I'd expected something else, something altogether more demonstrative. He was reserved, cooler than I'd thought he'd be, or was that me?

"How did Bernadette take it?" I imagined his sister would be peeved to see him go back to Dublin.

I had found over the years that the further a person lived from the city the more likely they were to regard it as either a beacon of cosmopolitanism and employment or a heaving den of danger and wickedness.

"She didn't put up too much of a fight. I'm sure she was glad to have the room back."

He paused on Amiens Street outside a takeaway and appraised a sign offering pizza and chips for €6, then shook his head and walked on, his expression briefly like a child's who'd denied himself a treat at Lent.

"How've you been?" he asked. "Have you much work on?"

"A bit."

I told him about Marina Fernandez and the case against her and he listened in his quiet way, nodding at the details.

"Is there much longer in it?"

"A few days I think, but it's hard to know." There was always the possibility that an agreement could be reached between them, though I doubted that would happen in this case.

"And any developments with the other business, in the Bots?"

"The murder?"

"Was it?"

"I think so. I can't see how it could be anything else. Though your lot don't seem to be in too much of a hurry." By his lot, I had meant the gardaí who hadn't been in touch yet to ask me about what I'd seen.

"It only happened four days ago, Bea. They'll get to you soon enough." Despite retirement, he remained defensive of the force.

"The funeral is next Monday," I said.

He replied but a Luas tram trundled by while he was speaking and I couldn't hear what he said.

"Pardon?"

"I said you'll be wanting to go to that, the funeral."

"I will." I waited for him then to offer his company but he said no more.

We had reached the car park and I began searching in my purse for the ticket and coins to pay for it.

"Here." He produced a few euro coins from his pocket and held them out on his palm. I took them. He smiled at me.

"Thanks." I turned and fed the machine and we made our way to the car.

I unlocked the boot and he put his bags in and closed it. We took our seats.

"You must be hungry. Will we go somewhere for something to eat?" I started the engine and reversed out of the space. "Or maybe you're too tired for that?"

He gave me a look, as if to say 'Don't start that' but he didn't voice it. I thought perhaps he might have heard enough of that in Donegal.

We reached the barrier and I fed the ticket into the machine. I drove out onto the road.

"If it's all the same to you, I'd like to go to Walsh's. I've missed their pint." He meant a pub near his home in Stoneybatter. So he was still drinking.

"I thought it was too hipster for you."

He laughed. "All the same . . ."

"Walsh's it is." I wanted to say something then, something about how I'd missed him, about how great it was to have him back in Dublin, but I couldn't work out what words to use that wouldn't make me sound like I thought he owed me something.

"Do you want to drop your bags home first or . . .?"

"No need. They'll be grand in the boot."

While we drove, he told me about his life in Donegal, how he'd been watching what he ate with the help of Bernadette and "easing off on the pints".

"I've been over and back to Letterkenny hospital but I'm due back to the Mater on Monday."

So that was why he hadn't offered to go to the funeral with me.

"Anything . . .?"

"Not at all. Just a check-up."

He said it as though he was indifferent to it but I knew that couldn't be true. I knew that every visit to hospital would be a private worry for him.

There was a small crowd in the Stoneybatter pub when we arrived and a gentle buzz of conversation was back-dropped with the voice of Clive Everton talking snooker on a large TV. Gabriel glanced at the screen as we passed it but chose a seat out of its view. I took my coat off and sat down. He threw his jacket over the back of a chair and went up to the bar for menus. The food was as I remembered from our last visit with pan-fried this and foraged that and hand-cut the other. He rubbed his chin.

"I suppose I'd better be good," he said, though there was a question mark in his eyes and I thought he was looking for me to guide his choice. But I wasn't his sister.

He picked the grilled lamb with boiled baby potatoes and salad and a pint. I chose a soda water and lime and what I took to be a stew though it wasn't called that.

"I've had more stew than I need for a lifetime, that and cod poached in milk," he said.

I winced in sympathy.

"Invalid food she had me on."

"Well you look good on it if that's any consolation."

He smiled and I smiled back for a bit longer than intended. He was the first to glance away and I felt myself blushing. There was a silence. I searched my brain for something to say, something that would let him know I had missed him, that I cared about him. But he got there first.

"We've a lot of water under the bridge, haven't we, Bea?"

I braced myself. "A fair bit."

"And we're good friends now, aren't we?"

"We are, Gabriel."

"I was thinking about it a lot this last while, you know, up above home, and I wouldn't want to do anything that . . ."

The barman arrived then and put our drinks on the table.

"Where were you hiding yourself?" he said. "We haven't seen you in ages."

"Up in Donegal for a while but I'm back now." Gabriel lifted the pint to his lips and took a swallow.

The barman paused as though he thought there might be more information forthcoming then gave up when there wasn't.

"Good to see you back anyway," he said, and left us.

"I didn't feel like explaining," Gabriel said.

"It's nobody's business but your own." I sipped my drink. "You were saying something about Glenties?"

"Yes, well, just that I had a lot of time to think up there." He took another sup. "And sometimes you can see things better, you know, when you're far away."

"Can you?" I didn't dare look at him. Instead I watched the cubes of ice in my glass, floating and dissolving at their edges.

"I think so."

"And?" This was difficult for him – I knew by the way he was picking his words and holding his pint glass and letting it go again without lifting it. And it was difficult for me too. I felt I knew what he was going to say and I wasn't sure I liked it.

"And just that I won't be ruining that – what we have as friends – I won't be bothering you anymore. I want you know that." He gulped a mouthful of stout then.

Bothering me? What kind of a woman was I that he could think that? I didn't know what to say.

"You know how fond I am of you, Gabriel . . ."

"Fond, yes, I know that. I've always known that. That's what I'm trying to say – we have a great friendship, a great fondness for each other, and I don't want you thinking I need anything else from you. I don't – not anymore. I appreciate what we have and I want to keep it the way it is."

"Well, that's clear anyway." I still couldn't bring myself

to look at him. I thought he might see into me, see what I was really feeling. What was it my mother used to say? That ship has sailed. And hadn't I stood like a fool on the dock and waved it off?

He swallowed back the remainder of his pint.

"I think I'll have another one of these. Celebrate my homecoming." He signalled to the barman.

Another pint was delivered and we clinked our glasses. "Welcome home," I said.

Our food arrived then. Gabriel's lamb was on a wooden board with a dangerous-looking knife, a side salad perched at its edge, and the boiled potatoes in a tin bucket. My stew was in a deep bowl, set into a plate with a chunk of sourdough bread on the side, more manageable at least.

"Ah, Jaysus," Gabriel said when the barman had left. "Could they not have put it on a plate?"

I took a spoonful of stew and tried to quell the ache in my stomach. He picked up his knife and fork and then put them down again.

"Have I been . . . Is it all right?"

"Of course." I mustered up a smile.

He speared a lettuce leaf with the tip of his fork and popped it into his mouth. "Right so. Good."

Chapter Seven

Saturday, February 25th

I lay on my back in the centre of the bed and thought about Gabriel. It was good, I decided, that he had been clear, that he had spelt out the parameters of our relationship. No, I corrected myself, our friendship. It was helpful to know that I need no longer worry about any misunderstandings between us. I would be in no danger of seeing that twinkle in his eye again. There would be no more complications. Ours would be a fraternal relationship. That was clear. Crystal clear. Life would be simpler for both of us and I would just have to learn to ignore that small voice that spoke to me about something I'd lost that I'd never quite had in the first place.

There had been no more discussion about it once we'd eaten our meal though we'd stayed on a while in the pub, talking about Paddy Hogan and what happened to him. And though he couldn't go to the funeral with me, Gabriel had agreed when I suggested we take a walk in the Botanic Gardens this morning. I'd dropped him to Oxmantown Road and handed him back his spare key. There'd been no reason for me to hold onto it. He'd taken it a little reluctantly, looking at it in the palm of his hand for a moment, before putting it in his pocket.

"Do you want tea or anything?" he'd asked as he opened the car door.

"Best let you settle in," I'd said.

And I'd watched him through the rear-view mirror as he opened the boot and took out his bags, closed it and put the suitcase down on the footpath near his hall door so that he could wave me off. I'd beeped the horn as cheerfully as I could and I had driven away with a small pain to the left of my solar plexus.

The Botanic Gardens was quiet when I drove into the car park, to the left of the main entrance gates, shortly after ten-thirty. I supposed that it was the cold wind and the spit of rain in the air that had kept visitors away and encouraged me to park there instead of on St Mobhi Drive.

I waited in my car for Gabriel to arrive and when he pulled up close by I got out and walked over to him.

"Thanks," was the first thing he said to me as he got out of his car, "for the fire and the bread and all that."

"You're welcome."

"No, really, you're a good friend, Bea."

That was who I was now – the "good friend" and that was who I would stay. I didn't respond or look at him and, getting no encouragement to continue in that vein, he said no more. I was relieved. It was a way of speaking that I wasn't used to from him – at least not when he was sober. And I wondered whether heart conditions made people more grateful for life and, by extension, more grateful for the people around them.

"You haven't been back inside the Palm House since, did you say?"

He was watching me and I knew he could sense my apprehension. I shook my head.

"It'll be grand," he said.

We made no pretence of going for a walk around the gardens and went briskly with our heads down against the wind, straight for the Palm House. At 65 feet, it was the tallest of the glasshouses in the gardens and was at the centre of a complex with two single-storey wings, one to the left and one to the right. Though I was wearing a warm coat I was grateful when we stepped inside, out of the chill and into the tropics. We entered through the Orchid House wing, to the right of the Palm House, the one where I'd read the closed sign two days earlier. I led the way through the structure, past rows of potted plants, some with delicate blossoms and muted colours, others waxen and gaudy, until we reached the connecting door. It was made of heavy, painted wood with a spring device at the top so that when we stepped through it and into the Palm House, it shut slowly and gently behind us.

"This way." I walked down three granite steps and led him round to the right, to the spot where Paddy Hogan's body had been found, directly below the cream-painted wrought-iron walkway.

"Just here," I said.

I knew the spot though there was no evidence left behind to prove it. The flagstones had been washed clean but I could still see him lying there, a red pool expanding out from him. The air around us was warm and moist with the cloying scent of some sweet flower I couldn't name. I shivered despite the heat.

"You okay?" Gabriel asked, putting his hand on my arm.

"I'm fine," I said.

There was no one else in the glasshouse. Gabriel stood and looked at the walkway for a long time. He rubbed his chin and pulled as his earlobe instinctively.

"Have you ever been up there?"

I said I hadn't. He took a few paces back and forward and from one side to the other, still looking up, until he found what he wanted.

"See it there? The door." He pointed to a door high up at the end of the walkway.

"Come on," he said.

I followed him out through another door which brought us into the grey stone lobby area I'd come in through on the day Paddy Hogan died. I shivered again at the memory of rushing in and I heard again that piercing scream.

"Let's try this direction," Gabriel said.

There was one magnolia-painted wall to our right with a window, effectively a room within a room and what looked like office space inside. The wall of this room stopped before it met the external stone of the building, creating a narrow corridor along its side.

"It must be here somewhere," he said.

I followed him down the corridor and around a corner to a door. He turned the handle and it opened. There was a steep staircase beyond it with another door at the top. We went up. That door, too, was unlocked and it swung out onto the walkway. And there it was before me – the last place Paddy Hogan had been alive. I reached for the handrail. It was tacky under my fingers, and there were shreds left sticking to it of Garda crime-scene tape that had been torn away when they had finished their work. The air was even warmer now and my skin felt as clammy as I imagined it might in a tropical rainforest. We took a few steps forward and stood above the spot where Paddy Hogan's body had lain. My head spun a little when I looked at the drop.

"See that." I indicated a patch of scratched paint on the handrail.

He leaned forward, bending himself over the rail.

"Careful!" I said.

"How tall was he?"

I closed my eyes and tried to imagine what his height might be but found it impossible. I guessed. "About the same as you."

He nodded and leaned against the rail again. "Belt buckle maybe," he said, running his fingers over the scratches.

I tried to picture it. Could Paddy have been leaning out, checking the irrigation and simply lost his balance? I watched Gabriel as he moved steadily along the walkway and back again. It would be difficult for someone to fall over those railings. But what if a person was reaching out, checking an irrigation nozzle – couldn't he easily tip off balance? Or a person could have a dizzy spell or a hangover or something. But then what about Paddy Hogan's grazed and bloody knuckles?

"Could he have grazed his knuckles on the way down?" I asked aloud but answered my own question. "But what could he graze them off? There's nothing nearby. What about when he hit the ground?"

"I don't think so – it wouldn't make sense," Gabriel said.

We were silent for a while and I almost expected to see

myself and Constance Anderson and George Delaney below looking over Paddy Hogan's body. It was a strange sensation, disorientating.

"If he didn't fall and he didn't jump, then someone must have pushed him," I said.

"It can't have been too easy to get him over." He leaned out again and looked down at the flagstones below. "Whoever it was must have been strong."

"And they must have known where to find him." I pointed out the places where strands of Trumpet Vine looked shorter than others. "Those must have been torn away by Paddy." As I spoke I had an image of him thrashing in the air, trying to grip something, anything, that might stop his fall. "He must have been terrified." I felt dizzy at the thought of it.

"Not a good way to go, definitely not." He leaned out again, assessing the drop. "Forty feet or more, I'd say."

I put my hand on his arm to bring him back, then we stood for a moment looking over the tops of the tropical palms, the giant bamboo, the banana plants and the bromeliads. The pathways below were obscured in places where broad leaves from one plant met the foliage of another. Could he have seen someone coming? If he did, and he was frightened of them, would he not have had time to go back down the stairs? It was possible he had not seen anyone. Or if he had and he stayed where he was, could that mean he saw only a familiar face, someone from whom he had perceived no threat?

"If there was anything else here the lads will have got it," Gabriel said, turning toward the door to go back down the stairs.

I was sweating now under the curved glass roof.

"Do you think it could have been an accident?" I asked.

He turned back to me and was about to answer when the door opened.

"What do you think you're doing up here?" It was George Delaney. "You shouldn't be here unsupervised." He spoke sharply. Then he noticed me standing behind Gabriel. "Oh, it's you. Beatrice, isn't it?" He looked confused. "You really shouldn't be up here, you know."

"Sorry, we just wanted to . . ." What did we want? I thought our actions must look macabre to him – rubberneckers at the scene of a crime.

He shook his head. "This door is supposed to be locked." He held it open for us to pass, glanced backwards at the walkway for a moment, then closed the door, produced a key, turned it and followed us down the stairs. He locked the door at the bottom too.

I waited for him to finish.

"Have you heard anything?" I asked.

"Nothing. The guards were here for a couple of days, forensics and that – photographs – and then they all left." He looked at me with his hazel eyes and the furrows of his brow deepened. "We're all supposed to get on with it – like as if nothing happened." He sounded bewildered by that and he turned his confusion into anger at Gabriel and me. "This isn't a peepshow, you know."

"I know that, I just wanted to . . . understand," I said.

He shook his head. "There's no understanding something like that." He made a gesture with the door key in the direction of the stairs then put the key in his pocket and began walking down the corridor.

We followed him.

"You had vandals the other day," I said.

"What? You mean the glass panes? Yeah, very disheartening," he said.

"Does it happen often?" Gabriel asked.

"Not in a long time. Senseless really, and a bugger to fix." He turned left and in through the main door back into the Palm House without saying goodbye.

We left by the back exit and made our way, quickly against heavier rain, to the little coffee shop behind the visitor centre. I liked it better than the large café with its stretch of glass looking out on the gardens, now half full with visitors who, I assumed, had opted to eat instead of trudging around in the cold and wet.

The coffee shop was quiet. We sat in the corner with tea and scones. I noticed that Gabriel took only one when he would have taken two or three before.

"What did you make of George Delaney?" I asked as he put the merest lick of butter and then jam onto the top half of his scone. He took a bite and then a slurp of tea before answering.

"Not sure. It sounded like he thought Paddy Hogan had jumped." There was jam on his chin and I handed him a napkin.

"I know – the way he said 'something like that', as though it was obvious." I watched him, waiting for his verdict.

"You'd want to be wilfully blind to think that," he said.

I nodded, relieved that he felt the same as I did, that he couldn't have fallen, that if he'd jumped he wouldn't have clung to the vines or had grazes on his knuckles.

He finished off his scone with another bite. I picked at

mine. It had too much soda in it. I was sorry I hadn't chosen the éclair instead but I was trying to set a good example for Gabriel.

"Were you able to get hold of Matt McCann?" I asked.

"No luck – I'm told he's on a few days' off." He paused to drink more tea. "Can I ask you something?"

I nodded and prepared myself.

"Do you think it's wise to be getting yourself involved in all this?" He knew me better than I knew myself sometimes.

"I promised myself I wouldn't and . . . I didn't find him on purpose, Gabriel, but I *did* find him. How can I not be involved?"

"You could try making your statement to the lads and then getting on with your life like an ordinary person?"

The way he said it, I couldn't tell whether he was making a suggestion or mocking me a little. I drained the last of the tea into my cup. "I do try to behave like an 'ordinary person', Gabriel, but . . ."

He sighed. "All right then, I'll call Matt again."

Chapter Eight

Monday, 27th February

I was glad that the Labour Court hearing was not due to start until two. It meant I was free to go to Paddy Hogan's funeral in Our Lady of Dolours church, opposite the Botanic Gardens. The pyramid-shaped church was vast and impossible to fill but there was a large crowd at it. The funeral was simple, with old-fashioned hymns of bygone times more suited to a man in his seventies – "Sweet Heart of Jesus", "How Great Thou Art" and "Hail Queen of Heaven". There was no eulogy for him and no glossy leaflet with his photo on the front. And, though the priest made an effort to individualise the service with a sprinkling of personal detail about Paddy in his homily, it was obvious he was talking about someone who rarely showed himself in the church and whom he didn't know. As his workmates carried his coffin back down the centre aisle and out, "Amazing Grace" was sung. Two women followed behind – his mother Rita Hogan and his sister Ava. They clung to each other, crying into their hankies, shuffling forward, a haze of incense around them.

Outside, in the cold of the car park, the pair stood close

by the hearse, the back of which was open showing Paddy's coffin and the many wreaths around and on top of it. I wondered if he'd grown any of the flowers himself. Though the priest had made no mention of how he'd died, there was talk now among mourners as they lingered to offer their condolences to the family. I recognised among the group a few familiar faces from the gardens and I saw Constance Anderson standing at the edge of the crowd. I supposed she was there for the same reason I was – to show respect for the man we'd found and see him laid to rest. There were no reporters that I could see and I wondered if that meant the word had gone around that the death was a suicide.

I joined the queue to offer my condolences to the family. Behind me, I heard one woman talking to another.

"I heard he leapt," she said. "Very sad, very sad indeed."

"Of course, he was never quite right," her companion replied.

I wanted to tell them to be quiet and to stop spreading lies but I didn't. When my turn came, I offered my hand to Mrs Hogan.

"I'm very sorry about your son."

"Who's this now?" she asked her daughter who was standing next to her.

The woman, in her mid-thirties, with thin dark hair to her shoulders and pale, bloated cheeks, shook her head.

"I don't know, Mammy."

I told her my name and said I'd found Paddy on the day he died.

"Barrington? Barrington, is it?" Mrs Hogan said, a little too loudly for a funeral.

Other people stopped talking and stared at us.

She narrowed her bird-eyes to look at me and I thought the look was a very hard one.

"And you found our Paddy?"

I said I had, along with two others and she nodded at me. Before she could say any more, a man came forward to speak to her.

"Rita," he said.

"Ah, Liam!" She put her arms out and he hugged her.

I walked away and stood for a while watching the crowd. I was about to leave when I felt a tug at my sleeve. It was Ava Hogan.

"Mammy wants you to call by some time to her . . . she'd like to hear . . . They haven't told her the details, but she deserves to know . . . He was her son." She sounded sad and angry and defiant but in that muted way of someone in the depths of grief.

"Of course I will. Where?"

She told me her phone number and gave me the address and I keyed both into my phone. She went back to her mother and the mourners began to get into their cars. They would wait for the hearse and the family's rented limousine to pull away so they could follow it. They were, the priest had said, going to stop for a minute outside the gates of the Botanic Gardens before making their way to Glasnevin Cemetery.

I left to prepare myself for work.

On the DART to Lansdowne Road I remembered that Gabriel had been to the Mater hospital in the morning. I got my phone out and sent him a text.

Hi Gabriel, how did the hospital go?

He wasn't long coming back with: **Grand, talk to you later**. I put my phone away and smiled to myself. What else had I expected him to say? His head could be falling off and he'd tell me he was grand.

At the Labour Court, Joe Waldron introduced his witness, Rosalind Griffin – a graphologist and document examiner. She was tall and thin and wore a large pair of glasses which she pushed up her nose at intervals though they didn't appear to be slipping. She told the committee she had a diploma in forensic graphology from the Cambridge Graphology Institute and qualifications in handwriting and forensic document examination. She also said she'd been accepted as an expert witness in numerous High Court cases.

"What does document examination involve?" Mr Waldron prompted.

"It's about the analysis and evaluation of documents to ascertain possible forgery and/or identify authenticity. By examining handwriting, I can review documents and establish, for example, if a signature is forged. Or as in this case, I can investigate line sequence, establish the writing instrument and ascertain whether it is consistent across a page or date."

Mr Waldron was quick to simplify. "So you can tell whether the same pen was used in entries on the same day or whether different pens were used?"

"Yes, I can."

"Yes. Now turning to Dr Dunboyne's diary – what where your findings in relation to it? If you could summarise, please?"

"Well, in summary, having examined the diary, I found that certain entries on particular days were made at a different time or date to other entries and that across a series of dates, these particular entries appear to have been made simultaneously using the same instrument."

"Which means?" Mr Waldron was keen that the witness spelt it out for the committee.

"That information was added to days in this diary at a different time to when earlier information was recorded, specifically information related to Nurse F, and that additional information was likely, with a high degree of probability, to have been added at the same time across a number of dates."

Ms Griffin went on to explain how she came to that conclusion based on ink type, handwriting flow analysis and indentation. The committee took copious notes. Mr Waldron looked very pleased.

"Thank you, Ms Griffin," he said. "Would you mind answering questions from Mr Taylor?"

There was a pause – long enough for me to stretch my fingers, which were beginning to ache.

Mr Taylor gave Ms Griffin a wide smile.

"You mentioned the Cambridge Graphology Institute as an institution you studied with?"

"Among others, yes."

"May I just pass these around?" he asked the chairwoman, waving a sheaf of pages.

She nodded and he passed them to everyone sitting at the table.

"This is a printout from the website of the Cambridge Graphology Institute – you will see that it's not actually in Cambridge. It is not affiliated in any way with any of the well-known colleges there." He looked at Ms Griffin.

"Is that a question?" she asked. "If it is, the answer is no."

"And neither is it a physical college. It is in fact an office over a shop in Eastbourne, Sussex. It offers distance learning courses."

Miriam Lynch raised an eyebrow and he smirked.

"Yes, it does," Ms Griffin said. "And it's affiliated to the British Institute of Graphologists. I also have a BSc from UCD here in Dublin. And I'm a member of the Chartered Society of Forensic Sciences."

Mr Taylor shook his head. "I really don't think I need to say any more than 'distance learning course'." His voice was dripping with contempt.

Ms Lynch nodded. "Mr Waldron, is there anything you'd like to add?"

"Only that Ms Griffin is a well-respected expert in her field and has given evidence at the High Court."

"In that case, I think we may adjourn for the day. Thank you, Ms Griffin." She looked around the room. "I'll see you all here next Thursday morning."

On the way home, I called my GP and got an appointment for six fifteen. My hands were sore and I thought my fingers looked puffy. I had to admit that I was worried. I picked up my car at Clontarf train station and drove the half mile to the surgery.

Dr Bernie Lewis was kind but after she examined me she didn't mince her words.

"I'm sorry but this looks like repetitive motion syndrome, Beatrice." She rubbed her fingers across my knuckles. "Your job's doing this to you."

"But . . . I have to work," I said. I'd hoped it was something temporary and easily dealt with.

"On the positive side we've caught it early so we have a good chance of getting on top of it. I'm going to prescribe some anti-inflammatories. Take them twice a day and rest your hands as much as possible. I'll see you in a month." She gave me a couple of leaflets to read.

"You've been a stenographer a long time," she said as I was leaving.

I wanted to tell her I was only in my late fifties and I wasn't ready to finish work yet. Besides, what would I do?

I filled the prescription in the late-night pharmacy and told myself I'd take the tablets but keep working.

At home I called Gabriel and told him about the funeral and the request from Ava Hogan that I visit her and her mother. And I asked him about his visit to the Mater hospital.

"What did the doctor say to you?" I was hoping for a little more than just "grand".

"He was very happy – blood pressure, heart rate, everything was fine. Told me to keep up the good work." He sounded proud of himself.

"I'm delighted for you, Gabriel." I wanted to say that I was relieved, too, to know he was well. I didn't mention my own problem. There was no need for that.

Chapter Nine

Thursday, March 2nd

Three days later, on the DART going to Lansdowne Road, the funeral and Paddy Hogan were on my mind. His death made me want to talk to Marina Fernandez. I had a feeling, when I saw her sitting in the hearing room, that she was thinking it was her last chance to fight for herself. I wanted to tell her that it wasn't. I wanted to tell her that it would be okay no matter what happened. I wanted to say "This is just a small episode in your life" and "You will have better days, you will have other chances".

I thought again of Laurence, who died by his own hand, and an old longing came back to me, that deep desire to go back and stop him before he ended his life. The feelings, I thought, were resurrected because of Paddy Hogan's death and I wondered if there was a part of me that felt it was suicide, a part of me that recognised it somehow at a subconscious level. But no, that wasn't right, that wasn't logical and, besides, Gabriel didn't believe it.

When I arrived at the Labour Court at twenty to ten the hearing room was empty save for one woman, middle-aged, sitting at the end of the long table. Her face was round and her lids were as heavy as a sleepy child's. Her straight blond hair rested on rounded shoulders and, overall, she gave the impression of someone who would rather not be seen.

When the legal teams arrived, Reginald Taylor stopped briefly to speak to the woman and I thought I noticed a sharp glance between her and Marina Fernandez.

Once the committee had settled, the young woman was asked to give evidence and she moved from her seat to one close to the committee.

Frances Parr was introduced as a nurse manager and former colleague of Ms Fernandez. She detailed her credentials and experience in various nursing homes.

"You work at High Hill Care Centre at present, Ms Parr?" Mr Taylor asked.

"Yes." She spoke with her bottom lip slightly protruding which gave the impression of petulance.

"And you were nurse manager while Ms Fernandez was employed there, between June and October 2015, is that correct?"

"Yes."

"And on October 8th, I believe you witnessed something. Can you tell us about it?"

"I saw Marina taking money from a patient's locker."

"Was that," he consulted his notes, "Mrs Claire Fitzmaurice's locker?"

"Yes. Lovely lady – she'd been with us a long time."

"Can you talk us through the details please, Ms Parr? What time was this?"

"It was in the evening and I was on my late drugs round. I'd left St Angela's ward and was going on to the next room when I realised I hadn't given Mrs Clinton her blood-pressure medicine . . . She'd been in the loo you see so I'd missed her."

"Yes. What did you do then?"

"I turned the trolley around and went back into the ward. I had to pass Mrs Fitzmaurice's bed to get to Mrs Clinton and I saw her then, Marina Fernandez, down on her hunkers with the bedside locker open and money in her hand."

There was a sound of disgust from Marina Fernandez and Caroline Brophy shushed her.

"Did you ask her what she was doing?"

"Not right away – I was in a hurry to finish the drugs round. But the following day at the beginning of the shift I did."

"And what did she say?"

"She denied it ever happened. But I saw her with my own eyes."

Ms Fernandez was shaking her head and staring at the witness.

"What did you do then?" Mr Taylor asked.

"I reported it to my boss, Michael Birch, and he decided it would be best if Marina was asked to leave. She left a short while later."

He turned to the committee. "Mr Birch is willing to give evidence if necessary but he's out of the country at present. There is a signed affidavit at Page 95 from him in your booklet. I don't think there's any need to read it into the record."

The committee members nodded and turned the pages of their booklet. Their lips moved as they read the document and they nodded in unison when they'd finished.

I took the chance to stretch out my fingers. They didn't feel as painful as before and I couldn't see any swelling. I supposed the combination of medication and a few days' rest had helped.

"Ms Parr, if you wouldn't mind staying where you are and answering questions from my opposite number?"

He nodded across the table at Joe Waldron who turned toward her.

"Ms Parr, do you believe that taking money from a patient's locker amounts to theft?"

"Yes."

"Then why did you not call the guards?"

"I wanted to but Mr Birch said no." She looked down at her hands.

"What reason did he give for not wanting to call them?"

"He said it would be damaging to the reputation of High Hill. We have an excellent reputation." She directed the last remark at the committee.

"Tell me about this theft."

He went through every detail of what she'd said again, where she was, how his client looked.

"And tell the committee, did the resident, Claire Fitzmaurice, complain about it?"

"No, but I wouldn't have expected her to. She has early-stage dementia and her memory is unreliable."

"Her family, then, did they complain?"

She shook her head. "She has no family . . . At least, they don't visit her."

"So the only evidence we have that this supposed theft ever occurred is that you saw it?"

She didn't answer.

"Ms Parr?"

"The records we keep of residents' possessions – they showed money was missing." There was a defiant tone in her voice now.

"And who keeps those records?"

"I do. It's my job to keep an eye on these things."

"I see." He glanced at the committee and back at the witness again. "Now, you said you were too busy to confront Ms Fernandez on the evening you witnessed this supposed theft?"

"It was very busy, as I say, and it was nearing the end of my shift . . ."

"When you did speak to Ms Fernandez, what did she say?"

"I already said. She denied it."

"She said something else though, didn't she? She accused you of something?"

"I don't see what that's . . ." She was blushing now.

"Ms Parr?"

"She accused me of being drunk."

"Had you been drinking on the job?"

"No way!"

He paused then to let the impact of the accusation sink in.

"Can you all turn to page fourteen in the blue booklet, please?"

A sound of rustling began and then stopped.

"This letter is dated October 13th, 2015. That is your signature at the end, Ms Parr?"

"Yes, it is."

"This is a reference supplied by you to Ms Fernandez which she subsequently gave to Chapels Nursing Home." He turned to the committee. "My client tells me she left

High Hill because Ms Parr had made it an unpleasant place to work and there were plenty of other jobs available." He turned back to Ms Parr. "You commend her work, her timekeeping and her care of residents. Where in this letter have you told prospective employers about her supposed thieving?"

The witness made a kind of growling noise.

"Pardon?" Mr Waldron said.

"I didn't. I just wanted to get rid of her."

He smiled then, knowing he had scored a point.

"Yes, she caught you drinking and you wanted her gone."

"No! That's not true at all!"

Mr Taylor intervened then.

"This is unacceptable. This woman came here to help the committee, not to be accused of wrongdoing."

"I have no more questions," Mr Waldron said.

Mr Taylor addressed Frances Parr. "Ms Parr, throughout your career has there ever been an occasion when you were reprimanded for drinking at work? Or indeed when you drank at work?"

"Absolutely not."

"Thank you." He turned to the chairwoman. "I think your diary allows for summing up next Monday, the 6th?"

Miriam Lynch checked her diary and spoke to the other committee members.

"Yes, I'm afraid that's the next available date with a start time of noon." She nodded to each side, rose and left the room with her colleagues.

On Thursday afternoon, having made an arrangement with Ava, I sought out St Teresa's Road and found it was a short terrace of two-storey red-and-cream-bricked houses. When I turned the corner, I was ambushed by its likeness to the buildings on Gabriel's Oxmantown Road and by a longing I didn't wish to name. The houses faced onto a granite wall, topped with a railing, beyond which was the Botanic Gardens. Number 15 had a green door with glass panels in it through which I could see another door inside. When I rang the bell, the inner door opened and Ava Hogan, as pale and drawn as at the funeral, stood looking at me for a moment before she reached for the handle of the outer door to let me in.

"Hello," I said without moving.

"Ms Barrington. Hi."

"Beatrice."

"Come in, she's been waiting. I'm Ava, her daughter." I wanted to say that I knew that, that we had met at the funeral. But then I recalled the blind haze that takes hold after a death, the blur of a funeral that can be like walking through a dreamscape and how difficult it can be to remember afterwards those seen or spoken to.

I stepped over the threshold and shut the door behind me. The hallway was narrow and dark, its walls covered in green, embossed paper that looked as though it had been painted over many times, smoothing out the pattern. There was a faint smell of boiled cabbage.

I removed my coat and she took it from me and laid it across the dark, wooden banister.

She took a step toward the front room, then stopped and turned to me.

"Mammy's very upset, you understand. She thinks a stranger like you shouldn't know things about her Paddy's end that she doesn't know herself." She looked at me to ensure I understood that there might be a barb in my welcome. "I know that doesn't make any sense but . . ."

I nodded and she walked ahead, leading me through a door on the left into a dimly lit front room.

Rita Hogan was sitting in an armchair close to an open, peat briquette fire. She was wearing navy nylon trousers and a heavy grey cardigan, at the collar of which I could see a high-necked blouse. I guessed that she was somewhere in her early eighties. Her grey, permed head moved slightly from side to side like a bobble toy that had been very gently shaken. Nearby, the mantelpiece was cluttered with Mass cards, images of the Sacred Heart and the Virgin Mary offering their consolation. There was a rectangular mirror above them, in which was reflected a mustard-velvet couch that sat under the window. The window itself was framed with heavy brown curtains. And though the mirror caught what light it could, the room was dim, as though it too was in mourning.

I extended my hand and Mrs Hogan stilled herself and took it. There was no warmth in the gesture.

"You'll have tea," she said, pointing toward an armchair opposite her.

I felt it had been positioned there especially for my inquisition. I sat. Between us a low, round table was draped with a white, oversized tablecloth, awaiting the tea things.

"I'll just wet the pot," Ava said and left the room.

"Quickly now, I need to talk to you. Close that door," Rita Hogan said.

Startled, I got up and closed the door. What might she have to say that she didn't want her daughter to hear?

"Now," she said as I sat down, "my Ava is . . . easily upset. She was always a delicate child. It wouldn't be good for her to be hearing all the details about Paddy. I don't want her to know everything. She couldn't cope, you understand?"

"Yes."

"But I'm his mother and I want to know everything. I'm entitled to know everything. I want to be able to see him in his last moments – they're all that's left to me."

I took a deep breath and began. I told her how I'd heard the scream and then run into the Palm House and found him. I told her who was with me and what we did next, how the paramedics came and then the gardaí.

"He used to bring me flowers from the Orchid House, you know. He loved those orchids. He was terrible like his father that way."

She leaned forward then and threw a briquette onto the fire, creating pinheads of light which sparked and faded.

"Tell me how he looked lying there – was he smiling?"

"Mrs Hogan, I . . ."

"Tell me. It'll help me with the prayers."

I didn't quite understand how it could, but I was about to go on when the door began to open and Mrs Hogan put her hand up for me to be quiet. Ava came through carrying a tray. She unloaded everything onto the table between us including a plate of chocolate biscuits. She poured the tea and offered me a cup. It shook in its saucer as she handed it to me.

"Would you ever get those Mikado biscuits for me?" Mrs Hogan said.

"What's wrong with the chocolate?"

"Please, Ava. I have a longing for them. They're in the press over the fridge."

"I know where they are." Ava sounded peevish, aware she was being sent on an errand to get her out of the way. But she left the room.

"Tell me – otherwise you're no use to me. Was he smiling?"

"No, there was no smile." I had seen the side of his face and remembered his open mouth now. I could almost hear the roar that must have come out of him as he fell.

"Did he look frightened?" She gripped the arm of her chair, bracing herself for my answer.

Had he looked frightened? What was the right answer to that?

I shook my head. "I couldn't say. It's hard to know . . . There was a lot of . . ."

"Blood, is it?"

"Yes."

She seemed satisfied with the response and was about to ask another question when Ava returned.

"Now, there's your Mikados," she said, and put the biscuits on the edge of the table.

"Oh thanks, love." Mrs Hogan nodded at her but made no effort to open the packet.

Ava poured herself a cup of tea and sat on the couch. She watched us, waiting for our conversation to continue. I said nothing, feeling that Mrs Hogan would admonish me if I did. The old woman didn't speak. I drank my tea.

"I'm after missing all that," Ava said resentfully. "Will you tell me what happened? I want to know." She gave me an imploring look and I wanted to tell her.

"I'm too tired to listen to it all again," Mrs Hogan said, shaking her head.

"But, Mammy . . ."

"Would you have me upset? I'm too tired, I said, I'm worn out."

Ava glanced at me and then briefly toward the ceiling, resigned to her mother's wishes.

"I should go."

Out of politeness rather than thirst, I finished the tea and then stood up.

Mrs Hogan didn't look at me or say goodbye. I thought as I left the room that she had wilted in her chair and I wondered whether I was right to have been so candid.

Ava closed the door behind us as we went out into the hall and then she gripped my forearm.

"When you found him, was he still alive?"

"No, I'm sorry, he wasn't."

She squeezed tighter. "And, tell me this, did it look to you like he'd jumped?"

"Well, I can't . . ."

"Tell me."

"I didn't think so."

"I knew he hadn't." She seemed to be appeased and took her hand off my arm.

I took my coat from the banister and put it on. She opened the inside door and then the outer door.

"You might call again sometime?" she said.

"If you want me to."

She looked at me for a moment. "You want to know what happened to him, too, don't you? I can see it in you."

"I want the truth to come out, Ava. That's what I want."

She nodded. "And you'll tell us if you find out anything?"
"All right."
"Anything at all."
I nodded and left.

Were the gardaí telling them that Paddy Hogan had jumped? I couldn't understand why they would be told such a thing. Was it simply an easy way to put an end to an investigation that the gardaí didn't have the resources to pursue or think was worth pursing? No, that couldn't be right. That would never happen. Would it? It must be just that the family were being told all avenues were being followed, that nothing had been ruled out yet. That would make more sense.

Once I was out in the light, I felt that what had happened in the house was strange – that I had been drawn into some sort of game the two women were playing. Mrs Hogan was hungry for every detail of her son's end. I supposed it was natural for her to want to fill the void of not knowing with all the minutiae she could glean from me but the experience had made me slightly nauseous and the claustrophobic atmosphere in the house was soporific.

And what was I to make of Ava, a grown woman, still cowed by her mother? Was she a little bit "delicate" as her mother had put it? She certainly didn't look delicate. But I couldn't say either that she came across as a very bright woman. There was something amiss. She had a vulnerability about her.

I walked along the road in a daze, to where I'd parked my car on Prospect Avenue. I sat in the driving seat and watched people going in and out of the Gravediggers' pub, next to the back gate of Glasnevin Cemetery. I felt an overwhelming urge to sleep. It was a while before I could start up the engine.

* * *

When I got home I called Gabriel. I wanted to tell him about the visit. He answered but his phone was making a whistling sound, as though he was walking in a strong breeze, and I couldn't hear what he was saying. I had to ask him to repeat himself.

"Hold on, I'll just . . ." he said and I stopped speaking. "Is that better?"

"Yes. Where are you?"

"In the park. I'm standing under a tree now, back to the wind."

I could picture him then on Chesterfield Avenue, the main artery through the Phoenix Park, his back against the generous trunk of a horse chestnut. He must have been on the way to one of his favourite pubs when I interrupted him.

"Are you going to Ryan's?"

"Ah no. Too early."

"Who *are* you?" This was a man who, before his illness, charted his day by the visits he made in the morning, afternoon and evening, to the pubs in his vicinity.

He laughed. "How were the Hogans?"

"Intense."

I told him all that had been said and the strange dynamic between Mrs Hogan and her daughter.

"I'm not sure what to make of them," I said.

"Grief can do funny things to people though, Bea."

"I know it can. But they seemed so wrapped up in each other yet so alone too, Gabriel. Do you know what I mean?"

"I think so."

"And it's as if no one from the guards is telling them

anything. They're being fed lines about Paddy having jumped. We know that's not right, Gabriel."

"Very doubtful, anyhow," he said.

"I'd really like to be able to help them if I can. I want to help them. I think I should."

He sighed then. "I thought you might say that . . . I was speaking to Matt last night . . ."

"And?"

"He says a Detective Inspector Rebecca Maguire is in charge out of Ballymun Station. He gave me her number. I'll text it to you."

"Do you know her?" I was hopeful he would have worked with her, too, and might be able to get some information that could help the Hogans.

"Afraid not. All I know is she has a reputation as a tough nut."

I wasn't sure what that meant. I had never heard him use it about any of the male officers he knew. Was it just that she didn't take any nonsense from "the lads"?

"There's a couple of others up there that I do know, though. I'll see if I can get anything out of them."

"It would be great if you could, thanks." I hung up and the phone beeped seconds later with Maguire's mobile phone number.

Chapter Ten

Friday, March 3rd

Shortly after ten I phoned Det Ins Rebecca Maguire on the number Gabriel had given me. That was my first mistake.

"Who is this?" she said, as though no one ever dared phone her on her mobile.

"My name is Beatrice Barrington. I was to make a witness statement about the death of Patrick Hogan." I waited. No response. "In the Botanic Gardens?"

"Oh, yes . . ."

"I was one of the people who found the body."

"Who gave you this number?"

"A friend . . ." I wasn't about to drag Matt McCann into things.

"You better come in then. You can call the station to make an appointment with me."

Her tone suggested I was already a great inconvenience to her and coming in to see her would be even more tiresome. Though I was tempted to hang up right then, I said a polite thank-you and goodbye, phoned the station and arranged to come in at lunchtime.

* * *

Ballymun, a suburb north of the Botanic Gardens, had been transformed when its high-rise towers were demolished. The concrete blocks had made way for compact council houses, relatively low-rise apartments and glossy glass offices. But it also had a multi-lane road running through its centre that, despite the shiny new buildings, gave the place an air of desolation. I parked my car outside a funeral home and walked the hundred yards to the Garda Station. The modern, granite, plaster and glass, four-storey office was marked out by a large aerial on top of its roof and by an old-fashioned black streetlamp, with a blue-glass top emblazoned with the Garda Síochána gold-and-blue symbol. It stood next to a heavy metal gate that led into the car park at the back of the building. The station's pedestrian entrance was further along and side-on to the road. I walked past three windows shut away from the world by ugly, vertical blinds and I went in through glass double doors to the public counter.

"I have an appointment with Rebecca Maguire," I told the young man who was sitting at a desk behind a large sheet of toughened glass. He furrowed his brow.

"You mean *Detective Inspector* Rebecca Maguire?" He emphasised her title.

I nodded.

"Your name?"

I told him and he wrote it down, mouthing it as he did.

"You can sit over there and I'll let her know you're here."

I sat on a cream plastic chair, which was one of half a dozen connected in a row, and tethered to the floor, designed, I assumed, to prevent some unhappy or impatient attendee from picking it up and attempting to use it to smash through the window at the public counter.

I spent the fifteen minutes I had to wait examining various posters attached to a noticeboard on the wall. There was one with advice on minding your belongings while travelling abroad, another about how to apply for a passport, a third on how to ensure that if your bicycle is stolen you get it back, and a fourth with the shadowed outline of a crying woman and a phone number for the nearest women's refuge. I remembered a woman I'd seen at a domestic-violence court case and thought how hard it must have been for her when she first walked into a place like this and told some stranger what the man she'd thought she loved had done to her. I was trying to remember the woman's name when, at one-thirty, Maguire appeared, or at least her head did, around a door that was at the side of the public desk. She had a heart-shaped face and blond hair scraped into a tight bun at the back of her neck. It was impossible for me to be sure what age she was and I wondered if the bun might have the effect of a temporary facelift.

"Ms Barrington?"

I stood.

"This way, please." She held the door open with an outstretched arm, which I bent down to pass under, and then let the door close with a click behind us. It was a very solid click and, for some irrational reason, it made me want to turn around and leave immediately.

On the corridor, she walked ahead. She was not in uniform, wearing instead a pair of well-cut black trousers and a pale yellow, long-sleeved blouse which clung to the muscles on her upper arms. She was solidly built and, if it had not been for her Doc Martens, if I met her on the street I might have thought she was a farmer or a midwife.

I followed her into a small room. Before she shut the door she slid a tile at its centre from "**Vacant**" to "**In Use**". There was strip lighting on the ceiling and magnolia-coloured walls, the kind of paint that blood or bodily fluids could easily be wiped off. There were wine-coloured carpet tiles on the floor that looked so full of nylon I imagined they would crackle with static if I walked on them in socks. In the corner there was a shelf with recording equipment and in the centre of the room was a plain, wood-coloured, plastic-topped desk with an A4 notepad and a blue biro on it. There were two brown-plastic chairs, one either side of the table.

"Please." She gestured to one of the chairs.

I sat down and she sat opposite me. Without looking up, she moved the notepad, which I could now see was designed for taking statements, toward her. Instead of picking up the biro she took a slim, expensive-looking pen from her blouse pocket, uncapped it and began to write. She kept her head bent while she filled out my name and the date in the places designated for that information on the top sheet. Her handwriting was neat and clear. She looked up.

"Well, now, you found the body." Her pen hovered above the page and her tone was flat, as though the whole matter was of little interest to her, but her green eyes caught my gaze and held it and I felt as though, just by looking, she might see into a person's soul.

"That's right," I said, my tone already defensive.

"Talk me through it from the beginning. As much detail as possible, please."

"Have you got the statement I gave on the day?"

"Never mind that." She waved her hand dismissively.

I didn't know whether that meant she had or didn't have the statement I gave the young garda or whether she thought it wasn't important.

I told her everything I could remember from the moment I heard the scream to the point where I walked out the gate of the gardens. I didn't mention the person I thought I'd seen running before the scream. I felt she would criticise me, as I had criticised myself, for not paying enough attention to the runner and I didn't want to expose myself to that. She wrote quickly and I could see that every word I said was taken down.

"That's everything, is it?" She stabbed a full stop with her pen and put the cap back on it, having filled three pages.

I hesitated. "Yes."

"Sure?" She raised a well-groomed eyebrow, waited a moment and then handed me the biro that had been on the desk.

"I'll give you a moment to read that and, if you're satisfied, sign the end of each page."

She left the room and I read over the pages. She had written down precisely what I'd said, word for word, no shortcuts, no simplifications, no additions. I thought that in another life she might have made a good stenographer. I signed the pages. When she returned, having left me a few minutes longer than was necessary, she didn't sit down.

"All done?"

"Yes, that's fine."

She took the pages and glanced over them, I assumed to check my signature.

"Right, thanks," she said and moved closer to the door.

I didn't move and after a couple of seconds she returned to the table, looked at me for a moment and sat down.

"Well?" There was impatience in her voice.

"I wanted to know, that is I wondered, because I'd heard . . ." I was apprehensive about asking but knew I had to.

"What?"

"You surely don't believe he jumped, do you?"

She tilted her head to one side and looked at me, her mouth tight with disapproval, and when she spoke her voice was firm.

"We need to get something straight right now. I'm *not* going to tell you what I think. It's your duty to tell me what you saw, no more than that and no less. I don't want to know your theories and I don't want you involving yourself in this case."

"But he had bits of vine between his fingers like he was trying to stop himself from falling. If he'd jumped, he wouldn't have done that."

"Now listen to me, Ms Barrington." The way she said my name made it sound foolish somehow or as if it was a false name I had given her. "I'm *not* Matt McCann. I'm *not* your friend and I'm *not* going to keep you abreast of my investigation."

So that was what she thought – that I was trying to interfere with her investigation. I had been right then, to feel defensive. She'd heard of me before we met and she hadn't liked what she'd heard. I wondered what the talk had been about – that I intruded in investigations, hampered them perhaps?

"Matt McCann never did that," I said, feeling suddenly insulted on his behalf. "All I ever did was try to help."

"I neither want nor need your help."

I should have walked out then, but I thought I would be letting Ava Hogan and her mother down. I had to tell her.

"There was something else I forgot to mention . . ."

"Forgot?" She seemed incredulous.

"Before I heard the scream, I'm pretty sure I saw someone running through the Cactus House. The one that leads from the main Palm House."

"Are you sure of that?" I could see she thought I might have made it up to prevent her from deciding that Paddy Hogan had jumped.

"Yes, I am."

She sighed and ripped off another page of paper from the notebook. She wrote my name and the date on the top again and then made a record of what I'd just told her.

"Go on." Her pen was poised to continue.

"That's it, really. Someone was running through the Cactus House and out, I suppose, or at least in the direction of the exit. But I didn't actually see them go through it."

"No description?"

"Just a flicker, a shape, a dark shape."

"Think, for goodness' sake. Man, woman, child?"

"Adult. It must have been an adult. I could see the person from the waist up, above the tables holding the plants, and a child would be too short for that." I closed my eyes, telling myself to be careful, not to fabricate just to please her. "Slim build, I think, dark clothes, possibly a man but not definitely. And I suppose whoever it was must have been reasonably fit to be able to run like that. That's all."

"Right then." She pushed the paper across the table to me. I read it and signed.

"You know it's an offence to give a false statement to a garda?"

"If you're suggesting I'm telling lies, just say so." I was getting tired of her attitude. I was only trying to do my civic duty.

"It would have been better if you'd told me about the runner in the first place, Ms Barrington."

There was nothing I could say to that. She was right. I pushed back my chair and stood.

"Paddy Hogan didn't jump."

"We'll see."

I walked out of the room, not waiting for her to direct me. She didn't try. But when I got to the door that led to the public office, I found I couldn't open it. I had to wait while she made her way up the corridor, at her own pace, to punch in the security code and let me out.

"Thanks," I said, not sounding at all grateful.

"You're welcome." Though her words were polite her tone suggested she was glad to see the back of me.

Chapter Eleven

I'd arranged to meet Gabriel at the coffee shop in the Botanic Gardens at three but arrived in the car park half an hour early. It was one of those days when sunshine, in between light cloud, felt warmer than it should for the time of year, when it was possible to open up once more to the possibility of summer. I got out of the car, stretched my legs and tried to shake off my overhanging irritation from the interview with Maguire. It had been brisk and intense, shorter in reality – forty-five minutes – than it had felt. I strolled in the direction of the Alpine Yard, a small courtyard with a little greenhouse in it that often contained pretty mountain plants. The sun was seeping in through the fabric of my winter jacket, soothing the tension in my shoulders.

Then I heard my name being called.

I turned and saw George Delaney coming toward me. I was wary of him, given our last meeting, and wondered briefly whether gardeners there were allowed to bar people from visiting.

"Hello," I said when he reached me.

We were standing together now within the walls of the

Alpine Yard. There was no-one else there and I noticed for the first time his gardeners' gloves and his heavy, workman's boots with their steel-capped toes. I felt vulnerable beside him.

"Have you got five minutes?" he asked.

I hesitated.

"It's just, I wanted to talk to you, to apologise. I shouldn't have been so rude the other day."

I nodded and followed him to a wooden bench that was fitted into a corner of the garden. It had a climbing rose growing on the wall beside and behind it. There were no flowers on the plant yet but there were buds forming and I remembered the blossoms would be yellow. It was sheltered there and warmer than I'd expected. We sat and he stretched his legs out in front of him, took his gloves off and put them between us on the seat.

When he spoke he didn't look at me but focused on the toes of his black boots, which were smeared with muck.

"I thought you were there just to gawp," he said. "It's hard, you know, when you lose a workmate like that – you get . . . I don't know, very protective of him or something. But I saw Ava yesterday and she told me you're trying to help her and her mother."

"I'm trying," I said, wondering what exactly Ava had said I could do.

"I was afraid I might have chased you away from this." He waved his hand vaguely and I took him to mean the gardens.

"No, Mr Delaney, you'd have a difficult job keeping me out of this place." I turned to give him a reassuring nod, but he remained looking straight ahead. "It must be very hard for you, and all the staff, to think a colleague could have been killed here."

He did look at me then, a perplexed expression on his face.

"Killed? Ah no, he jumped."

I was astonished at his certainty.

"Ava doesn't think so."

He shook his head and his tone suggested I didn't understand. "You don't know Ava. She's . . . naive and gullible. And families always want other explanations for suicide, don't they? It's easier to think some stranger took his life than accept that he took it himself. You can see that, can't you?"

"But you said you understood I was trying to help the Hogans . . ." I was mystified now.

"No, I know you're trying to help, but the best help you can give them is to accept what happened to Paddy."

I held his gaze for a moment. "What makes you so sure?"

"Look, Ms Barrington –"

"Beatrice."

"Beatrice. I don't mean to be rude but you didn't know him. He was always a bit . . ." He hesitated to find the words. "A terrible worrier. And sometimes he'd have these days when you just couldn't reach him."

The Hogans had said nothing like that to me. "I didn't get that impression from Ava or her mother."

He gave me that look again as though he thought I came down with the last shower.

"They wouldn't, would they? They'd never want to admit that. And Ava's . . ."

He'd already said "gullible and naive" – what else would he come up with?

"She's vulnerable."

"Is it possible that people here would prefer it was suicide?" I knew I was being blunt but I wanted to turn his theory about families and what they wanted on its head. Could it be a case of what was best for the gardens? Or was this personal? Had he got something to hide?

He didn't take it well. He stood up and growled at me.

"Think what you like, Beatrice, but you needn't be spreading fairy stories. We've had enough of the guards snooping around here and you needn't be giving them more cause, do you hear me?"

He was standing above me now. What was this? Had Ava told him I was going to make a statement to the gardaí? Was he trying to intimidate me?

"What do you mean 'fairy stories'? And don't tell me what I can and can't say to the guards. I was there too, remember?"

I stood up to face him. I was angry with him. How could he not have seen what I saw? How could he be so willing to conclude that Paddy had taken his own life? They were supposed to be friends, weren't they?

"I thought you were his friend," I said, looking for a moment directly into his hazel eyes.

He said nothing, but picked up his gloves, turned his back on me and walked away, his temper evident in the weight and speed of his stride.

My phone beeped just then and it was Gabriel.

"I'm in the coffee shop."

It was ten past three.

"Sorry," I said when I found him, sitting at a table for two at the back wall.

"Are you all right?"

I sank into the chair, aware now that I was trembling and not sure whether it was from fear or anger.

"I'll get you a tea," he said.

He went to the counter, ordered and then came back.

"He said he'd bring it down."

He sounded astonished and I was, too. The coffee shop had always been self-service. I glanced at the counter and saw there were three people behind it for what was a quiet day. Perhaps that was why they were now offering table delivery.

Gabriel wasn't long seated when a man in his mid-40s, whom I hadn't seen before, came to our table carrying a tray with a pot of tea and a plate with a large chocolate-chip cookie on it. He unloaded it and offered his hand to Gabriel and then to me. He had a nice smile and black wavy hair that reached to just below his ears with a few streaks of grey through it. I thought it made him look like an ageing hippy though he was too young for that.

"I'm Bob Richmond. I've just taken over managing here after years of working in the kitchen, so I'm celebrating." He pointed to the large biscuit. "That's with my compliments. I hope I'll see you again."

"That's kind of you, thanks," I said.

"No problem." He walked back toward the counter, calling "Leila!" as he did, to one of his staff and signalling for her to clear a recently vacated table.

"That's good business," Gabriel said, breaking the biscuit in two and eating one half before pushing the plate across to me. "You look like you need the sugar."

He waited while I milked my tea and ate some of the biscuit.

"Well? What was she like?"

I had trouble for a moment remembering who he was talking about. The encounter with George Delaney had been so unsettling that I'd temporarily forgotten Maguire.

"Well, you were right about her being tough." I told him about Ballymun Station and her dismissive attitude and suspicion of my motives. To my surprise, he laughed a bit.

"Sounds like you're getting a reputation for yourself there, Bea," he said.

I didn't think it was funny. "God almighty, I haven't done anything wrong. All I did was find a body. It's not my fault that happened." I sounded more irritated than I'd intended.

He put up his hand in a defensive gesture. "Take it easy. I'm not saying it is. Are you not going to eat that?"

I pushed the remains of the biscuit back toward him thinking he would finish it as he always did but he didn't touch it.

"I bumped into George Delaney earlier. That's what delayed me."

"George Delaney?"

"You remember? The gardener who caught us on the walkway – the one I was with when we found Paddy Hogan."

"Oh right. What did he have to say for himself?"

I told him about the encounter.

"I just can't understand why everyone is so determined to label it a suicide. Are they all blind?" It made no sense to me. "I mean if Paddy Hogan was one of your friends or workmates you wouldn't just assume, would you?"

"He does know more about him than we do, Bea."

He had a point, I knew, but I wasn't prepared to concede it.

"But so do his family." I was thinking of him standing over me, and his sinewy hands and the steel-capped toes of those boots.

"He'd be strong enough," I said aloud.

"But why would he do it?" Gabriel asked.

I looked at him and I knew he knew what I was thinking – that we ought to make some effort to find out.

"Will we see if anyone else will have a word with us?" he asked.

I finished my tea and we left, agreeing that we would be better splitting up to talk to people. I said I'd try the receptionist in the visitor centre and Gabriel opted to try chatting to one of the younger gardeners he'd spotted on his way into the coffee shop.

"I'll see you back at the car park in half an hour," I told him.

The reception area was reached by walking through the visitor centre foyer, where there were toilets and stairs to the floor above, and then through another glass door. There was shelving inside the reception area with books for sale, then a reception desk of grey granite with a leaflet stand. At the end of the room there was a glass door leading directly out to the gardens. And a third door, to the side of reception, opened into a large café with its wall of windows from which the Curvilinear House could be seen.

I approached the desk, browsed through the leaflets and picked one up, for a lecture called "Botany for Beginners", and began to read it.

The young woman behind the desk glanced in my direction after a few moments and moved away from the cash register to where I was standing.

"Can I help you at all?" She had shoulder-length, wavy red hair held back from her face on one side with a silver clip. There were signs on her round face, which had barely any make-up, that acne was an issue solved in the recent past.

"I'm thinking of going to this lecture on Sunday. Will it be any good?"

She thought that was funny and showed it in a wide smile. Taking the leaflet from me she pointed out the name of the lecturer.

"That's Professor James Christakos. He's supposed to be very good, the best, though I haven't heard him myself."

She looked around her and then leaned forward confidentially. "You should see him in here with all his students, the girls hanging off him."

I wondered if that was the man I'd seen briefly in the coffee shop. "Thanks, I'll give it a go. Can I ask you a question?"

"About what?"

"Paddy Hogan."

She moved away from me and shook her head as though she was deeply disappointed. "We were told not to talk to reporters."

"I'm not a reporter. I'm a family friend." It wasn't entirely untrue, not now anyway. "I just wanted to know if he was happy here."

She didn't answer immediately, still wary of me.

"I didn't know him well enough to be able to tell," she said. "But he was never grumpy, if that's what you mean, not like some people." She tidied the leaflets on the desk though they were already neat enough.

"So he'd be in and out of here, would he?"

"All the staff get a discount in the restaurant, so . . ."

She pointed her thumb in the direction of the door to the café. Then she looked behind her and in both directions and dropped her voice. "He talked to me the morning he died. He was really upbeat, I thought, excited even. Hard to believe he's gone."

"Do you remember what he was excited about?"

"I wasn't really paying all that much attention, to be honest. But I think it was something about some plant he liked, and then a woman came by with a big buggy and he held the door open for her. That was the sort of man he was. And then he waved at me and went out that door over there." She pointed in the direction of the door that opened out into the gardens and froze for a moment, as though she could see him still waving at her now.

"It's hard to believe a man like that could . . ." She looked upset by the memory.

"Maybe he didn't," I said.

Her eyes opened wide at me in a way that suggested she was startled by the idea that someone else might have helped him over the railing of the Palm House.

"Did he get on well with all the staff here?" I asked.

She opened her mouth to speak then shook her head as though she'd changed her mind. "I couldn't say. I really wouldn't know anything about that." She moved away from me, back to the cash register.

I waved the brochure at her.

"Thanks for your help. I think I might give this a try." I put it in my handbag.

I wandered around for a while outside hoping to speak to other staff but I didn't manage it.

Eventually, I found Gabriel standing beside an empty

flower bed. A gardener was down on his knees with a trowel in his hand and a wheelbarrow at his elbow. He was talking and Gabriel was nodding. I kept going, making my way slowly to the car park, wandering through the Teak House with its pelargoniums, each one gaudily painted in shades of pink and purple.

I scanned the car park for Gabriel's car but couldn't see it, so I sat into mine. A few minutes later the passenger door opened and Gabriel got in.

"I walked," he said before I had time to ask.

"How long did that take you, an hour?"

"Not at all – 45 minutes."

"I'm impressed."

I put the car into reverse and was about to pull away when I remembered I hadn't paid for parking.

"Oh, I have to go back – I forgot to pay."

I took the ticket from my bag along with my purse and went back into the gardens to the payment machine next to the visitor centre. I scanned the ticket, put two euro in the slot and had turned back toward the car park when I noticed Bob Richmond in the Teak House talking to a woman. I stood outside for a few moments to admire the Snow Glory just coming into bloom. I couldn't hear what was being said and I didn't recognise the person he was talking to, but I assumed she was a gardener from her overalls. She had short dark hair cut in a fringeless bob which accentuated the cheekbones under her almost black skin. The two had their heads together and were talking intently and at the same time. The woman had one hand on her hip. Just then a handful of visitors stepped into the Teak House along with a tour guide who began telling them about the gardens. Richmond and the woman walked out.

I turned quickly so that they couldn't see me and went back to the car.

"Machine on the blink?" Gabriel asked when I opened the door.

I told him what I'd seen as I reversed out of the parking space and pulled up to the barrier. I put the ticket in, the barrier lifted and we drove out.

"Did you think they were arguing?"

"It looked like that . . . but I've no idea what about . . . that glass is thick."

"It could just have been about work. Maybe he gave her the wrong coffee or sandwich or something."

"Maybe." But they seemed so intense. "Do people get that animated about a sandwich?"

"Some people might."

As we made our way down St Mobhi Drive I saw Constance Anderson standing at her gate, talking to someone in a black leather jacket. It was the young man I'd seen her with before. He had something on his shoulder that looked like a bag of fertiliser and when she turned to go up her drive, he followed her.

"I've seen him before," I said.

"Who?"

We were out of sight of him by then.

"That young man talking to Constance Anderson – tall, dark-haired, black leather jacket, black jeans – on the day Paddy Hogan died . . . oh!" I thought then of the figure that had been running through the Cactus House, the dark blur at the corner of my eye, just before

Constance screamed. He was the right build and his monotone clothing fitted.

"What are you thinking?" Gabriel asked.

I told him. "Might be worth saying it to Maguire next time you see her," he said.

I said I supposed I should though I didn't relish the idea of another encounter with her.

We talked about the gardens for a while.

"Who runs the Botanic Gardens anyway?" I asked.

He googled the question.

"Office of Public Works and there's a director living on site."

I thought for a moment what it would be like to wake up every morning and look out at the gardens – the privilege of it, almost as good as waking up to a view of the sea.

"What about the gardener you were talking to, had he much to say?"

"Plenty to say about dahlias but when it came to Paddy Hogan not very helpful. Told me he prefers to mind his own business and I should do the same. Would you mind dropping me on Fairview Strand? I've got to meet someone in Gaffney's."

"So you haven't given up the pub scene entirely then?"

"I'll probably just have a coffee."

I stopped the car when we reached the pub – an old Victorian hostelry which was typical of Gabriel's tastes.

"Talk to you later," he said, stepping out of the car without further explanation.

I watched him stride across the road and push open the door of the pub before I drove away.

* * *

At home I considered whether I should phone Maguire to tell her about the young man I'd seen Constance Anderson with. I should tell her, I knew. Constance had been in the Orchid House on the day Paddy Hogan died, hadn't she? And what if that young man had been with her? What if it was he I saw running through the Cactus House? I should call her but I couldn't bear to. Instead I wrote a brief email describing him and what I thought and sent it to her. There was no response.

Chapter Twelve

Sunday, March 5th

The Botany for Beginners lecture was on at the Botanic Gardens at eleven. I arrived twenty minutes early to ensure I'd get in. I went to reception to pay for a ticket but the young woman who had spoken to me on Saturday wasn't there. Instead, there was an old man who seemed to be a caretaker, in sagging overalls, a coarse-looking pullover visible at the neck. His cheeks looked as though someone had let most of the air out of two pale yellow balloons. He didn't look up when he took my money.

"Thanks," I said when he handed me the ticket.

He looked at me then, smiled enough to reveal the nicotine-stained teeth of a long-term smoker and said, "That's no bother".

There were already quite a few people in the lecture theatre, which was on the ground floor in the visitor centre, when I arrived. To my astonishment, there were also two cameramen, a woman with a control board at the back of the theatre whom I took to be a sound engineer and a third man speaking loudly in an American accent to them all who I assumed was a film director of some sort, complete with a blue baseball cap that had "*LA Dodgers*" written across it. The theatre had tiered seating and a small podium with a wooden lectern, and a table and chair.

I made my way upwards past rows of men and women predominantly of late middle age. To my eye, they all looked like amateur gardeners who were probably retired. I had to check my own thinking then and remind myself that I was neither a gardener nor retired but I was there too.

I took a seat in the centre of the eighth row, with a good view of most attendees, next to an elderly man. He rubbed his two hands together as though he was excited and leaned in to me in a conspiratorial way.

"*Natural World*," he said.

"Pardon?"

"You know, the magazine? And they do programmes, too."

"Yes, but . . ."

"That's who they are. They're making a programme about the professor."

"I'd no idea he was that . . ." I didn't know how to end the sentence. Important? Well-known? Worthy? Good entertainment?

The man clapped his hands together again and rubbed them palm to palm. "We're lucky to be here to see this." He leaned forward, put his hand into the back pocket of his trousers and produced a comb which he ran through his silver, flicked-back hair.

"They might fillum the audience," he said, winking a blue eye at me and for a moment I caught a glimpse of the young man he had been.

By eleven the lecture theatre was full and the film director stepped onto the podium and leaned one elbow on the lectern.

"Hello, people. My name is Mason Bryant. You probably know already that we're from *Natural World* and we're filming this lecture as part of a documentary on the great professor."

The audience murmured. He put his hand up and there was silence.

"We're hoping that you all will co-operate with us. If you can keep your seats throughout the lecture and try not to cough that would help en–*or*–mously. Also, if you could be a little patient? We hope not but there may be a need for retakes. That's all folks, thanks."

For reasons I didn't understand the audience applauded. The director smiled, lifted his baseball cap and bowed theatrically before getting off the stage.

I checked my watch. The lecture was supposed to be an hour long but we could run until lunchtime if retakes were needed. I shouldn't have worried though. Professor James Christakos was the ultimate professional. And when he stepped up onto the podium I recognised him immediately from the coffee shop. He was the tall, tanned man who had set the female students fluttering. There was no denying he was handsome, and I hadn't even noticed those dark brown eyes before. I thought he would not have looked out of place on the stage of the Abbey Theatre. I'd expected too that a botanist might wear corduroy and a tweed jacket with elbow patches but he was wearing an expensive-looking dark-blue, three-piece suit. The waistcoat had an unnatural number of buttons, all of which were done up, giving the impression of containment.

He looked up into the audience, waited a moment until there was silence, and said "Morning, guys".

Some people around me mumbled a good morning back.

"Ah come on, we can do bedder than that. *Good morning, guys!*"

The people around me laughed and repeated "Good morning" loudly. I cringed. There was nothing I liked less than interactive theatre and this had all the makings of just such an experience.

"Excellent." He smiled widely, showing off teeth so white they could not have been made by nature. And he turned his head from one side of the room to the other to take in the whole crowd and the cameras with his beam. "For those of you who don't know already," here he made a small smile as though it was very unlikely, "my name is Professor James Christakos. I know what you're thinking – Greek, right? Well yes, half, and an eighth Irish, but way, way back. I'm from New Hampshire." It sounded more like "New Hampshah" when he said it. "And before I arrived in this fair isle I was working in a little college you might have heard of – Berkeley and before that, Dartmouth."

There was a murmur of appreciation for his credentials.

"This morning, I'm gonna walk you through the basics of botany. This is the kind of talk I give my students on their first day, so very basic stuff. But interesting, I promise. All righty? Good."

He took off his jacket, laid it across the table behind him and turned back to the podium.

"Throughout history, the study of plants, or botany, has made a vital contribution to our understanding and quality of life." He picked up a control, turned and clicked and a screen unfurled behind him. A Venus flytrap filled the screen.

"Did you know plants can move, feel, kill? That they can counteract pollution and can even solve crimes?"

I settled back and let the lecture wash over me for the most part, as he ranged from the general to the particular, focusing only now and then on a few things I hadn't heard before. His delivery was good and, I had to admit, entertaining with anecdotes of just the right length and amount to elevate some of the more mundane information he shared. The two cameramen moved back and forth, occasionally coming between the professor and his audience but he continued as though they didn't exist. At one point, he remarked on the warmth of the room.

"Gotta take this vest off," he said, unbuttoning the many buttons of his waistcoat and breathing out as though his broad chest had been trapped inside it. Then, as though he was going to embark on some physical task, he rolled the white sleeves of his shirt up above his elbows where they strained over his biceps. He came out from behind the lectern, bringing the microphone with him.

"That's bedder," he said.

When it was over, the audience clapped for a longer period than was necessary until Mason Bryant said "*Cut!*". He walked back onto the stage and said something in the professor's ear.

He responded quietly, then turned and, gesturing to a queue that was beginning to form, he said loudly "No, no, you must give me a few moments to talk with my guests".

I thought I saw Bryant roll his eyes, but he got off the podium and signalled for his team to follow him out.

I took a place at the very back of the line behind people I imagined wanted to ask his advice about plant problems or get books they were holding signed by him. I hoped to catch him alone so that I could ask if he knew Paddy Hogan. Just in front of me, a woman was talking to the next person in the queue, making comments about the weather and the quality of the lecture.

"I've been to all his public lectures here. He has such magnetism, doesn't he?" the woman was saying. She was getting little or no response from the man to whom she directed her remarks but she continued anyway.

I recognised then the grey bob and the voice. When she stopped talking to catch her breath, I touched her elbow and she turned around.

"Constance, isn't it?"

She blinked a couple of times but couldn't place me.

"I'm Beatrice. I met you when we found that man."

"Of course. I just couldn't remember your name. How are you?"

"Fine. You?"

"Fine. I enjoyed the lecture. He's terrifically entertaining to listen to, don't you think? And what a clever mind. They're making a programme about him." She said it as though I hadn't been in the theatre.

"Yes," I responded.

"I have his book on orchids. It was published last year. I went to the launch. I've signed up for his short course too – 'All about Orchids'. I can't wait."

"He gives courses?"

"Yes. He lectures the horticultural students here, but he runs short courses for us amateurs. The orchid course is starting at the end of the month. If you're interested you'll need to apply soon. It's very popular."

"I'll bear that in mind. By the way, I saw you on TV after . . ."

"Oh," she said, putting her hand to one cheek, "you know what reporters are like. I couldn't get away from photos of myself in all the newspapers either." She allowed herself a small, satisfied smile but dropped it quickly. "It was a dreadful thing though, wasn't it?"

"Terrible. I suppose the guards have been on to you?"

"No." She paused as though considering what this meant. "I gave them a statement at the time. I'm sure that was enough for them. It was hard to believe though, wasn't it, a man like Paddy Hogan jumping like that?"

"You knew him then?" I didn't try to hide my surprise.

"Oh yes, I know all the gardeners here. I'm a regular, you see." She said "regular" in the same way some people say "business class" when they talk about flying.

We shuffled forward as the queue shortened.

"It must have been a terrible shock for you to see him like that?" I said.

"It was *very* distressing. And he was such a generous man, very patient when I asked him about plants and," she looked over her shoulder and lowered her voice, "he sometimes gave me cuttings." She made it sound as though he was supplying her with illicit drugs. "I'm afraid I didn't have much success with them. I'm not as green-fingered as I'd like which, you can imagine, is a great disappointment to me. I told him so and he even called over once or twice to show me how to pot-on a few seedlings. As I say – very kind."

I had a feeling Constance was holding something back,

behind her chattiness. Could it have been about the young man in the black jacket that I'd seen her with?

I was about to try bringing him into the conversation but her turn came to speak to the professor.

"Excuse me," she said to me and turned away to focus her attention on him.

"Ah, Constance!" he said.

"Hello again, James."

Their voices dropped then and I couldn't make out what was being discussed.

While I waited, I thought back to our discovery of Paddy Hogan. Had Constance given any intimation that she'd known him? I couldn't recall. I didn't think I'd heard her say his name. If it had been someone I knew, I felt sure I would have called his name involuntarily when I saw him, just as George Delaney had. Unless I was right about the young man who'd been with her – that he had something to do with the death and she knew it.

Constance finished and left with a quick goodbye to me.

As I stepped forward to speak to the professor, he glanced at his watch and began to roll down his shirtsleeves.

I thanked him for the lecture, in particular the section on crime detection. It was an area of particular interest to me, I said.

As he put his waistcoat back on and buttoned up, he responded by telling me about a case he'd been involved in that helped police in the US.

"I was asked to help trace this rare pollen found on the clothes of a murder victim." He rubbed his right thumb and index finger together to demonstrate just how tiny the pollen was. "Pinpointing the location of that pollen led them to the killer." He said it almost in singsong, and I thought it must have been a well-worn dinner-party anecdote. Yet he had gone to the trouble of bringing it out for me, the last woman in a long queue of well-wishers. There was, I had to admit, something generous about that.

"Can I just ask you something? A man died here last month, Paddy Hogan . . ."

"Yes, poor guy."

"Only, I found him. And there were tendrils between his fingers from the vines above, like he had grabbed at them to stop himself falling. Do you think that's what he might have done?"

He looked at me, startled. "Well, that's not a question for a botanist." He began to pull on his jacket.

"I know – sorry. Did you know him at all?"

"Sure I did. Paddy helped me out lots of times with preparation and stuff for my lectures. He was a good guy. Great eye for detail, actually, really great eye." He pointed the first finger of his left hand up to emphasise his words.

"Did you see him that day?"

"What? No, I didn't. I had a late start that day and by the time I got to the gardens . . . they told me what had happened to him." He ran his left hand across his mouth and back again. "He had vines between his fingers? I hadn't heard that . . . that's awful."

I noticed he had become pale under his tan.

He lifted his eyes to mine and looked at me for a moment.

"And you found him, did you? Poor you."

I felt unexpectedly moved by his sympathy and didn't know how to respond so I extended my hand. "Thanks for your time," I said.

He took it with his right hand then covered both our hands with his left and shook. His grip was tight and deliberate, the kind of handshake given to a mourner and I felt he wanted to convey an understanding of how distressing it must have been to make that discovery.

"You're welcome, Ms . . . what did you say your name was?"

"Beatrice, Beatrice Barrington."

"Right. I gotta go, Beatrice, but good talking to you." He gathered up his papers and walked ahead of me out of the theatre, his notes clutched to his chest like a shield and his long stride rapidly putting distance between us.

I followed as far as the entrance to the visitor centre and stood there watching him go past the sleeping flowerbeds and across to the house belonging to the director of the gardens where the film crew was waiting.

Mason Bryant nodded and one of the men hoisted his camera onto his shoulder. The professor paused at the low gate for a moment, looked around him, then opened it and strode up the path to the white front door, with its sunburst window above it. He knocked, the door was opened by a man I took to be the director of the gardens and he stepped inside. The cameramen, sound engineer and director followed.

"If that fella was a biscuit, he'd eat himself."

I turned round and the old man who had served me at reception was standing there. He was leaning on a sweeping brush and must have noticed my confusion at his change of duties.

"I was only standing in for the receptionist till they could find someone else. She rang in sick this morning."

"Oh, do you mean the smiley young woman with the red hair?"

"That's her."

"I was only talking to her on Friday. I hope she's all right."

"You know these young ones – they go out on the razz on a Saturday night and then they're surprised when they can't get out of bed in the morning." He didn't say it in a bitter way – he seemed to view it with equanimity, as though it had been the same in his youth and it would always be the case.

"She was very kind to me yesterday. We had a chat about Paddy Hogan." I watched him as I said the name and tried to measure his wariness, but could detect none.

He blessed himself. "Poor Paddy, Lord have mercy on him."

"Could I buy you a coffee?"

"*Ehmm* . . ." He looked at me speculatively. "If you want to wait a few minutes . . ."

I said I'd wait for him in the coffee shop around the back of the visitor centre. It wasn't long before he followed me in and I went to the counter and bought a pot of tea, which was what he said he preferred. There were some chocolate biscuits and I put a couple on a plate.

Bob Richmond was on his own behind the counter and a queue was forming. "Do you need a hand with that?" he asked.

I thought it was kind of him to offer even though he was busy. "I'm fine, but thanks," I said.

I carried down the tray and unloaded its contents onto the table. When I sat down, I stirred the pot before pouring tea into two cups.

The caretaker added the tiniest splash of milk into his,

sat back in the chair and crossed his arms.

"First of all, what is it you're after? Are you a journo?"

I shook my head. "God forbid. No. I'm . . ." I hesitated. Should I obfuscate? He seemed the type it might be better to be straight with.

"I should have said, my name is Beatrice Barrington –"

"I'm Seamus Lennon."

"Mr Lennon –"

"Seamus."

"Seamus. I'm just going to come out with it – last month I was with one of the gardeners, George Delaney, when we found Paddy Hogan's body. And his family have asked me to help them find out all I can about his death."

"Terrible thing."

"Did you know him?"

"Course, everyone knew him – sure wasn't he the maestro's son?"

"You mean Jackie Hogan?"

He nodded. "Can be hard to be the son of someone like Jackie, d'you see? He was exceptional, one of the best gardeners they ever had here and that's saying something."

He took a biscuit and broke it in two, leaving one half on the edge of his saucer and dipping the other half into his cup before rushing it to his mouth. He washed it down with tea.

"There was always something a bit soft about Paddy – I don't mean touched now, just soft in his ways and the way he treated others. You'd think he felt things too deep." With his words came unexpected colour to his sagging cheeks. He blinked and coughed and took more tea. "Some of them in here think they're god's gift to the gardens and the world in general, some of them, but they forget the Bots was here before them and it'll still be here when they're long gone."

"Who do you mean?" I tried not to sound too eager for information. I sipped my tea.

"Some of them teachers over in the college there, and one or two of the gardeners – they think they walk on water some of them and look at the likes of me as though they'd scraped me off the sole of their shoe." He had a look of distain on his face. "Not Paddy, mind, he always took the time to say good morning or ask 'how are you?'. And we'd have the occasional drink after work. 'Did you see the match?' he'd say, that sort of thing. Ordinary fella really." He leaned forward and lowered his voice a little. "The only time the Yankee professor ever spoke to me was when one of his students puked their guts up in the lecture room and he needed someone to clean it." There was a bitter edge to his words. "You may as well be invisible to the likes of him."

I had to admit to myself that I was disappointed – I had expected better from the professor.

"And now with this filming going on, God almighty, I'm surprised he can get his head through the door." He paused for breath.

I poured myself more tea, though it was deep red now and no longer very hot, then topped up his cup. I was about to ask him more about Paddy Hogan but I didn't get a chance.

"They say he killed himself," he said, shaking his head. "If you're going to do it, there's easier ways."

"Do you think he did?" I was hoping for some doubt, some possibility that at least someone in the gardens had ideas other than suicide.

He leaned back in his chair, the front legs of which lifted off the ground. "It's hard to understand, isn't it? A man like him, gentle sort, a bit timid, but brave enough to throw himself over that railing? If he did do it, whatever he was trying to escape, it must have been unbearable."

Before I could ask any more questions, he drank back the dregs of his cup and stood up.

"I'd better get back to it. Thanks for the tea."

"Thanks for your time, Seamus."

He nodded and left, pushing the glass door hard so that it swung back with a clang. He hadn't said he thought Paddy had killed himself exactly but he'd seemed to imply it was possible. I was sorry I hadn't got a chance to ask him whether the guards had been in touch. I was beginning to think Maguire wasn't too bothered about Paddy Hogan.

Chapter Thirteen

When I got back, I made myself lunch, did some laundry, and sat on the couch with some tea. The sky over Dublin Bay was a painting of blues, whites and greys. I thought at one moment it might open up and pour, and then at another I was sure I would be able to get the clothes dry that I'd put out on the line in the garden.

The Hogans were on my mind, the father and son, the mother and daughter. It seemed to me that they lived almost claustrophobic lives, the men both in the same place of work so near their home, the women entwined intensely with each other. But then how could I really judge when I was seeing them at their worst? Wouldn't all families cling together after such a traumatic bereavement? For a while anyway, I supposed. I thought of Seamus Lennon's description of Paddy – "he felt things too deep". What did that mean exactly? Did it mean he was more likely to take his own life?

I wanted to able to talk it all over with Gabriel. I knew he would help me see things more clearly. Where would he be now? I was certain he would have gone to Mass in Aughrim Street church. His stay in Donegal would have reinforced his religious practice. But I wasn't sure whether or not it had broken his habit of getting Sunday lunch in one of the local pubs. Though we'd eaten in Walsh's on the day of his return I'd garnered from him that it was an exception now rather than a habit. But he was hardly cooking for himself every day?

I considered whether he might be in Hanlon's but dismissed that idea given his past experiences there. He could be in Walsh's or Kavanagh's. I checked my watch. It was four-thirty. He might even have had his quota and be at home by now. I let his phone ring five times before giving up.

What now? I felt listless and in need of something, so I got my coat to go for a walk. When I opened the hall door, though, he was standing there, just about to knock.

"Are you off out?" He stepped into the hall. "If you give me a minute I'll go with you – just need the jacks." He made for the stairs.

I waited, marvelling at how much better I suddenly felt.

"How was Mass?" I asked when he came back downstairs.

He gave me an impatient look. "Are you starting on your anti-church hobby horse already, Bea?"

I shrugged. "I was just asking." I closed the door behind us.

"It was grand. I said a prayer for you."

"You've no car?" I wanted to ask if it was because he'd had a few pints.

"No, I'm trying to keep up the walking."

"All the way? That's impressive."

"Nice morning for it."

I felt guilty then dragging him out for another walk but he didn't seem to mind. We crossed the road and strolled over the grass verge to the path that ran alongside the low wall which was holding back the sea. It was busy with Sunday ramblers.

"How was the lecture?" he asked.

"Interesting."

I told him about the professor and about meeting Seamus Lennon and Constance.

"She seems to know plenty about the gardens," he said.

"The thing is, I had a feeling she was holding something back, like there was something more about Paddy Hogan than she was saying."

"Are you sure? By the sound of it she doesn't seem the kind of woman who can keep information to herself."

I thought about that, about how much she had seemed to enjoy talking to reporters and journalists. Who was it that had interviewed her on TV? Was it the crime correspondent? No, one of his stand-ins, a younger man. She was talkative, I agreed, but she was a clever woman and I felt sure she was capable of keeping her mouth shut if she really needed to.

"Don't you think it's strange that she never said she knew Paddy Hogan?" I said.

"A bit," he admitted.

"I would have liked the chance to ask her about that young man who was with her . . . Gabriel, I wonder if you happened to bump into her in the gardens or somewhere and got her talking, might she have more to say? Or at least something different to say?"

He raised his eyebrows. "I think you might be getting a bit too devious for your own good, Bea."

"It wouldn't be me being devious, it'd be you." I grinned at him.

He shook his head. "Honestly, I don't know what's happened to you in the last few years. You used to be so . . ."

"What?"

He wavered, picking his words. "Careful."

I didn't respond immediately but I knew he was right. I had been. In everything I did I'd been afraid of the world. Was that because I'd been taught such a hard lesson in my twenties? Perhaps.

"I suppose we've both changed, Gabriel, haven't we?"

"We have, Bea, and for the better."

I knew he was talking about his own health in particular and the way he was looking after himself, but it felt like he was talking about our relationship too. He was saying we were better together the way we were now. I felt a little pinch of pain under my left breast. Oblivious to the impact of his words, he pointed toward the Wooden Bridge and the Bull Wall ahead of us, which both jut out into the sea to form one of the arms built to shelter Dublin port.

"Did you know the captain of the *Bounty* – from '*Mutiny on the Bounty*' – had a hand in bringing the Bull Wall to Dublin?" he asked.

"Did he?" I knew the history of the wall well and Captain William Bligh's connection to it but I didn't say so. It was easier to let him go on talking about it, telling me things I didn't need to respond to, while my poor heart soothed itself.

We walked out across the bridge and onto the Bull Wall and talked about other, inconsequential things. He said he was going to give his house on Oxmantown Road a fresh paint and maybe even get some new curtains and asked if I might help him choose them. I said I would though I didn't really want to – it felt too intimate a thing to do for him now.

On the way back rain in large round drops began falling on us. We quickened our pace and I thought about the washing on the clothesline in my garden. Soon it would be limp and dripping and smelling of salty water. But what did it matter?

When we were back and dried and I had taken in the washing and put it back into the machine, we took bowls of soup into the living room and continued talking about nothing and everything. He said he'd been feeling time heavy on his hands since he came back to Dublin. I feared he was going to tell me he was going home to Glenties for good, but he didn't.

"I think I need to find some part-time work for myself. A few hours a week would do me."

"What would you like to do? Security or something?" I knew a lot of retired gardaí went into security.

"Maybe. I'll put the feelers out."

"Or what about something in the courts? A lot of ex-guards work there."

"Ah no. Too much politics involved. As I say, I'm just thinking about it."

We sat in silence for a while half-watching TV or at least that's what I thought we were doing until I realised Gabriel was half-watching me.

"What?" I asked.

"How are you doing, Bea? I don't mean to be . . . but you've more time on your hands than you're used to."

I sighed. "I know . . . there isn't a lot of work around at the moment. Actually, I was thinking of taking up a hobby."

He looked at me with curiosity. "Like what?"

"Something that might require me to spend more time in the gardens . . ."

He nodded then, seeing where I was going with it.

"Constance told me the professor is giving a course on orchids. Maybe I'll sign up for that."

"Good idea. But do you know anything at all about orchids, Bea?"

I thought about that and checked the time – seven-thirty. "When does Raheny library close?"

He googled it. "Eight."

I stood and grabbed my bag. "Are you coming?"

The rain stopped as we made the short drive to Raheny library in my car.

"Constance said the professor wrote a book on orchids," I told Gabriel. "If they have that I'll borrow it. If not, I'll find something else."

The red-bricked building on Howth Road was still busy when we got there ten minutes before closing. I went straight to the desk and asked for any books available on orchids. The librarian tapped on her keyboard.

"Yes, we have a few. You'll find them in the sciences section under Botany."

"Thanks."

We went to the section she indicated and scanned the shelves. There were three orchid books, one of which was the professor's. *World Orchids: The Rare and the Beautiful*. I couldn't help thinking, as I read the title, that there was a touch of soap opera about it. Gabriel picked up a Dorling Kindersley from the Royal Horticultural Society that promised to teach simple steps to growing orchids successfully. And the third book was called *The New Encyclopaedia of Orchids*.

"I'll just take the professor's. That should be enough to get me started."

We checked the book out just as the library closed.

In the car on the way home, Gabriel managed to find his favourite – Johnny Cash – on the radio and it made me smile to hear him. I had to admit that, though I used to complain about the singer, I'd missed him while Gabriel was away. There was something honest about his singing, something from the guts that I realised now reminded me of Gabriel.

He hummed along and leafed through the professor's book.

"Plenty of glossy photos in this anyway," he said. "And very long descriptions of the plants – where he was when he first saw them, how he felt about them."

"That's a bit self-indulgent, don't you think?" I said.

"It's the cult of the personality, isn't it, Bea? That's what people want now. You can't just be an expert – you have to offer up a bit of your personal life, as well."

"Well, I think it gets in the way." Was I being unfair saying that? Had I forgotten how I'd enjoyed the professor's lecture in part because he had enlivened it with personal anecdotes?

Back at home I set the book down on the kitchen table and put the kettle on.

Then I sat beside Gabriel and we began looking through the book. The orchids in the photos were beautiful and each had its own perfect symmetry. I thought I recognised some from the Botanic Gardens though I'd never looked closely enough at the labels in the Orchid House to be sure.

"Ah, for god's sake!" I said after turning a page and seeing one plant called *Platanthera christakii*. "If that's not self-indulgence I don't know what is. Just look at that."

The kettle came to the boil as I spoke and I got up to make tea and sandwiches, only realising then how hungry I was.

Gabriel began reading aloud.

"'This is among my favourites for obvious reasons. I had the privilege of travelling on a field trip to the Azores with colleagues. It was a three-week visit and we were based largely on Pico island. But it was on Sao Jorge that I made the discovery. My team and I had already been walking for three hours along a trail across a lava plain, known locally as a faja. We had moved into higher ground, I won't say where precisely, when we stopped for a short break. Leaving my rucksack with the team, I wandered on alone. And then I saw it – the most delicate and beautiful Platanthera. It was immediately obvious to me that this was distinct from other orchids on the island and as yet unknown to the world. We set up camp and began our detailed work. Later, on publication of our findings in the esteemed Portuguese Journal of Botany, I graciously accepted a suggestion from my team that the plant should bear my name.'"

"I see what you mean about ego," Gabriel said.

He turned the pages until he came across an Irish orchid and began reading again.

"'This was a four-day visit to the wonderful Burren in the West of Ireland. I was leading a group from the Irish National Botanic Gardens, with guests from Ireland, the UK and US, and we were staying with Eileen and Peter

Cassidy at their lovely guesthouse on the edge of the national park. The third day we had rain, relentless rain. Now this was Ireland so it wasn't unexpected, and everyone was prepared for it. But it was tiring. So instead of exploring until 6pm as planned, a decision was taken to return to our guesthouse at half past four. I walked with the group until we were almost there and then something, to this day I can't say what, told me to go back. Now I have to point out that we did have a permit to leave the designated trails. So I walked back, some three quarters of a mile I would say, and I wandered a bit and the rain slowed and I decided to examine some growth right at the side of a flat, bare rock. I was down on my hunkers, dazzled by the violet of Pinguicula vulgaris when I saw something else, just at the edge of my vision – an elegant creamy-green orchid, Platanthera bifolia. I knew it lived there but it was still a privilege to see it. I stayed, it must have been for more than an hour, just admiring it. I took some photos, made some observations. And though the sky was grey, the cloud low, and the rain still pitting the limestone around me, it was as if the sun had come out.'"

"He has to be the centre of everything, doesn't he?" I said, putting the tea and plate of sandwiches on the table.

"Is this all you're having?" Gabriel asked as though he felt guilty sharing what I had to admit was a meagre evening meal.

"It's enough."

We ate in silence for a while. I thought about Paddy Hogan and how he must have tended orchids as part of his work. Did all of his duties involve planting and nurturing or were there other things too, like recordkeeping and form-filling? I picked up my cup, holding it with both hands.

"Would the gardeners in the Botanic Gardens have other jobs to do besides the physical stuff, do you think?"

"Most jobs involve a bit of admin these days, don't they?"

I put the cup down again without drinking.

"So if a person has to carry out some form of admin, say ordering seeds or fertiliser or something, he'd probably have to have access to a computer."

"Now, Bea!" He knew what I was thinking – that we should try to take a look at Paddy's computer if he had one.

On my phone I googled Paddy's name and then @botanicgardens.ie and his email address popped up. I showed it to Gabriel.

"If he has a work email address then he must have access to a work computer," I said.

"Even if he does have one, it'd be hard to find and getting into it would probably be impossible."

I understood his reluctance – technology was not his forte.

"Couldn't we just try? Tomorrow maybe?" I said.

"Aren't you working tomorrow?"

I checked and found he was right. "But not until midday . . ."

He didn't respond and I took his silence as acquiescence.

"I'll see you at the gardens at nine," I said before he went home.

Chapter Fourteen

Monday, March 6th

"We need to find out where the gardeners' office is," I said to Gabriel.

It was nine o'clock and we'd both left our cars in the car park and were standing next to the Teak House.

"We'll just have to ask," he said.

I followed him toward the visitor centre, thinking I could ask the receptionist. But when we got inside Seamus Lennon was mopping the floor.

"Hello again," he said.

"Morning, Seamus. You couldn't point us in the direction of the gardeners' office, could you? We're looking for a word with George." I tried to sound as casual as I could.

He shrugged. "Not sure you'll find him there now but . . . do you know the sensory garden?"

I said I did.

"It's just round behind that."

"Thanks, Seamus."

We moved away then before he could ask any questions. He leaned on his mop and watched us go.

We found the building, a creamy brick house with a

slate roof and a single chimney, with little difficulty. It was smaller than I'd expected with two windows and an unruly clematis growing up to its windowsills. I thought there might only be one room inside. Its green door, set at one end of the building, was ajar and voices were drifting out.

"We may as well get the lay of the land," I said and before Gabriel could object I pushed the door open and went inside.

We were in a narrow hall with two doors off it to the left. Both were open but there were sounds coming from only one of the rooms, nearer the back. We walked toward it and as we passed the other room I glanced inside – there were about half a dozen desks with computers on them. There was no one in it.

In the back room people were sitting at tables in what looked like a basic canteen kitchen with a sink area, a kettle, toaster and microwave. Mugs dangled from a wooden cup tree. Even from where I was, they looked brown inside, as though they'd never been properly scoured.

"Are you all right there?" one of the gardeners said, coming toward us as we stepped into the kitchen, his hand wrapped round a mug of tea.

"We're just looking for George Delaney," Gabriel said, having quickly scanned the four faces present to be sure one of them wasn't George.

"Over in the Palm House, I think."

"Right, thanks."

We turned and left.

"Let's go to the sensory garden for a while," I said when we were back outside.

"You go on. I'll be back in a minute. Just need to . . ."

He signalled in the direction of the visitor centre and walked away.

I took it that he needed the gents'.

The sensory garden, a little pocket of scents and sounds and textures, was shaped like a curved teardrop with a narrow entrance widening at the end and shielded on one side by trees and on the other by a wall and planting. There were no visitors in it and I could stand discreetly close to a silver beech and see the door of the gardeners' office. I watched as the gardeners that had been in the kitchen left. One, two, three . . . four.

I waited for thirty seconds but Gabriel didn't return. Then I came out from my hiding place and tried the door of the office. It was closed but not locked. I twisted the dented brass doorknob and let myself in, shutting the door behind me.

Inside there was no sound. I walked quietly to the kitchen door, opened it slowly, put my head around. Empty. Good.

I checked the other room with the desks and computers. It was empty too. I stepped inside, leaving the door slightly ajar. I could see then that the desks were really just basic wooden-topped tables of the kind that might be used in a school exam hall, with no drawers. Each one had an extension cable on the ground beside it where the computers were plugged in and there were baskets, or document trays, beside each computer with papers in them. How could I identify the computer Paddy Hogan used? There were two in each row and I worked my way from the front to the back of the room looking over the papers in the trays – there were lists of plants and invoices mostly with the occasional brochure of seeds or equipment. At the third computer in the middle row I found a pile of papers and an empty envelope with Paddy Hogan's name on it. I couldn't believe my luck.

I turned on the computer. It clicked and pinged into life. The screen showed a large purple-pink orchid. I pressed enter and it asked for a password. Of course it did. What had I been thinking? How would I know Paddy Hogan's password? I tried 1, 2, 3, 4 and then his name and then his mother's name and then . . . What was that? A voice?

"Yes, I can hear you . . ." It was coming from the hallway.

Who was it? I strained to listen. I couldn't hear any reply. Whoever was in the hallway, he was speaking on the phone.

"Yes, yes, I'm here."

The voice was familiar but I couldn't quite place it. I could hardly call out "Who's there?" And I couldn't walk out without being seen. The door to the room I was in was slightly open. I moved as quietly as I could around the tables and stood to one side of the door, pressing myself against the wall. If he came into the room he would open the door wider and I would be hidden by it. Hopefully. I stood very still and waited. And while I waited, I listened.

He spoke in a low voice but his words were heavy with anger as though he would have shouted them if he'd been able to.

"You think you've got something on me? You think you can hold that over my head?" There was menace in his tone and his breathing was ragged. "No, listen to me! I've got too much riding on this to let you fuck it up."

He seemed to be pacing up and down the hall. I heard

someone reply, a crackle of electronic voice, but I couldn't make out the words.

"You'll have to wait. I'll have money for you after," he said.

More crackling speech.

Suddenly I could feel a sneeze pushing its way out through my sinuses into my nostrils. I moved my arm to my nose and tried to smother it in the crook of my elbow.

"Hold on," the man said. He stopped pacing.

I held my breath and pushed myself against the wall as though that might make me invisible, as though I might be able to sink into the plaster, melt into the brick.

"*Shush*," he told the caller. "I heard something."

He pushed the door back and stepped into the room.

"Hello? Hello? Who's there?"

Was I breathing too noisily? I stopped breathing entirely for what felt like minutes.

He went back into the hall.

"It's okay, it's nothing," he said into his phone.

I could hear the electronic voice again and then he almost growling.

"You do know what I'm capable of?"

I shivered and felt sure at that moment that I knew. But the caller didn't seem to be deterred. And after a moment there was a groan.

"Five then, that's all I can manage. But you'll have to give me time."

The caller said something else.

"No. I'll call *you* when I have it. And don't ring me while I'm at work again."

The phone beeped as he ended the call.

"*Fuck! Fuck! Fuck!*" he said.

Then I heard him walk away to go out the front door. I exhaled and crossed to the window just in time to see Bob Richmond walking back toward the visitor centre.

I went back to Paddy Hogan's computer and was just about to try another random password when the front door opened again. I froze.

"*Bea, where are you?*" It was Gabriel.

"*In here!*"

"*Feck sake!*"

"I was trying to get into this computer. I think it's Paddy's."

He took one look at it and shook his head. "Not a hope of getting into that. Come on out of here before anyone catches us."

I supposed he was right. I followed him out and we walked quickly away from the building to the car park.

"Where were you?" I asked him.

"I got waylaid by Seamus Lennon there, complaining about the TV crew all over the place, annoying everyone, he said."

"I can imagine."

"Seamus said he heard the professor boasting that once the programme airs he'll be made and the Botanic Gardens will be famous."

It certainly would be good publicity for the gardens but then I thought of what Seamus had said to me – that the gardens were here before all the people now working in them and they would still be here after they'd gone. The gardeners and the college staff, the director and the important visiting professors, they were only custodians.

"Gabriel . . . something happened while I was in there."

"What?"

I told him then about the angry, one-sided conversation I'd overheard.

"And it sounded like Bob was giving someone money?" he said.

We had reached my car and we stood there, speculating.

"It sounded to me like he was being blackmailed . . ."

"But no clue about who was doing it? Man or woman?"

"No." I wondered if Bob Richmond could have had some part in Paddy Hogan's death. And maybe someone knew that and wanted payment for their silence.

"Blackmail's a dangerous game," Gabriel said.

I checked my watch – it was just after ten.

"I need to go and get organised for work. I'll call you later."

At the Labour Court, the committee said it would work straight through to 3.30pm with a brief coffee break to make up for the late start.

Reginald Taylor began by summarising the reasons behind Marina Fernandez' dismissal. He highlighted the evidence given by "the well-respected Dr Dunboyne". Then continued, "We also heard from Frances Parr, her previous manager, and a statement from the owner of High Hill Care Home. These are all upstanding, well-regarded professionals. I hope you will give due weight to their evidence."

He went over what each witness had said and told the committee that Ms Fernandez was lucky she had only lost her job.

"It was only Dr Dunboyne's compassion that prevented him from calling the guards," he said.

It was a wonder the words hadn't caught in his throat.

It seemed clear to me that Dr Dunboyne's only interest was in protecting the reputation of his nursing home.

The committee took a short break when he'd finished and I took some air. I wanted to rest my fingers, which, though much better than before I started the treatment, were still not quite right. Was this how it was going to be now? I took my place back in the hearing room just in time for the committee to reappear.

"Mr Taylor," Miriam Lynch said, "could you tell us whether Ms Fernandez had any representation when she was formally questioned about the thefts during the employer's investigation?"

The barrister looked momentarily confused. "Ms Fernandez was not questioned during the internal investigation. She was written to and she responded."

The chairwoman looked at him steadily for a moment before saying "I see" and then "Mr Waldron?"

Joe Waldron did his best to dissect and damage each allegation against his client. I noticed his suit, which was normally creased, looked like it was fresh from the dry cleaner's and I thought he must have made a special effort for the final day. He handed in written testimonials from Ms Fernandez' employers in the west of Ireland and in the UK.

"I won't read these into the record but you can see that these people had complete faith in my client. They have nothing but praise for her."

"All right, thank you, Mr Waldron, we'll give them due consideration," Miriam Lynch said.

He criticised management at Chapels Nursing Home for its lack of proper investigation into the thefts and for its unfair treatment of Ms Fernandez.

"My client has been wrongly accused," he said. "And I'm sure you'll agree with me that it's very telling that no one called the guards at any stage though they allege property was stolen. I believe fair procedures were dispensed with by Chapels Nursing Home when my client was effectively branded a thief and unfairly dismissed." He paused for breath and looked down at his notes. "True, she was the nurse on duty at night and, as such, was responsible for the patients in her charge. But any number of people had access to the lockers, including the patients, and who really knew what had happened?" He looked at each member of the committee in turn. "All we do know is that Ms Fernandez was held responsible and, without proper inquiry, sacked by management, and that was a travesty."

He went on to suggest that each of the witnesses had their own reasons for being untruthful.

"The timing of Ms Fernandez' suspension makes no sense unless she was suspended after she made a complaint about Dr Dunboyne. No one has explained why it took so long to suspend her after the alleged thefts. But I think we all know why."

He gave the committee that look again.

"I would like it on record that it has taken Ms Fernandez four months to find another job and she was suspended from that once news of her Labour Court case became known. *This episode is ruining her life.*" He paused and looked at his client. "Ms Fernandez wants you to know that she will walk out of here today with her head held high – she has done nothing wrong."

When his speech was over, Miriam Lynch thanked him.

"We'll need some time to consider these issues."

She consulted a diary on her desk and then whispered to the committee members either side of her.

"We hope to have a decision for you by Wednesday the 15th. Let's pencil that in and if there's any change we'll let you know."

While I packed up I watched Marina Fernandez walk out of the room. I thought she looked tired. And I couldn't help wondering why she hadn't given evidence in her own defence.

Chapter Fifteen

Tuesday, March 7th

The morning held echoes of midwinter with a clear blue sky and frost on the ground. I'd intended going for a walk in the gardens and asking about the professor's course on orchids but decided to have tea and do a little thinking first in the coffee shop opposite the gardens' entrance gate. I parked in St Mobhi Drive, fixing my scarf and gloves before getting out of the car. My breath was visible, a small ball of white fog that drifted upward toward the houses, the grey roof-slates of which were glistening with frost. Only Constance Anderson's roof was dark, the slates wet from having thawed. Underfoot the path was slippery and I walked round the corner with care.

The window of the coffee shop was steamed up on the inside from customers' breaths on the cold glass. Inside all nine tables were occupied.

I was glancing around, trying to assess whether any of the occupants were near finishing, when I spotted Constance alone at the back of the room close to the counter. She was holding a newspaper and wearing a pair of reading glasses which she now slid down her nose to look at me. Then she beckoned me over.

"You can sit here if you wish," she said.

"Thanks." I pulled out a chair, which was wooden with a straight back and a Laura Ashley floral-cushioned seat. I was about to sit down when she shook her head.

"You need to order first." She said it as though I had committed a terrible faux pas.

I went to the counter, asked for tea and a slice of fruit cake and paid.

"I'll bring it down," the young woman who served me said.

As soon as I sat I realised Constance had almost reached the end of her coffee.

"Would you like another one of those?" I asked.

"No, no. I've had quite enough caffeine for the moment." She had placed the newspaper, folded to a quarter of its size, beside her cup. I thought she looked pale and a little worried and wondered if, like me, she might be dreaming about Paddy Hogan.

"How have you been, Constance?"

"Fine, I've been fine, thank you."

My tea and cake arrived then. I thanked the waitress and she left.

"Has Paddy been on your mind? He's been playing on mine . . ."

She looked at me doubtfully as though she couldn't understand why I was attempting to stray away from small talk.

"Not really," she said.

I wondered if I'd be better off sitting in silence but tried again in small-talk territory.

"How are your plants coming on?" I asked.

"What?" Her response was surprisingly sharp and I thought I saw a flash of anger.

It seemed I couldn't say the right thing.

"You said you were trying to grow flowers in your garden . . ."

"Oh yes." Her features became benign again. "I'm having some success with my orchids but not so much with other things."

"Orchids?" Here was something we could talk about. "Did you get some tips from the professor's book? I got it from the library."

She smiled. "Great, isn't it? He's just so accomplished. And with *Natural World* making a programme about him – it's just so exciting to know him."

"Yes." I lifted the cup to my lips to smother a desire to cringe.

She sniffed and finished her coffee.

"I have to go now," she said.

She put her newspaper into a straw-weave tote bag that had been hanging from the arm of her chair. She stood up to put her coat on, wobbled, put one hand out to steady herself and then sat down again.

"You're very pale," I said.

"I just felt a little . . . I'll be all right in a minute."

"I hope you're not coming down with something."

She rested her left elbow on the table and put her hand to her forehead.

"It's my nephew . . ." she said almost to herself.

"Your nephew? What about him?"

She shook her head. "He visited me yesterday and he

had a bad cold – probably gave it to me."

I pictured a child with a runny nose, sneezing on her as he kissed her cheek.

"Would you like me to walk back home with you?" I asked after a short while.

She looked toward the door and then nodded. "If you wouldn't mind."

I finished my tea and we left, walking slowly round the corner through the cool air, her breath coming in little puffs like a slow steam engine.

When we got to her house on St Mobhi Drive she stopped and leaned against the white gate pillar.

"I'll just catch my breath," she said.

I'd intended leaving her there but changed my mind. Despite the cool air around us she looked flushed and a little sweaty.

"Okay now," she said after a minute.

We began walking up the long driveway which was bordered by a privet hedge on one side and a lawn on the other. When we got to the door she said she was still feeling a little light-headed.

"Would you like me to make you a hot drink?"

She put her hand on the door frame to steady herself. "If it's not too much trouble."

I followed her down a narrow, dim hallway into a bright kitchen with a large window that looked out onto a garden with a greenhouse at its end.

She sat down at a heavy, pine table – a large table, I thought, for a woman who lived alone. It also seemed a little too large for the kitchen, which was of a country style with a dresser and cream presses and an Aga stove.

"That's not lit," she said when she saw me look in its direction, perhaps thinking I might attempt to boil a kettle on it.

Despite that, the room was warm and I wanted to say that it felt like the cooker was lit. I filled her electric kettle and switched it on and as I did my phone buzzed in my handbag. I took it out. It was Gabriel.

"Do you mind?" I asked Constance. She shook her head and I stepped out into the hall.

"I thought we might take a walk around the gardens this morning – where are you?" he asked.

I explained, and he said he wasn't far away.

"I'll park outside and wait for you," he said.

When I went back into the kitchen Constance was sitting with her eyes closed.

"Do you have any Lemsip?" I thought the soothing drink might help her temperature.

But she shook her head. "I can't abide it. Tea will be fine – you'll have one with me? And I think I have paracetamol somewhere."

She indicated a drawer near the sink and inside I found a pack of the tablets along with clothes pegs and a neatly folded plastic-bag collection. I gave her a glass of water and the blister strip. She swallowed two.

I made the tea in a china pot I found, located cups and saucers and put a set at her elbow. She opened her eyes.

"Important call?" she asked.

"Just a friend. We were going for a walk. He's waiting for me outside in his car."

"It's too cold to leave anyone sitting in a car. Ask him to come in."

I hadn't expected her suggestion but I was glad to agree. I'd been hoping for an opportunity to introduce them.

Gabriel was listening to Johnny Cash – "Sunday Morning Coming Down" – and tapping out its rhythm on the steering wheel when I knocked on the car window. He opened the door.

"I'm going to sit with Constance for a bit – do you want to come in and meet her? She suggested it."

"Right so." He switched off the engine, the music stopped abruptly and he hopped out of the car. He took the driveway in a few strides and I had to walk quickly to keep up with him. He'd got fitter since his visit to Donegal.

In the kitchen, Constance had put an extra cup and saucer and a plate on the table, in the same floral pattern, with chocolate biscuits on it and napkins at each placing. She seemed considerably improved. I had no idea paracetamol could work so quickly and I wondered whether the prospect of male company had perked her up.

She smiled at Gabriel and put out her hand for him to shake in an almost regal way. He obliged.

"Are you feeling better now?" I asked her, after pouring the tea.

"Much. I don't know what came over me." She sipped from her cup and smiled at Gabriel when he took a biscuit.

We made polite conversation about the day's cold weather compared to the mildness the previous Friday.

"That's Ireland for you," Gabriel said.

Constance agreed enthusiastically, as though he'd made an observation worthy of Copernicus. She asked him whether he had any interest in gardening and what his favourite plants were.

"I'm very partial to a good orchid," he said.

I tried not to laugh – I knew he preferred roses.

Constance smiled. "You're a man after my own heart. I have a greenhouse filled with orchids."

"Did you grow them yourself, Constance?" He sounded enormously impressed.

"I did my best. I'm not as green-fingered as I'd like to be so they're nowhere near as lovely as the ones in the Botanic Gardens." She gestured toward the kitchen window. "I'll show you when you're finished if you like."

It seemed to me that she addressed her offer only to Gabriel so, when they both eventually stood up to go outside, I didn't follow. She glanced over her shoulder at me as she went out but didn't invite me to come along. I could see them from the window, talking as they walked together down a narrow path which cut through the middle of a plain but well-trimmed lawn. It surprised me that a woman so interested in horticulture would have nothing but grass in her back garden.

I got up, stretched and decided I needed to find a bathroom. Taking my handbag with me, I made my way out into the hall and up the narrow staircase. At the top there was a typical landing, small and dark with a door in the ceiling to reach the attic. I thought from up there that the house smelled a little bit sour or musty. The bathroom door just at the top of the stairs was ajar, making it easy for me to find.

After I'd washed my hands and topped up my lipstick in an unkind mirror, I walked back down again, admiring as I did a selection of botanical drawings positioned on the wall. They were elegant and made a handsome collection. At the foot of the stairs there was a photograph of a group of people, all in rain gear, smiling. I recognised Constance and the professor standing just behind her. I took out my phone, took a quick photo and as I did I heard the back door opening. I put my phone away and walked back into the kitchen.

Constance gave me a curious look as though she was suspicious that I had been snooping.

"I hope you don't mind – I needed the bathroom."

"Not at all." She nodded. "But there was no need for you to go up, you know. There's a little loo tucked under the stairs there."

"I didn't realise," I said, feeling I had been accused of crossing some social boundary.

Gabriel didn't sit down but took his coat and walked into the hall. I followed.

"Can I just say those botanical drawings are lovely?" I gestured to the five drawings framed in white.

"Well, thank you. They're my own work."

I took a few steps back up the stairs to look at the drawings more closely and Gabriel joined me. The images were all orchids.

"You're very talented," he said.

Constance puffed up like a courting pigeon and her cheeks reddened.

"I'll do one for you if you like – maybe of the *phalaenopsis* you so admired?"

"That would be very generous of you, Constance, thank you," he said.

It took all my effort not to grin at him. He knew how to charm when he needed to and he had really turned it on for her.

"That's a very interesting photo," I said, indicating the framed picture at the foot of the stairs as though I'd only just noticed it.

She peered at it closely, reminding me for a moment of a mole. "Yes, happy days. There he is." She pointed out Paddy Hogan.

I hadn't recognised him.

"Poor Paddy," she said.

"Where was it taken?" Gabriel asked.

"On a field trip to the Burren with a group from the gardens. I was one of the paying guests."

"Lucky you . . ."

"Yes, I was very lucky to be included – it was mostly professionals, experts really in their field." She sighed. "Oh well, we just have to get on with things."

"Are you feeling okay now?" I asked.

"I'll be fine. I'm sure it's just a head cold. But thank you for looking after me."

We said goodbye and left her standing at the door, watching us as we walked down the driveway.

Clouds had rolled in while we were inside and now it began to rain sharp icy drops.

"I think we'll have to give the walk a miss?" he said.

I followed him to his car and sat into the passenger seat.

"She certainly took a shine to you," I said.

"Ah now – she's lonely, that's all. Where are you parked?"

"Down there a bit – interesting though, wasn't it?"

"What, the photograph?"

"That, and everything else – very interesting. I took a photo of it." I opened my phone.

"I thought you might have."

There were nine men and five women in the photo, arranged in two semi-circular rows, all in boots and rain jackets and jeans or waterproof leggings. The men were mostly standing in the back row. Above the group, the sky was heavy with cloud in various shades of grey and they seemed to be standing on a limestone plateau. I stretched the photograph with my fingers so that I could look more closely at it. Besides Constance and Paddy Hogan, I recognised the professor and George Delaney. And I thought one of them might have been the woman I saw arguing with George in the Teak House.

"I wonder if that was the trip to the Burren the professor mentioned in his book."

"Could be."

"She really does know lots of people from the gardens, doesn't she?"

"Seems to."

"Doesn't it make her reaction when Paddy Hogan died even stranger?" I couldn't reconcile her not calling his name. "Shouldn't she have said 'Paddy Hogan is dead' when she came running out of the Palm House? Isn't that what you'd say naturally?"

"It's a bit odd, sure enough. But . . . I'd like to know a bit more about that trip."

"Maybe you could call back to Constance on your own, turn on the charm again and she might tell you."

I was half joking, but he responded seriously.

"I suppose I could do that if I have to . . . I could call in tomorrow and ask her for some tips on growing orchids."

I stifled a laugh.

"Well, if you want answers, Bea . . ."

He sounded a bit cross, and I said no more. I did want answers.

I put my hand on the door and put one leg out.

"Let me know how you get on," I said, standing up.

He had driven away by the time I got to my car.

I went home and resolved to enquire about the professor's orchid course another day.

Chapter Sixteen

Wednesday, March 8th

At breakfast, I logged into my emails on my laptop to check if there were any work offers. I would be back in the Labour Court on March the 15th for judgment in the Fernandez case and after that I had nothing lined up until a commercial case two weeks later. I'd been told that case was likely to run for two weeks, but then it was impossible to know. I looked at my hands, my fingers, each bony knuckle. All was perfectly normal now. But what would they look like if I was in court every day for two weeks? How much work should I do? How much should I not do? It wasn't that I was worried about money. I had no mortgage and, though I wasn't frugal, I wasn't the kind of person who needed a lot of things. I appreciated a new suit when the season turned, good shoes but not high fashion, a few classic basics, nothing extravagant. There were also some savings, accumulated over busier years, I had not as yet tapped into. So money was not the issue. What mattered was being busy, feeling useful. What else was there? I scanned down the list of emails – there was a lot of spam but no job offers.

The phone buzzed with a text message then from Gabriel.

Are you around? Can I call over?
I said I was. I would be glad to be distracted.
See you in fifteen.
I checked the time, ten-thirty. Before he had the episode with his heart, he would have been standing outside the door of Hanlon's or some other pub near his Stoneybatter home waiting for opening time. I was glad that his long rest in Donegal had broken that habit. It wasn't an addiction, I felt, merely a social routine.

By the time he called to the house I had made some tea and wholemeal toast for him. He sat at the table and in his usual manner spared no time helping himself.

"Well?" I asked, watching him with fascination as he stretched a tiny portion of butter across a slice of toast.

"I went back to Constance's." He took a bite and then added another sliver of butter from the dish and spread it carefully.

"When?"

"Last night."

"I thought you said . . . Never mind."

"She said the trip they were on was for four days a couple of years ago – May 2015." He swallowed some tea. I suspected his toast was still too dry. "There's the four we know – Constance and the professor, Paddy Hogan and George Delaney. Another four came over from the US university the professor had links with. Three were visiting from Kew Gardens in London – there were two Irish guests, and one of the other gardeners from the Bots, Kaya Nkosi, was there as well."

"Kaya Nkosi – she must be the woman I saw arguing with George Delaney." I counted on my fingers. "That's fourteen on the trip."

"But there was someone missing from the photo, someone who was holding the camera." He ate more toast, enjoying himself.

"Who?"

"Ava Hogan."

"Oh!" I hadn't expected that. She'd never given the impression that she was involved with her brother's work in any way. "I wonder why she never mentioned going on a trip with the gardens."

He chewed for a minute. "Why would she? She's probably forgotten about it."

"I'm sure you're right." Still, I felt as though we were missing something. "Anything else?"

"They stayed in Hazelgrove Lodge – that's a guesthouse on the edge of the Burren – and every day they went out on the Burren to look at the flora. Constance had a particular interest in the orchids, obviously. But they looked at everything."

"And that was it?"

"Meals were included, she said, so they all ate together. There was very little free time, talks organised in the evenings, that sort of thing. There was a visit to the nearest pub one of the nights. It was a seven-mile walk, she said, and they only did it the once. It rained a lot of the time."

"It sounds a bit . . . intense." The Burren in the rain looking for flowers all day. It didn't exactly sound like fun to me.

He gulped some tea. "They seemed to be long days, right enough – up at six-thirty, in bed mostly at ten. She found the whole thing enjoyable, she said, but a bit too short."

I fetched the professor's book and found the page that described the Burren trip.

"Here it is." I read aloud: "'*This was a four-day visit*

to the wonderful Burren in the West of Ireland. I was leading a group from the Irish National Botanic Gardens, with guests from the UK and US, and we were staying with Eileen and Peter Cassidy at their lovely guesthouse' – yes, that must be the trip, when he spotted the *Platanthera bifolia*. Did Constance say anything about that?"

"Never mentioned it. Maybe she didn't know."

"Or didn't think it mattered."

He rubbed his chin in the way he often did when he was thinking.

"I was wondering about the Burren," he said then. "Ever seen it?"

"Years ago, I think."

My phone rang then from the living room where I'd plugged it in to charge. By the time I got to it, it had stopped. The number was not familiar and I didn't call it back.

In the kitchen, Gabriel pushed his chair back from the table, stretched his arms above his head and yawned. I thought it was a bit early for him to be tired.

"When was the last time you were out of the city?"

I tried to remember – had it been when I'd stayed with Georgina O'Donnell in Ballymoney?

"A while," I said.

"We could both do with a bit of country air," he said.

I wanted to remind him that he wasn't long back from Donegal.

"What are you doing at the weekend?" he asked.

What was I doing? Some housework, laundry, perhaps finally call my former colleague Janine Gracefield and find out how she was. Not a lot.

"Only I was wondering . . ." He looked at me a little

warily. "Would you be interested in a weekend away? I wouldn't mind trying that Burren guesthouse – Constance said it was lovely – and you could probably do with a break."

I hesitated. What was he asking me? Were trips away to be a part of our reconstructed fraternal relationship? He noticed my delay.

"I'm not . . . we'll get two rooms, Bea."

I smiled – doing my best to give him the impression that I was relieved at that.

"Yes. Why not?" I said.

And suddenly the thought of getting out of the city for the weekend with Gabriel seemed very attractive even if the ground rules were crystal clear.

"I'll book it," I said.

I googled the guesthouse and gave them a call. The man on the phone, who introduced himself as Peter Cassidy, said they had rooms available.

"You're lucky it's March – you'd not normally get anything at such short notice," he said.

I made the appropriate noises of gratitude, thinking that he was a bit too full of his own importance for my liking.

"Check-in is at two o'clock," he said.

"Fine. See you then."

"Grand," Gabriel said when I told him. "I'll pick you up Saturday morning. You don't mind if I drive, do you?"

I laughed at him – as if I had a choice.

Just as I had loaded the dishwasher with our cups and plates, my phone rang again. It was the same unfamiliar number. I answered it.

"Are you Beatrice Barrington?" It was a woman's voice. African, I thought, perhaps South African.

"Yes?"

"Ava Hogan gave me your number. My name is Kaya Nkosi. I worked with Paddy."

"You're one of the gardeners at the Botanics?"

"Yes. Could we . . . would it be possible to meet?"

"What's this about, Ms Nkosi?"

"Ava asked me to speak to you. They are all saying Paddy Hogan killed himself but I do not think that is right . . . Can we meet? I could call to your home?"

"My home? Yes, all right."

I gave her my address and she said she would call by at half seven.

Kaya Nkosi knocked on the glass of the hall door instead of ringing the bell and it made me wonder if she was nervous about visiting me. When I opened the door though, I could see she was not the nervous type. She was tall with dark-brown skin, dark eyes and short, dark hair in a fringeless bob. She seemed to radiate confidence and she was definitely the person I'd seen arguing with George Delaney as well as the woman in Constance Anderson's photo. She tucked some hair behind her right ear and extended her hand to me.

"Hello."

I shook her hand and opened the door wide. "Come in, please."

She stepped into the hall and undid the buttons on a black rain mac. She was wearing a lilac, silk-sheen shirt dress underneath. She caught me looking at it.

"I have to meet someone later." She smiled and there

was a sort of sparkle in it that made me think she was going on a date.

I led her into the living room and she sat on the couch, resting a black quilted handbag on her lap.

"Can I get you something? Coffee? Tea?"

"No, thank you. I cannot stay for long."

I sat down on the armchair. "Ava asked you to talk to me about Paddy?"

"Yes. Did you know him before he died?"

I shook my head. "Unfortunately not."

"He was a good man. He was the kind of man who would help you if you asked for help. Or even if you did not ask for it, he would help you." She played with the handbag's silver clasp as she spoke. "When I came to the National Botanic Gardens I was not that long in Ireland and I had few friends. I came over here because I want to specialise in orchids – you know the Botanic Gardens is famous for its orchid-growing?"

I nodded though I hadn't known.

"And it was also very good that Professor James Christakos was there too. I thought I could study his work and learn from him." She waved her hand. "That does not matter. What I wanted to tell you is that Paddy made everything easier. He was kind to me when other people were indifferent. Those first two months, I think I may have left if he had not helped me settle in. He explained how the gardens worked – not what they tell you in the office or when they interview you for the job – the real things. And he helped me find accommodation that would not take all of my money."

"I see." I was waiting for her to get to the point of her visit.

"That is why I cannot believe them when they say he killed himself. He was not an unhappy man."

"How can any of us really know what's going on inside another person's head though, Ms Nkosi? People can seem outwardly fine and still be suffering." I didn't know why I was saying this now, when what she was telling me was what I believed.

"I know that." She shook her head. "But Paddy was not inside himself."

I must have looked confused because she turned her palms upwards in a gesture of exasperation.

"I'm saying he had plans. He spoke to me about some book he was working on. He was excited about it."

"A book?"

"Yes. And I want to say this – I heard him arguing not long before he died." She twisted the clasp on her handbag again, open, shut, open, shut. "Do you know the coffee shop in the gardens?"

I nodded.

"I was on the other side of the wall – the wall that separates the coffee-shop courtyard from the rest of the gardens?"

"I know it."

"I was walking toward the arch," she made a shape of an arch in the air with her left hand to emphasise the entrance to the courtyard, "and I heard the voices. Paddy was saying something about being silent or silenced and then I think he said, 'This has to stop' and I heard someone say 'Weasel'. I could not recognise the other voice, not from that one word. When I walked into the courtyard Paddy was alone and going toward the door that leads into reception."

"Did he say anything to you about it?"

"No. I don't think he noticed me."

"And the other voice, was it a man?"

"I think so . . . I cannot be sure."

"Have you told the guards – the police – what you heard, Ms Nkosi?"

"The police did not ask me any questions."

I got a piece of paper and a pen and wrote Detective Inspector Rebecca Maguire's email address on it. "Please, if you want to help the Hogans, send this detective a message. She's looking into Paddy's death."

She took the paper from me, opened her handbag, put it inside and twisted the clasp closed again.

"There is something else," she said. "I asked Paddy to help a friend of mine – Celine Deegan – a student I met at choir. He said he would. It could be that is what led him into difficulties."

"What do you mean? What sort of help?"

She shook her head. "It is not my story to tell. Let me give you Celine's number. She told me she will speak to you." She took out her phone and sent me a text. My phone pinged.

"Thanks," I said. "Can I ask you something?"

She nodded.

"I saw you arguing with George Delaney a few days ago. What was that about?"

She hesitated, then stood up and put on her coat. "I was reminding him about Celine – when you speak to her you will understand."

I saw her to the door.

"I hope you have a nice evening," I said. She gave me

that smile again and though I knew I shouldn't, I asked, "Is he very handsome?"

"Yes, and useful I hope!" She spoke over her shoulder as she walked away, her expression serious again.

I called Ava as soon as she left.

"How did you get on with Kaya?" she asked.

"Fine. She seems genuine."

"She is and she really liked Paddy. She told you, did she, that she doesn't think he . . .?"

"She was very clear on that," I said. "Can I ask you something? Was Paddy working on a book?"

"A book? You mean his drawings? I think he was going to try to get them published."

"What are they of, the drawings?"

"Flowers, just flowers. Would you like to see them?"

I said I would and she said she'd call by with them when she had a chance.

"Mam's a bit . . . off at the moment," she said.

"Whenever suits just send me a text." I wondered what "off" could mean. It seemed to me that Rita Hogan was difficult enough already and I felt sorry for Ava with no one to share that burden.

After the call I texted a message to the number Kaya had given me. Celine Deegan came back within ten minutes and asked if I could meet her after choir practice on Thursday.

Chapter Seventeen

Thursday, March 9th

I'd agreed to meet Celine at three o'clock in the lobby of the Helix Theatre in Dublin City University where her choir was practising for a performance. It was only a fifteen-minute drive from home, so I'd arrived a little early and when I entered the building and heard singing I followed the sound into the theatre and took a seat at the back. There were lights on the stage but otherwise the room was dark and nobody noticed me.

They were midway through "Amazing Grace".

A young woman with honey-blond hair and a round, almost angelic face was singing the solo. The group behind her, a blend of men and women, were humming.

"*How precious did that grace appear the hour I first believed!*"

The song swelled and the voices harmonised and there was something beautiful and moving in the music as it filled the near-empty auditorium. I was transfixed by it.

"Lovely, lovely, see you all tomorrow," a voice said, I assumed the conductor, when the song had reached its end.

The group began to break up. I got out of my seat and

slipped back to the foyer and waited. I was there for ten minutes when a woman approached me – the same woman I had seen singing the solo in the choir. She had lively blue eyes and the plump cheeks and creamy skin of a cherub.

"Are you Beatrice?" she asked.

"Yes."

She put out a hand and shook mine and then pulled back quickly. "Sorry, I forgot – sweaty palms. It happens to me every time I have to sing a solo." She shoved her hands into the pockets of a black wool coat, the kind with no buttons that's tied at the waist. There was a silk-sheen gold scarf at her neck.

"I didn't notice," I said.

"Do you have a car?"

"Yes."

"I've an hour until I have to go to a lecture – would you mind if we went somewhere to get food?"

"Where would you like to go?"

"Do you know the Rise Café?"

I said I did and we walked together out to the car. I was curious about the choice – the café was at the more expensive end of the market and I imagined as a student she would be struggling financially. Perhaps she had banked on my paying, which I would. She told me about DCU while I drove and how she was studying to be a nurse. The choir, she said, was her way of winding down. It helped her relax after lectures and, when she was on work experience, it enabled her to close the door on the challenges and shocks of hospital life.

At the café we found a table for two tucked into the corner where a wall filled with wine bottles met the window.

"Would you like coffee? A sandwich?" I handed her the menu.

I signalled to the waitress who came to our table with pen and notebook in hand.

"Tea for me, please, and the smoked ham sandwich," I said.

Celine asked for soup, a chicken wrap and a Diet Coke. The drinks arrived promptly and before the food. I milked and stirred my tea.

"What did Kaya tell you?" Celine asked, pouring Coke into her glass and causing the ice to crackle and fizz. Her nails were long and painted a sparkling gold, matching her scarf.

"Just that she'd asked Paddy to help you and she thought it might be good if I knew why."

"And you're going to find out about Paddy for his family, is that it?"

"I'm trying anyway."

She sipped her drink. "I'm from Clones, you see, in County Monaghan, and being a student in Dublin is expensive . . . Rent and food and books."

I wondered if she would ask me for money in exchange for information and she must have seen that in my face.

"I'm not telling you this because I want money from you – it's to help you understand why I did what I did."

I nodded and drank some tea. "Go on."

"And I can't keep asking the parents – they don't have all that much."

"I understand," I said.

"It was a friend of mine, Julia, who introduced me to it. She studies in DCU too and she's from Monaghan as well. She told me it helped her make ends meet."

"Yes." She was taking a while to tell me what it was she'd been doing and I took it that she was ashamed or embarrassed about it.

She sat forward in her chair and lowered her voice. "It's a website – *OnlyFans* – do you know it?"

I hadn't heard of it and was about to say so when the food arrived. Celine sat back.

"Soup and wrap?" the waitress asked.

"For me," Celine said. "Thank you."

The waitress put my ham sandwich before me, I thanked her and she left.

Celine began eating her soup.

"Go on," I said.

She leaned forward again. "So people, men I think mostly, they find you on this website and they subscribe to your feed and they get to watch you do things and sometimes ask you to do things." She waved the soup spoon in the air as she spoke.

"Your feed?" I asked.

"Yes – the images and stuff you post?" She waited for me to nod my understanding. "They can see you through a webcam but you can't see them. If they like what they see, they go on subscribing."

I bit into my sandwich. I wasn't sure how to respond – it was the online equivalent of a peep show.

"Do you not feel . . ." I wanted to say demeaned but she assumed I was thinking of her security.

"Frightened? No. I'm in my bedroom – no one touches me or knows me. I call myself 'Lulubell', like a country and western singer. Doing it means nothing to me and it's perfectly safe. That is . . . I thought it was safe." She paused to finish her soup.

I thought there must have been other ways a student could make money. Could she not get a job in Pennys? Or with her voice, find a gig with some band?

"I can make a couple of hundred in an afternoon this way," she said.

"I can see the attraction." She wouldn't make that in Pennys and it was none of my business how she earned her money. "Where does Paddy Hogan come into this?"

"Right. One day I was with Kaya at the Botanic Gardens. We were having coffee and a man came over to our table, he worked there. His name was Bob Richmond. Kaya introduced us and said I was a student at DCU. I knew straight away that he'd been looking at me – I could see it in his eyes. He didn't say anything but I knew."

I finished my sandwich, waiting for her to continue. Bob Richmond again.

"The night after that I saw him on campus and then the following day, when I was coming out of my apartment block, he was there, leaning up against the wall, just staring at me."

The thought of that made me shiver and I picked up my tea for comfort.

"That must have been frightening."

"He never spoke to me. Then he messaged me on the website, asked me to do things, called me by my real name. I had to block him. After that, he showed up on campus a lot and sometimes he'd walk behind me. I shouted at him a few times to leave me alone but he kept coming back."

"What is wrong with people?" The words came out of me involuntarily.

"I told Kaya about it and she said I should tell the guards but I didn't want to. You can understand why."

"Of course."

"She suggested I should meet Paddy Hogan. She said he was a nice man and that he'd help me. And he did. He told me Bob Richmond has a partner and a baby on the way and he'd 'talk sense into him'."

"And do you think Bob might have fought with Paddy?"

She shook her head. "I only know that Paddy did something because Bob stopped following me."

She finished her Coke and dabbed her mouth with her napkin.

"Thanks for telling me, Celine. I don't suppose you'd be willing to tell the guards?"

She shook her head.

"You haven't spoken to Bob Richmond since, have you? On the phone or anything?" I was thinking of the conversation I'd overheard that sounded like he was being blackmailed.

"God no. Why would I?"

I believed her.

"And I suppose you finished with the website?" I was sorry I'd said that as soon as the words were out.

A flash of irritation crossed her face. "Not until I finish college and find a proper job." She spoke from between clenched teeth, stood and put her coat on, wrapping the gold scarf round her neck. "It's not important to me, do you understand? It's harmless."

I wasn't sure how to respond. I couldn't say I thought it was harmless.

She shook her head. "Thanks for lunch anyway," she

said. Then she walked out of the café.

I had an urge to follow her and apologise for not saying what she wanted to hear. But I was worried about her safety. Did she not understand that in a relatively small city like Dublin, or anywhere else in Ireland, anyone could find her if they really wanted to?

I paid the bill and left.

Chapter Eighteen

Friday, March 10th

On Friday morning I awoke gasping from a dream about pelargoniums and the sound of my mother singing. The purple petals of the plant had moved on a breeze from the windowsill in my childhood kitchen to the floor of the Palm House in the Botanic Gardens and they lay on the stone path around the head of Paddy Hogan. It was a strange sensation to wake up catching my breath and still to feel like the child who heard my mother's singing. What could that have been about?

I got out of bed, put on a dressing gown and stood for a while at the window. The sea outside was calm and grey, reflecting a uniformly dark sky that sat over the city. And though the view had the power to lift my spirits no matter what the season, it didn't seem to have that effect this morning. I was glad Gabriel had suggested the weekend trip to the Burren. I considered calling him then to tell him about Kaya and Celine but decided it would be better to wait until the drive down. A part of me feared, given the way things were between us now, that I might becoming too reliant on him and I didn't want that.

I went downstairs, had some breakfast and, without getting dressed, set up my laptop on the kitchen table. Still no offers of work. I knew that demand for stenography had waned but, even so, there were still companies managing to survive. Where was I going wrong? Had I lost my reputation for excellence? Had my involvement in the Stephen O'Farrell trial three years before meant I was sullied by it? If that was the problem, I decided, there was nothing I could do about it. I examined the knuckles of my hands. How would I manage anyway, I asked myself, if I was commissioned for a lengthy trial now?

I went upstairs, got dressed and began to think about Kaya and Celine and Bob. My mind was fizzing with questions and I decided to call Gabriel after all. Sitting on the edge of my bed I pressed his number. I let it ring twice, three times, four times before stopping it and letting it drop onto the duvet. As I did, it buzzed. I picked it up expecting something from Gabriel – an explanation perhaps, a message saying he'd call me later. But it was a text from Ava saying she'd drop by with Paddy's drawings sometime in the afternoon. I gave her my address, pleased that I'd have something new to focus on. In the meantime, what I needed was a long walk by the sea to help me think. I put on my warmest wool coat, wrapped a red scarf round my neck and went out the door. I didn't bring a bag but put my phone in my pocket and set off in the direction of the Wooden Bridge. I walked parallel to the sea beside the low wall that edges it. There was a stillness in the water that is rare particularly in March – it had the quality of mirrored glass with the birds and the clouds reflected in it. There were people walking by me, with dogs or attached to their phones, but they, like the birds, seemed subdued to me, and I wondered if there might be a storm on its way.

I was thinking of Kaya and Celine and had almost reached the Wooden Bridge, which links Clontarf Road to the Bull Wall, when I saw a familiar face walking toward me.

It was Bob Richmond. I nodded at him, expecting him to walk on, but he stopped and though my head was filled with what Celine Deegan had told me about him, I stopped, too.

"Is this your neck of the woods?" he asked.

"It is. And shouldn't you be at work?"

"I thought I'd give myself a couple of hours off this morning. Sometimes I just need to be beside the sea, you know? Helps me get my head straight."

I could understand that. "I do know," I said. "And how is the coffee shop going for you since you took over management?"

"All going to plan so far anyway." He looked out in the direction of the Poolbeg Chimneys and then back at me. "I hear you were the one who found poor Paddy."

"Were you two friends?"

"Friends? I suppose – he came in to me every morning for his coffee – I liked him."

I wondered why he was telling me that. Surely he didn't like him all that much after Paddy warned him off harassing Celine?

"He seemed like a nice man," I said. "I haven't found anyone prepared to say a bad thing about him."

"Yeah. I'd heard you were asking about him."

Were people complaining about me? "Who told you that?" I struggled to keep a neutral expression on my face.

"Doesn't matter who." He shuffled his feet as if he was going to walk away but changed his mind. "Look, I don't mean to overstep – but for his family and that, for the people who worked with him, don't you think it would be better to just leave him in peace?" He looked intently at me as though he thought if he stared long and hard enough he might force me into agreement.

I wanted to say 'Don't lecture me, stalker', but I said, "I . . . I think his family would prefer to know the truth. They're entitled to that." I tried to sound firm though his presence now, a little too close to me, was unsettling.

"I think you'll find they know it already."

"Do they though, Bob?" I was tempted to mention Celine's name but thought it might be too risky, given I was alone with him and so close to the sea. Perhaps it was better if he didn't know I knew about that.

"No-one wants you around trying to dig up dirt, understand?" Suddenly his tone was laced with menace.

I didn't respond.

He stood for a moment longer then nodded and walked on.

I took a seat on a nearby bench. I was shaking a little and it took time to get my heartbeat back to normal. Was I angry or frightened? Probably both. Why did he think he could speak to me like that? Was he afraid I'd stumble across his secret once I started "to dig up dirt", that I'd find out what he'd done and that Paddy had confronted him about it? Well, he was too late with his threats. But might he have argued with Paddy? Could he have pushed him? Or perhaps this was just some kind of attempt at closing ranks. I thought about the gardens now more like a tight family than a place of work – a family that resented outside interference.

A seagull swooped down beside me and attacked a half-eaten sandwich someone had discarded. What did I really know about Paddy Hogan anyway? Maybe he was in some kind of difficulty of his own. Maybe Ava Hogan was deluded about her brother. Or maybe she wasn't but nobody cared.

I recognised in myself then that little knot of stubbornness forming, that resistance to being told what to do. And, too, I had a sense that there was something going on that wasn't quite right, an attempt to protect the reputation of the gardens even at the cost of the truth. No, I wouldn't be letting Bob Richmond put me off.

When Ava knocked in the afternoon she refused to come further than the hall. She didn't even close the front door. Cold, damp air seeped in from behind her and I could almost smell the rain on it though it wasn't yet raining. She looked harried and some of her dark hair had escaped from a messy ponytail, as though she'd tied her hair back quickly before running out the door.

"I'm sorry, I need to get back – Mammy's not feeling the best," she said when I offered tea. "These are Paddy's." She handed me a supermarket carrier bag filled with papers. "Mind them, won't you? And I'll get them off you next week."

"I will, of course. Are you managing okay?"

She sighed and it sounded as though the noise came from her feet up.

"It's hard. I always thought when someone dies you're sad and then you get less sad as the days go by . . ." She put her hand on my arm. "I'm not stupid. She tells me I am but I'm not. I was too small when Daddy died . . . I just didn't know what grief was like."

"None of us know until it comes to us," I said, patting her hand on my arm.

We said goodbye. I had wanted to ask her about the trip to the Burren but that would have to wait.

I stood and watched her go down the garden path, her shoulders rounded against the cold. There was a taxi waiting for her and when it drove away I closed the door and thought of the dim living room in the house on St Teresa's Road where she was going, and Rita Hogan demanding in her armchair and I had great sympathy for her.

I took the bag she gave me and brought it into the living room, gently sliding out its contents onto the coffee table. I caught my breath at the sight of a series of botanical illustrations, watercolours on stiff card. They were far from the simple drawings I'd imagined when Ava had told me about them. Each one had a detailed description of the plant's parts in copperplate handwriting. There were also pages of typed notes to go with each. In the bottom corner of every illustration was a signature "*P Hogan*".

I examined one after another – the level of detail amazed me. I had seen botanical art before but never so perfect, so delicate. I felt I could put my hand out and pick up each bloom, brush the pollen from each stamen. I thought of Constance's drawings of orchids then – how crude they seemed in comparison to Paddy's work and how strange that they both shared an interested in botanical drawing. I handled the illustrations carefully and read through the typed pages. There were detailed descriptions of the plants, their origins, nomenclature, classification. There were also pages overwritten with red biro corrections that looked like some sort of introduction and a page that appeared to be a working title for the collection – *Selected Plants of the National Botanic Gardens of Ireland.*

I spent a long time looking through the pages, until my eyes were sore.

I remembered Paddy Hogan in death, the fingers that made these works, entwined with vine, immobile on the flagstones. It seemed even sadder to me somehow that such talent was lost.

Chapter Nineteen

Saturday, March 11th

On the drive down to the Burren, Gabriel said he was sorry he hadn't had a chance to phone me back on Friday.

"I needed to talk to a few people – might have a bit of work on – can't tell you about it at the moment," he said.

"You don't have to tell me. I don't own you," I said, too quickly, too sharply.

He didn't respond and I was cross with myself for souring the atmosphere so early in our trip.

"Don't mind me – I'm not sleeping too well," I said.

He nodded.

"I have a few things I need to tell you," I said.

I told him about Kaya Nkosi's visit and about Celine Deegan and Bob Richmond and *OnlyFans*. He hadn't heard of the website.

"What will they think of next?" he asked, throwing coins into a basket at the toll booth. "She must be rightly stuck for a few quid."

I didn't say what I was tempted to say.

"Then yesterday morning, I was walking on the seafront when I bumped into the man himself."

"Bob Richmond?"

"Exactly . . ."

I recounted what Bob had said and how threatened I'd felt by him.

"Do you think he's capable of killing Paddy, say if Paddy threatened to tell Bob's partner about Celine and they argued?" I asked him. I was picturing the two men pushing and shoving each other and then Bob pushing a little too hard.

"It's not impossible," Gabriel said, one hand on the steering wheel now and the other rubbing his chin. "But it would have had to be some accident."

"Okay. Well, just say then you had been using this website and then following a girl and then you were caught . . ."

"Me?"

"Try to imagine it. What would you do if a colleague found out? You'd be mortified, wouldn't you?"

I glanced at him and thought I noticed a brief blush. I didn't want to know what that meant.

"I'd certainly be mortified."

"And if you had a partner – like Bob Richmond – and a baby on the way, wouldn't you be desperate to shut someone up?"

"I suppose I would." He pressed his lips together. "But if the price of Paddy's silence was that Bob should leave Celine alone, and he did leave her alone, then what would they be fighting about?"

It was true Bob had left Celine alone and Paddy wasn't asking for much.

"We only have Celine's version though, don't we? Maybe Paddy warned Bob off her but also looked for something from him – money maybe?"

"That's possible. Though he doesn't sound like the type..."

"Well, somebody fought with Paddy and somebody pushed him over. I'm sure of it."

If not Bob, then who? That young man I saw with Constance Anderson? Or perhaps George Delaney – he was able, I thought, but why would he do it?

We stopped for lunch close to Glasson before crossing the Shannon at Athlone. From a table at the window of the Wineport Hotel, we watched the wide, wind-blown river as it passed. I wondered how the water could still have a hint of blue though the sky, hanging low over bare trees, was slate grey. A lone heron stood on the near bank, straight among reeds that were bending with the wind. The beauty of it reminded me of Paddy Hogan's illustrations and I told Gabriel about them.

"I'd like to see those when we get back," he said.

I finished my vegetable soup and watched him pick the last bits of flesh from the bony frame of a grilled plaice. I was impressed that he was keeping to his healthier diet and I said so.

"I like being alive," he said. "And I'm glad you agreed to come away this weekend. It'll do you good. Isn't it good to get out of the city?"

"It is. Tell me something – do you miss Donegal more now after your stay?" Was he wistful for it?

"Sometimes I do. You know I love the city and Stoneybatter but there isn't always enough sky. I definitely miss the sky and the stars, Bea. I'd nearly forgotten what the stars looked like."

I felt a small pain in my heart when he said that. I wanted to tell him that the stars weren't everything.

"And your friends there, do you miss them?"

"There aren't many left – most of them upped and moved the same as myself. You can't eat the scenery."

"And what about your family?" Why was I pushing this? What was it I suddenly longed to hear?

He laughed a bit. "The thing about families, Bea, they're great in small doses."

I didn't ask any more questions. I watched him across the table finishing a glass of water and told myself that would have to be enough. His company would have to be enough.

We reached Corofin at a quarter to three and went out the road in the direction of Kilinaboy, in search of Hazelgrove Lodge. Rain spat at the windscreen, and around us the landscape transformed from fields trimmed with stone walls to a patchwork of limestone and low bushes all forced to grow in one direction by the prevailing wind.

"Barren might have been a better name than Burren," I said. It seemed desolate to me.

We turned right before Killinaboy and went on a couple of miles until I could see a building that looked like Hazelgrove Lodge in the distance.

"Is that it over there?" I asked.

Its yellow walls stood out, alien and gaudy in the dull greys. We drove on until we found a fingerpost in brown with "*Hazelgrove Lodge*" written on it in white lettering. We turned left and Gabriel eased the car down a narrow, tarmacked lane, its centre sprouting grass. On either side of us there were low hedges and beyond them I could see raised areas of grey stone, pockmarked and darkened now with rain.

The lane ended at an open gate with stone pillars either side.

"This must be it."

The car rattled as Gabriel drove it from rough road onto the smooth, clean driveway that led up to the lodge.

The building was sheltered on one side by a hazel hedge and its yellow walls didn't seem quite so gaudy now – more of a butter colour. It was shaped like two wide cottages joined back to back by a low, glass corridor and there were Velux windows in its tiled roof. We parked alongside an old, boxy, green Range Rover and as we got out the front door of the lodge opened.

"You found us okay?" A woman emerged and crossed to us, one hand extended.

She looked in her late sixties with short, wavy straw-coloured hair and a round face on which the flesh hung generously, merging with her neck. She was wearing a yellow blouse tucked into a pleated brown skirt and flat, brown lace-up shoes. She reminded me of a nun in civvies. Then she smiled at us and was the picture of kindness.

"I'm Eileen Cassidy and you must be Beatrice and Gabriel. Get yourselves in before it starts again." She glanced at the sky and walked inside.

We followed her with our bags. I wondered what she meant by "starts again" – it was spitting rain and had been for ages.

She stopped halfway down the tiled hall and looked back at us.

"It was two rooms you wanted?" She tilted her head to one side as though she thought she might have made a mistake.

"That's right," I said.

"Grand, so."

We followed her on into a wide living room where a low table had been set with a china tea service. There was a plate at its centre with buttered fruit scones.

"I'll just wet the tea – you must be dying for a cup."

She disappeared and we sat down on a plump, beige couch and looked around. There was a turf fire in the grate and a painting of the local landscape above the mantel. In the corner, an upright piano had photos and ornaments on it, giving the impression it had not been played for a long time. Shelves beside the fireplace held books and more photos.

Eileen returned with a pot of tea under a knitted cosy. She placed it on a round brass trivet.

"There now, let it draw for a minute or two. I'll go and get your room keys for you."

I took the lid off the pot and stirred before pouring out into two china cups. Gabriel helped himself to a scone. I drank my tea and admired how he managed the delicate cup, its fine curved handle incongruous in his hand.

"It's a nice place, anyway," he said.

I tried to imagine it filled with the group from the Botanic Gardens. They must have taken their wellingtons off at the door before trouping inside onto the cream, plush pile carpet.

Eileen reappeared.

"You must have plenty of space here," Gabriel said.

"Twenty-two rooms, would you believe?" She smiled with pride. "Peter did all the renovation work himself."

"He did a great job."

She nodded her appreciation. "Do you think you might want dinner tonight?"

I glanced at Gabriel who nodded.

"That would be lovely," I said. "We didn't realise you did evening meals."

"Oh, we do. There's always been call for it cos we're a long enough drive to the town. Now, here are your room keys – eleven and twelve, at the back, and they've lovely views."

I took them from her.

"I'll leave you to it, so. Seven-thirty is dinner time."

She left and we finished our tea.

"We should go for a walk while we still have the light," I said.

"I'll be glad to stretch my legs after the drive." He stood, stretched his arms above his head and yawned. "Bit of fresh air will be good."

We carried our bags to our ground-floor rooms.

"I'll knock when I'm ready," I told Gabriel.

My room was bright and comfortable with the same cream carpet as the rest of the building and a double bed with crisp white sheets and a red throw. There was a window next to the bed looking out on the Burren.

I unpacked my few things, freshened up, then put on a thick jumper, a heavy coat and scarf and knocked on Gabriel's door.

He opened the door and went back inside to fetch his car keys. His room was much the same as mine with the same desolate, beautiful view.

We took wellies from the boot of the car and set off walking in what was still a fine drizzle. We were not going anywhere in particular. We wandered down the drive and out onto the road until we found a sign to indicate a walking trail near Lough Avalla. We followed it through a sodden meadow and then through a copse of clustered, bare hazel trees painted with moss, and holly trees with wizened berries, and leafless, prickly hawthorn. There were signs along the way for visitors, highlighting some of the flora. I looked to see if any of them featured the orchid the professor wrote about in his book and had been so pleased to spot – the *Platanthera bifolia* – but it wasn't there.

After a while the terrain opened up, and sky and plateaued limestone seemed to dissolve into each other at the horizon. There was something moving about it, about its desolation, and I allowed myself to imagine the people who walked there a thousand years before seeing just what I was seeing now.

"There isn't much colour around, is there?" Gabriel said.

"Too early for it." To my eye there seemed to be nothing but low-growing scrub and patches of moss in the soil between the stones. What did we expect to find wandering in the Burren in early March?

We walked on until what light there was began to dim. It was six and close to sunset.

"We should get back," Gabriel said.

We took another branch of walkway and after a time we found ourselves on the road again. We could see Hazelgrove Lodge in the distance. We walked single file, facing into any oncoming traffic. A solitary car passed us, slowing down as it did, and the driver gave us a small wave. About a mile from the lodge, at a T-junction, we saw a sign for Brothery's Bar.

About half a mile further on Gabriel stopped.

"That's very sad." He indicated a wooden cross with a teddy bear tied to it and a bunch of wilting flowers at its base. There was a small plaque attached and he read the inscription aloud. "*Daisy Cassidy aged 11 years, 26th May, 2015* – poor little thing."

"That's heart-breaking. I wonder if she was anything to Eileen and Peter?"

We said no more and walked on briskly to Hazelgrove Lodge. It was almost dark and I suddenly wanted to be off the road.

Chapter Twenty

When we appeared for dinner in the dining room, though there were more than a dozen round tables, only one was set with a white tablecloth and silver cutlery. It was positioned in a bay window so that there was glass on three sides. The curtains were still open but there was only blackness with no moon or stars visible and all we could see was our own reflections. I sat side on to the window and Gabriel took the seat opposite me. We were settled when Eileen and her husband Peter arrived. They were both wearing aprons and Peter's was tied at the front, like a proper chef. Eileen introduced him.

"He does the cooking and I do the running around," she said, smiling at him.

He shook hands with us and I thought he had delicate fingers for such a broad man. I took him to be about the same age as his wife, late sixties. His hair was almost entirely white and in need of a trim, and he had the leathery face of someone who spent a lot of time outdoors. His eyes were amber behind round-framed glasses, more fashionable in the 1980s. He pushed them up to the bridge of his nose.

"I have a bit of salmon if you want, or some lovely fillet steaks, reared down the road."

"I'll have steak, thanks. Medium if that's okay?" I said.

"Me too, well done," said Gabriel.

"Good." He nodded and left for the kitchen, appearing satisfied that his pitch for the meat had had the correct impact.

"There's only the two of you tonight," Eileen said. "You have the place to yourselves. Would you like if we joined you for dinner?"

"That'd be very nice," I said.

"Are you sure now?"

"Yes, that would be lovely."

She gave me that kind smile of hers again and followed her husband out, before scurrying back in again.

"I'm sorry, you'll be wanting wine. Red?"

"Yes, please," Gabriel said.

"Just water for me, thanks."

She fetched a bottle of Merlot and a jug of water that had ice, mint and slices of cucumber in it. She put glasses on the table along with soda brown and crusty white bread in a basket and a dish holding curls of golden butter. We both took a slice of bread.

"I didn't realise I was so hungry," I said.

"It's the change of air." Gabriel poured himself a glass of wine and said hastily, "I'll just have a little blowout tonight, on account of the occasion."

Eileen returned with two steaming bowls of soup.

"Ham and pea," she said, putting them down. "We'll join you for the main course."

As we ate the soup I looked around the room. There

were paintings on the walls, all landscapes, some of which appeared to be for sale. And beside the door there was a large framed photo. When I'd finished the soup I got up to look at it. A more youthful Eileen and Peter both smiled out at me. A young woman with Peter's eyes stood between them, a baby in her arms. To the right of Peter, was a young man, perhaps in his early twenties, with the same smile as Eileen's. And to the front, a boy of about sixteen gazed with serious expression on his face. As I was admiring it, Eileen walked in with more bread on a chopping board. A waft of frying onions followed her. She stopped to see what had caught my eye.

"That's a lovely photo," I said.

She let out a sigh. "'Tis. They're all scattered now. Joseph, our youngest there, is in Seattle working for an IT firm, Steven's away in London and Nicola is up in Dublin."

"You must miss them."

"I do."

I followed her back to the table. She added a few more slices of turnover to the basket and took away our bowls.

"The soup was delicious," Gabriel said.

"I'm glad you liked it. Peter won't be long." She turned away.

"Are you enjoying the wine?" I asked Gabriel when she had gone.

"It's grand." He took a drink from his glass to demonstrate its grandness. "How's the water?"

"Flavoursome."

He grinned at me and the door from the kitchen opened again. This time, Peter came through, two plates in his hands.

"Medium," he said, putting a plate before me. "And well-done." He gave Gabriel his.

"Looks lovely," I said. And it did. The steaks were garnished with roast cherry tomatoes, fried onions and mushrooms.

Eileen appeared with two dishes, of mashed potato and broccoli, and a small jug of pepper sauce. She arranged them on the table.

Peter went back to the kitchen then re-emerged without his apron and with plates for himself and his wife. Gabriel filled their wineglasses and they sat down, Eileen to my right and Peter to my left, his back to the window.

We ate with enthusiasm and, initially, without speaking except to make appreciative noises.

"Are ye liking the Burren?" Peter asked after a while, leaning back in his chair, his half-empty glass in his hand.

"It's lovely, even this time of year," I said.

"This is the time I like it best," he said. "I have it nearly to myself. When summer comes round again it'll be crawling with tourists."

I thought there was a hint of resentment in his voice and I wondered at it, given the business he was in. He must have guessed at my bewilderment.

"I don't mean . . . I just meant I like it best when it's peaceful."

"I'm sure. Up home in Glenties when the tourist season is over there's a big sigh of relief, dependant and all as they are on the dollars," Gabriel said.

"Is it Glenties you're from? I've a second cousin – Beecham – out the Letterkenny Road."

They talked for a few minutes about possible mutual acquaintances in Donegal. Then they moved on to whether the county would ever win the all-Ireland football final again.

I turned to Eileen. "You must get all sorts down here because of the Burren."

"We do, and from all over the world. We're very proud of it really. Did you go as far as the lake when you went on your walk earlier?"

"More wine?" Gabriel asked and she extended her glass. Then he topped up Peter's and his own.

"We did," I said, turning back to Eileen. "We went out the drive and down the road a bit, then to the left in a big loop. It was really breath-taking."

"That's a good walk, all right." She took a sip of her wine and then put a last piece of steak in her mouth.

"It was and very enjoyable. The landscape is so otherworldly. When you're in Dublin it's hard to imagine it."

"I suppose so." She looked at me a little sceptically.

"Do you get up to Dublin much yourself?"

"Not since . . . Not in a while." She drank again and watched me as though trying to make a judgment about my character. "Did you notice it on the road, the cross for Daisy?"

"I did yes. A very sad sight. Was she one of yours?"

She nodded. "Granddaughter."

"I'm so sorry, Eileen."

"That's why we don't go to Dublin. Our daughter won't see us anymore." She drank from her glass again, swallowing back more than just wine. "She was down here for a holiday, Daisy I mean, while Nicola and her husband went away for a few days. She was mad about this donkey, down below in O'Brien's and we let her go out the road by herself . . ."

"Eileen?" Peter looked at his wife now.

"Sorry, I didn't intend to . . . it just came out." She took the napkin from her lap and dabbed her eyes with it.

"We try not to talk about it too much anymore. It was eating us alive," Peter said.

But Eileen continued. "She went without telling us some time during the night." Her voice was quiet now, almost inaudible. "She must have wanted to feed the animal."

"God, that's awful, I'm so very sorry," I said.

Gabriel emptied the remains of the wine into Eileen's glass.

Peter let out a sigh. "Can we not do this?" he asked her.

He got to his feet and began clearing the table. She did the same.

"Sorry," she said. "I've spoilt your evening."

"No," we both answered.

I glanced at Gabriel, signalling that perhaps we should finish up.

"It was a lovely meal. I don't think I could eat another thing," I said.

Peter stopped what he was doing. "Ah no. There's chocolate cake – Eileen made it."

She lifted her head and gave me a watery smile.

"I couldn't refuse chocolate cake," I said.

"Good. And we'll have another drop of wine."

"Will you join us?" he said to me.

"Tea for me, please," I said.

He took the plates back to the kitchen and Eileen followed him with the dishes.

"Their hearts must be broken," I whispered to Gabriel.

"A desperate thing to happen," he said.

And I knew he was thinking of the families he had brought terrible news to in the course of his work.

Peter came back to the table with another bottle of

wine to go with the chocolate cake and a pot of tea for me.

We talked for a while about the lodge and the landscape around it and how locals complained about tourists blocking up the roads.

"Not this time of year, of course," Peter said, retrospectively excusing us from the criticism.

I took a forkful of cake which was luscious and melting.

"This is lovely," I said to Eileen.

"I do a lot of baking these days," she said.

Peter and Gabriel began talking about the impact of the *Wild Atlantic Way* branding on tourism.

Eileen continued talking to me, in a low voice. "I find it calming, the baking, it soothes me somehow. Do you know when you wake up too early in the morning and for a few seconds you think everything is all right and then you remember and your stomach knots? That's when I get up and bake."

I remembered that feeling well and found myself telling her about my brother Laurence who died young and at his own hand. I told her about Leo Hackett having swindled him out of his money and about my parents fading away afterwards. It had been so long since I'd said Laurence's name out loud. I felt for a moment as though he had only died the day before and I held my napkin tight as an echo wave of pain washed through me.

Eileen could see it.

"That's the way with grief," she said. "It creeps up on you." She lowered her voice further. "Sometimes I feel as though I might lose my reason if I don't talk about it." Then she said loudly – "If you'd like to see the kitchen, I'd be delighted to show you."

The two men looked at her.

"We'll be back in a minute. I just want to show Beatrice the double-burner."

They went back to their conversation as if it was perfectly normal for someone to have an interest in a double-burner. I followed Eileen, who had taken her wine with her, out the door, and into the kitchen. It was a large square room, fitted out with stainless-steel work surfaces and splashbacks.

To one side there was a small square wooden table with four chairs.

She pulled a chair out and sat down, sipping from her glass.

I sat next to her.

"Do you want a drink?" she asked.

"No, I'm fine, thanks."

"He doesn't like to hear me talking about what happened to Daisy. Silence is his way of coping with it. I think he's afraid it'll wash him away entirely if he says any more about it. But I need to let it out every now and then."

"Of course." I could sympathise with Peter – my default position too was to bottle up, push down emotions in the hope that they would fade.

"It's a funny thing, isn't it? That longing to put things right?"

She was not looking at me now but over my shoulder to some past time and place I couldn't see.

"I can't tell you all the hours I've spent going over that evening in my head and trying to figure out what I should have done."

"I can imagine." And I could imagine – I had been through that when Laurence died.

"It was very busy that day. We had this crowd up for a few nights. They were a noisy enough bunch and a few of them were picky with the food – so demanding as well." She paused and rubbed her temple. "They were from the Botanic Gardens up in Dublin, some of them, but there was an English lot with them, and a few Americans."

My heart thumped in my chest.

"Up to all sorts, I can tell you." She took a drink from her glass. "I heard Daisy crying one of the nights they were here – the second night I think – so I went in to her and on my way back didn't I see one of the men creeping into one of the women's rooms!"

"One of the Irishmen?"

"I think so, yes."

"Which woman, do you remember?"

She thought and drank and shook her head. "Well, I knew who it was at the time because of the room number but I can't remember her name now."

"She was Irish too?"

"Yes."

I didn't dare press her any further on the matter. I sipped my water. "You were telling me about Daisy."

"Yes . . . we were both very busy and Daisy had been at us to bring her up the road to say goodnight to the donkey. She used to worry, you see, that the animal would be hungry if she didn't feed it. No use telling her it survived before she arrived and would after she was gone." She made a choking noise in her throat and coughed and drank some more wine. "Anyway, by the time they all went out and we cleaned up, it was coming on to eleven and I was very tired and I said she could go up first thing in the morning. I tucked her into bed, Beatrice, and I kissed her little forehead and I told her I'd see her bright and early." She let out a sob. "We knew nothing till Ger O'Brien knocked about half six in the morning. He was after finding her on the road. She was in her little nightie with a cardigan over it and her feet in sandals, lumps of carrot scattered on the road. When I think of her lying there alone all night . . ." She covered her mouth with her hand and closed her eyes, anguish like an aura around her. "They got the driver a few days later. A fella from beyond Doolin out for a few drinks. He turned himself in. Told the guards he thought he hit an animal . . ."

I gasped at that, the coldness of it – to hit a child and keep on going.

"That's horrifying," I said.

"Nicola and her husband didn't last after that. They were both tormented. And she stopped speaking to us entirely."

"You must be a very strong woman to keep going, Eileen," I said.

She gave me a look of resignation. "What choice do I have?"

We heard the kitchen door open then and Peter walked in carrying plates and forks and the remains of the cake.

"There ye are," he said, "I was about to get a small one for Gabriel."

Eileen, with her back to him, quickly wiped her eyes and stood up. "I think I'll go on up, love."

She gave me a nod and went back into the dining room where I heard her bidding Gabriel goodnight.

"Would you like a drop?" Peter asked me.

"No, thanks. I think I'll go to bed myself."

"I'll see you at breakfast so."

While he got the drinks I went back to the dining room and told Gabriel I'd see him in the morning.

He gave a lopsided smile. "Goodnight, honey Bea," he said.

It had been a while since he'd had so much to drink and it must have gone to his head.

In bed under a heavy duvet, before I drifted off to sleep, I thought I heard the floorboards on the corridor creak with footsteps that stopped briefly outside my door before moving on. But I might have imagined that or confused the natural sighing of the house with the story Eileen had told me about the man who'd been creeping around late at night during the Botanic Gardens trip to the Burren.

Chapter Twenty-One

Sunday, March 12th

At breakfast, shortly after eight o'clock, Gabriel looked tired.

"Did you stay up much longer?" I asked.

"We just had the one," he said as though I'd been asking about his drinking. "But we did talk for a good while . . ."

"You can tell me on the way home," I said.

We both had a full Irish breakfast though I'd half expected Gabriel to look for porridge instead given how healthily he'd been eating. I supposed the few drinks had given him an appetite. We didn't speak much and I looked out the window at the continuous grey drizzle and the landscape with its gnarled trees and slabs of stone and wondered how the Cassidys could bear to remain in the place after what had happened.

"Did you get enough?" Eileen asked as Gabriel wiped up the last of his egg with a bit of toast.

"Plenty," he said, pushing back the chair and stretching his arms above his head, making the tail of his shirt come out from the waist of his trousers.

She smiled at that and he quickly straightened himself, tucked in the shirt and stood up.

I finished my tea and got to my feet.

"Thanks for everything, Eileen," I said.

She hugged me for a moment and I thought I felt the grip of grief in it. I wanted to tell her to sell up and move away, to find a new life some place where there weren't any memories.

"You should visit us in Dublin – you'd be welcome any time," I found myself saying.

"Maybe we will," she said, though I knew she didn't believe her own words.

We went to our rooms, got our bags and left.

"Safe journey," Peter said as we loaded the car.

The couple stood in the doorway and waved at us as we drove away.

"God love them," Gabriel said when we were on the main road.

I recounted what Eileen had told me the night before about Daisy's death.

"And the group from the Botanic Gardens were there at the same time," I said.

"Peter told me much the same," he said.

"Did he really? And Eileen said he doesn't like to talk about it."

"Whatever came over him, he wanted to talk last night."

He turned onto a wider road and, though I hadn't realised I was tense on the narrow lanes, I relaxed a bit.

"But Eileen mentioned something about the Botanic Gardens group," I told him. "She said she saw one of the men going into one of the women's rooms during the night. 'Sneaking', she said."

"Did she say who?"

"No. She couldn't remember who either of them were but she thought both of them were Irish. I wonder is there any way we could find out. It could be useful to know." I thought for a few minutes. "If you ask Constance, I'll ask Ava . . ."

"Worth a try," he said.

"When you were talking to Constance a few days ago, she never mentioned any relationships on the trip, did she?"

"No, but . . . we talked about a lot of things, not just the Burren." He looked toward me for a second and then back to the road. We were nearing the motorway.

"I see." I bit my lower lip to prevent myself from laughing.

But he detected it anyway. "Ah, feck off, Bea, will you?" He turned on Johnny Cash singing "Cry, Cry, Cry", then drove onto the slip road for the M6 and accelerated into light traffic.

We didn't speak for a while. And I thought of Eileen and Peter and how strong they must be just to keep going and stay together. The death had broken up their daughter's marriage and it could have done the same to them. They must have had their own private recriminations – the "why didn't you's" that eat away even when they are unspoken.

"Maybe I'll call Ava now and see if she's free when we get back," I said.

He turned down the music and I took out my phone as we drove past Athlone through a curtain of rain.

When Ava answered the line had an echo on it and it seemed to accentuate her hesitancy in agreeing to meet me. I wasn't sure whether that was because her mother was in the room or if there was something else. I didn't mention the Burren and only said I thought we ought to talk that evening if possible. She agreed but said she would rather meet at a local pub, the Tolka House. I told her I could be there at seven.

"Best if I don't come along, I suppose?" Gabriel said when I hung up.

"Probably. She sounded, I'm not sure . . . nervous or something. I'll call you after."

The Tolka House pub was next to the river of the same name, the same one that passes through the Botanic Gardens. When I opened the door shortly before seven, a wave of warm air and chatter poured out along with the smell of evening dinner. I had parked at St Mobhi Drive and though it was only a short walk, the drizzle and damp that had followed us back to Dublin from the Burren had infiltrated my bones. I closed my umbrella, stepped inside the pub and was grateful for its warmth. It was full of families but I found an empty table for two, next to a fireplace at the back of the lounge, which I hoped would give us a little privacy. I left the dripping umbrella by the table, got tea from the bar and sat down.

I had just taken off my coat and settled myself when Ava appeared. She stood for a minute or two, shaking the rain off her yellow, hooded raincoat and scanning the room intently for me. I waved when she looked my way and she came over.

"I think I'll get a hot port. Would you like one?"

"No, thanks, I'm fine with this." I indicated my tea and she nodded.

She took off her coat and put it on the back of her chair. Her hair looked damp despite the hood and I thought she might not have washed it for a few days. I noticed too that the blouse she was wearing had a stain on the front. She went to the bar to order and returned with the glass of ruby, steaming liquid cupped in her hands, a paper napkin wrapped around it so that it wouldn't burn her, and placed it carefully on the table before sitting down.

The smell of the hot port drifted toward me, a mixture of sweet grape, lemon and cloves. I thought fleetingly of Christmases past.

"I like this drink. It reminds me of Liverpool – that's where I tasted it first," she said.

"Liverpool? When were you there?"

"A couple of years ago. I went on my own."

"Oh." I thought it a curious place to visit alone. "Are you a big Beatles fan then?"

"Beatles? No, not really." She looked confused by the question and there didn't seem much point in discussing it further.

"How's your mother?" I asked.

"Up and down – you won't tell her what I said about Liverpool? She thought I went to Wexford to visit my cousin."

"No, of course not." I wanted to say 'You're a grown woman and you ought to be able to go where you like without telling your mother' but I didn't think that would be of much help to her.

She sipped her drink. "Mammy wants answers and she's not getting them. It's very frustrating for her. I called that detective, Maguire, and asked for news. She said she'd come back to me in an hour – I'm still waiting."

I could almost hear Gabriel then explaining how busy Maguire must be, making excuses. I wasn't about to do that.

"That must be very annoying," I said.

"It is. I don't know who killed Paddy but somebody did." Her hot port was half empty but she declined my offer to buy her another one. "He didn't jump – there's no way he jumped."

"Can I ask you something?" There were things I needed to know.

She nodded.

"Were you on a trip a couple of years ago to the Burren with Paddy and people from the gardens?"

"I was. Why?" She sounded defensive.

I topped up my tea from the stainless-steel pot I'd been given with its ill-fitting lid. Liquid dripped on the table and I put a beer mat on the spill to soak it up.

"I hadn't realised that you were involved in Paddy's work – you never said."

"Involved? I wasn't." She finished her drink then took the paper napkin off the now-cold glass, twisted it between her fingers and began tearing pieces off it. "Paddy told me about this trip with a few places for guests and asked if I'd like to go. I hadn't been to the Burren before so I went. Who told you about it anyway?"

"Constance Anderson. She seemed to enjoy it."

"She would."

"Did you not enjoy it?" I thought I saw a flicker of something across her face when I asked that. Then it disappeared. I wondered if there had been trouble there or something.

"It was okay."

"Did everyone get on?"

"They had to – they worked together. The professor

was going around a bit full of himself but I don't think it bothered people too much." She had made a small pile of shredded paper now and began picking up each piece, rolling it between finger and thumb and dropping the bits into her empty glass. It was almost as if her hands were moving independently of her.

"And did Paddy get on with everyone else? I mean there weren't any arguments or anything?"

"I don't remember any arguments." She finished her paper task and let her hands rest in her lap.

"What about you? Did you get on okay with other people on that trip?"

She looked at me suspiciously. "It wasn't some chummy holiday and it was only for a few days – it was fine – are you trying to say something happened there?"

"No, I'm only trying to help . . . I just thought if there were tensions you might have noticed . . . but, never mind . . . I wanted to thank you for showing me Paddy's watercolours. They're really beautiful."

She smiled for the first time. "They are, aren't they?"

"Works of art. Could I hold on to them for a day or two? I'd like to show them to a friend of mine."

"Okay – but be careful with them."

"I will. Can I ask you one more thing about the Burren? Late at night in the guesthouse, you didn't see a man going into the room of one of the women, did you?"

"*What? No!*" She looked absolutely shocked. "Are you suggesting it was Paddy? Did Constance say something?"

"No, no, she didn't – and I didn't mean Paddy."

"So, who did?"

"Look, I don't know, it doesn't matter." Why had I

asked such a clumsy question? I hadn't meant to upset her.

It was time to go. I said I'd call her if I had any news.

We both stood and put our coats on.

"I'm just going to the . . ." I indicated the door at the back which led to the toilets and she said goodbye.

In the ladies' I washed my hands and examined my knuckles. They seemed fine again. I topped up my lipstick in the mirror. The result was unsatisfactory. Cold weather was hard on middle-aged lips, drying them, chapping them more easily than when I was a young woman. I wondered what it would be like to visit one of those clinics and have my lips plumped but quickly dismissed the idea. The trouble with getting one part fixed was that, just like redecorating one room in a house, it made everything else look a bit shabbier.

When I was leaving the pub I glanced to my left and saw, at a corner table, Constance Anderson with a man whose back was turned to me. I waved and she waved back and the man turned round and looked over his shoulder at me. It was George Delaney.

I stood for a moment before making up my mind to go over. They both looked uncomfortable as though I'd caught them at something furtive.

"I didn't know you drank here," Constance said, her tone curt.

I wanted to say 'It's a free country', but instead said "Once in a while".

"It's a nice spot," George said, smiling without showing his teeth.

What was a married man in his thirties doing in a pub on a Sunday night with an older woman? His hands were clasped together in his lap and he was so uneasy I almost felt sorry for him.

"It is – nice and cosy on a miserable night like tonight. I'm just back from the Burren – it was even worse over there."

"The Burren?" Constance said, her eyebrows raised.

"Yes. Oh, I forgot – we were only talking about that the other day, weren't we?"

She nodded and glanced at George.

"You were both on a trip to the Burren a couple of years ago, weren't you?" I said to George.

He looked uncomfortable.

Constance gave me a sharp look. "You know very well he was – I showed you that photograph."

"What about it?" George asked.

"Was there any trouble? Did Paddy get on okay with everyone?"

"Fine. Everyone got on fine on that trip. Why are you asking about it?"

"I was just curious. There can be tensions when work colleagues spend a few days together. Was there any . . . professional jealousy, say, when the professor went off alone and spotted that rare orchid?"

He laughed. "Not at all. It was rare but most of us had seen it before in the Burren. Sure, we have an example of it in the gardens. It was just that it was the first time for the professor seeing it in its habitat – that's why he bigged it up in that book of his."

Constance looked pleased with his response. "I told all this to Gabriel," she said. "Did he not tell you?" She gave me a sly smile.

I had a ridiculous urge to slap her face. "Just one other

thing then . . . did either of you see one of the men in the group going into a woman's room late at night?"

They looked at each other again and smirked.

"Don't be ridiculous," Constance said. "The men on that trip were all married."

"Except Paddy Hogan," I said.

"Well, yes, but Paddy wasn't . . . the sneaky type," she said.

I thanked them and left. When I glanced back, as I went out the door, their heads were close together and Constance seemed to be chastising George.

Chapter Twenty-Two

Monday, March 13th

In the morning I woke to a text message from Ava.

I'd like to collect Paddy's drawings today, if that's okay?

I said it was fine and asked what time she'd call though I was sorry to have to let them go. I understood, though, how hard it must have been for her to part for long with anything belonging to Paddy.

About one if you're home, she replied.

I called Gabriel then and asked if he'd like to come over and see the illustrations before Ava took them away.

He arrived at the door at eleven with a bag of croissants.

"I thought you might like them for your breakfast," he said.

I could have told him that I'd breakfasted more than three hours earlier and had spent the remainder of the time checking court listings for work, but I didn't.

"Thanks," I said, wondering if he thought croissants were a good low-fat breakfast. "Go on into the living room – the watercolours are spread out on the table. I'll call you when I've made the tea." I had no intention of bringing tea and croissants into the living room with the illustrations there. If anything happened to them I'd never forgive myself.

When it was ready I went back into the living room. Gabriel was going through Paddy's watercolours.

"This is very skilled work," he said. "They're top notch."

"Aren't they? Come and have your breakfast."

He followed me reluctantly into the kitchen.

"They must have taken him months to paint, years even," he said. "And they weren't finished. It's hard to believe a man with the dedication to work on something like that would have . . ."

He didn't finish the sentence but I knew what he'd meant to say.

"But you don't believe that? You know it doesn't make any sense."

"What I mean is, if there was evidence needed that he had plans, that he had things he wanted to continue – you only have to look at them."

We finished our food and I told him about my meeting with Ava and seeing Constance and George together at the pub.

"I asked them both about the Burren and whether they'd seen anyone sneaking around at night. They said they hadn't . . . Unless George was sneaking in to visit Constance?"

He raised an eyebrow.

"Each to their own, I suppose," he said. "Come back inside. I want to have another look at those watercolours before Ava arrives."

We went back into the living room, sat on the couch and looked at each illustration in turn. I recognised the Venus flytrap, labelled as *Droseracae Dionaea muscipula*.

Paddy had drawn the flower, pale-petalled and delicate, but also the leaves that formed the trap, red on the inside, green on the outside and edged with fine filaments that looked like teeth. It was so vivid that I imagined if I touched those leaves they would snap shut around my fingers. Gabriel handed me another illustration.

"This is the one from the Burren, isn't it?" he asked.

It showed a white orchid, almost translucent with a large petal like a hood at the top, two petals that looked like thin wings and a third growing down, long and narrow, and tinged with green. The flower was small and delicate and I thought that, if I touched it, it would feel like wax. Paddy had drawn its stalk and leaves separately, and labelled each plant part. In the top corner of the page he had written *Orchidaceae Platanthera bifolia*. There was a separate page describing the plant structures in detail and where it could be found.

"Yes. That's the one in the professor's book. I have to say I prefer the illustration to the photograph. It seems to capture it better somehow."

"I know what you mean."

"Three of them aren't finished," he said. He handed me another illustration incomplete this time. It had been drawn but not yet coloured. I recognised it instantly though I hadn't known its proper name – it was *Geraniaceae Pelargonium zonale*. My mother would have called it a geranium.

On another page there was a rough outline of petals and a stalk, but no detail. The label said *Orchidaceae Platanthera christakii*.

"That's the professor's orchid," I said.

The third incomplete illustration was labelled *Rosaceae Dryas octopetala*. The petals had been drawn but not coloured. There was colour at its centre though, a pale yellow and it reminded me of the flowers on a strawberry plant.

"There's another six pages, as well, with notes on plants that Paddy never drew," Gabriel said.

"If you'd done all this work and gone to all this trouble wouldn't you want to complete it before . . ." I said.

"I think you would," he said. "The other thing I'm wondering about – what was his system? There's all sorts of plants here from all over the gardens but there doesn't seem to be any system to it."

I thought about that for a while. "Maybe he chose rare plants." But no, that couldn't be right. The *Pelargonium zonale* was in almost every house in the country. "Or maybe he just chose his personal favourites."

Gabriel nodded. "That makes sense. What was he calling it? '*Selected Plants of the National Botanic Gardens*'? So he could pick and choose what he wanted."

"I wonder how many people knew he was doing this. Maybe we should ask about it . . . maybe George Delaney knew. Or the professor. We should definitely ask him."

I thought Gabriel gave me a strange look then – a mixture of bewilderment and something else I couldn't quite identify.

"If you want, we could ask him," he said without much enthusiasm.

My phone pinged then with a message from Ava.

See you in ten?

I responded: **Okay.**

I gathered up all of the illustrations and papers and put them back into the carrier bag in which they'd arrived.

"I'm glad we got to see them," I said to Gabriel. "I feel I know Paddy a bit better now."

Ava arrived, dripping. "Can you believe I could get so wet just running from a taxi?"

I hadn't noticed until I opened the door to let her in that rain was coming down in heavy sheets, bouncing off the path and battering the shrubs in the front garden. There was a cold wind behind it and it took a little effort to shut the door again.

Ava shook herself and droplets sprinkled on the walls.

"Let me get you a towel. Go on inside. Gabriel, the friend I mentioned, is there."

When I returned Ava was standing in the living room talking to him. He was praising Paddy's work.

"Thanks," she said and reached for the bag.

"Can I ask, do you have any idea when he planned on finishing these?"

She shook her head. "He'd been at them for a few years. It took him ages to even do one. Look, sorry, I can't stay any longer. I need to get back to Mammy."

I followed her into the hall.

"He was very talented," I said.

"I know." She swallowed and blinked to steady herself.

When I opened the door, the rain had eased off to a benign drizzle.

She stepped out.

"I'll be in touch," I said and closed the door.

When I turned around Gabriel was at my shoulder.

"I've a few things I have to do this afternoon, but if you want, I suppose we could go and see the professor tomorrow?" He sounded half-hearted but resigned.

"It can't do any harm," I told him. I didn't ask what the few things were that he had to do and he didn't tell me.

Chapter Twenty-Three

Tuesday, March 14th

I took the professor's book on orchids with me when I went to the Botanic Gardens the next morning. I sat in my car, in the car park, waiting for Gabriel. It was mild enough to roll down the window and listen to the birds welcoming the stirrings of spring.

When Gabriel arrived at a quarter past nine, we walked together to the visitor centre to ask where we might find the professor.

The receptionist, the same young woman I had spoken to about Paddy Hogan, checked her computer for us.

"We keep a copy of the college timetable here," she said as she tapped. "You'd be amazed how many students forget which lecture they're supposed to be in." She gave me a second look. "Did you catch the professor's lecture in the end?"

"You have a great memory. Yes, I did."

She tapped a bit more.

"He'll be out of his first lecture at ten and he has another one at ten-thirty. They're in the Teagasc Horticulture College. Do you know where that is?"

"I think so."

"If you head toward the rose garden you can't miss it. I'd imagine he'll be in his office in between lectures so you should be able to catch him there."

"Thanks. Does he have his film crew with him today?"

She shook her head. "I haven't seen them around. I think they're more or less finished with him. There's great excitement about it, though. Everyone says it'll be brilliant publicity for the gardens. They're having a party here next Sunday to celebrate."

Other visitors approached her then and she turned her attention to them. We went to the Teak House to admire the pelargoniums in bloom, their vivid pinks and purples vying for attention. I picked out the one I thought Paddy had chosen to draw.

"I think that's Paddy's one," I said. "Maybe he would have finished it this week . . . he might have been waiting for it to be in full bloom here." That thought made me sad. How cruel it seemed that the plants would go on flowering without him.

I rubbed the leaf of another variety between finger and thumb and then breathed in the lemony scent. "Lovely."

"Not very keen on them really. They can get very leggy," Gabriel said.

I had a sudden image of my childhood kitchen with a row of pots on the windowsill, the pelargonium leaves patchy green, my mother in an apron overwatering them, a smile on her face.

"Bea?"

"What?"

"I was just saying, all that publicity for the gardens –

they wouldn't want anything like an inconvenient death to get in the way."

"I don't suppose they would."

"Would they go as far as covering things up, though?"

"They might." I checked my watch. "Have we time for tea?"

We went to the coffee shop and up to the counter together. I wanted to admire the cream cakes.

Bob Richmond was at the counter alone.

"Hello again. Two teas, is it?" he asked amiably.

I thought of the way he'd spoken to me on the seafront at Clontarf and how angry he was with me. It was as though all that animosity had melted away. Was it because Gabriel was with me now? I found it hard to like men who treat women differently when in the company of other men, whether better or worse. When I looked at him, I couldn't help thinking of Celine Deegan too, and how he had stalked her like prey. But I kept my views to myself. If he could play at being polite, so could I.

"Hi, Bob – yes, please," I said, in as friendly a manner as I could.

"Sit down and I'll bring them over to you."

We sat near the exit. Around us most of the tables were empty. Bob arrived quickly with our tray and after he'd unloaded it, he sat down.

"Look, I'm sorry about the things I said to you last time, Beatrice. I had no right to speak to you like that." He seemed sincere.

I was instantly disarmed. "Apology accepted, Bob," I said.

"I had a few things on my mind and I guess I took it out on you."

"Business worries, is it?" Gabriel asked.

"Something like that. Anyway, I'd better get on with it. He stood up. "See you again."

Shortly before ten, we walked past the director's house and round behind the rundown, cordoned-off Victoria glasshouse to the Teagasc College buildings. They were tucked away in a hollow close to the River Tolka and at the edge of the gardens. Clad in timber and stone, they seemed to be doing their best to blend in and looked as though they could have been built out of the slope. We stood on the footpath looking down at the buildings, their roofs planted with something low-growing and tinged with red.

"I suppose we can find his office easily enough," I said. We walked down the slope and over to what looked like a main entrance and went in through glass double doors.

Inside, students were chatting together in groups or strolling to their classes.

"Excuse me. I'm looking for Professor Christakos' office," I said to a young woman who was passing.

"Down there, up the stairs, take a left, second door, I think, or third. Anyway his name is on it."

"Thank you."

We walked in the direction indicated, up the stairs and into a corridor then left until we found a door with his name in blue ink on an acrylic sign. I knocked twice. No answer. I tried the door. It wasn't locked.

"We may as well wait for him inside," I said.

"Strictly speaking it's breaking and entering, Bea," he said, following me inside.

"How is it if the door is open?"

He gave me a look but didn't argue further.

The air was spicy in the office, like the scent inside a log cabin. There was a long bookcase on one wall and a filing cabinet on the other alongside an abstract painting of greens and browns. A small round table with two plastic green chairs were set up in one corner where I imagined he gave tutorials to some of his students. A tidy desk, devoid of papers, sat in the centre of the room. There were two expensive pens on it, a long, thin letter opener, an old-fashioned calendar, of the sort that requires flipping over a page from one day to the next, and a brass desk lamp with a green shade. It seemed self-consciously chic to me. The back wall was entirely tinted glass and looked out at the high boundary fence of the gardens. Though I couldn't hear them, I imagined the cars passing on the busy road beyond.

"Nice, isn't it?" I said, going over to look at his books. "I suppose he had most of these shipped from home." Where was it he'd been before the gardens – Berkeley College in California was it?

On the bottom shelf I spotted something familiar. It was a copy of his book on orchids. I pulled it out and flicked through the pages. It was identical to the edition I had with me except in hardback with a glossy dust jacket. As I was putting it back, the door opened.

"What's going on here?" The professor was startled. He looked at me, crouching by the bookcase, and then at Gabriel by the window. "What d'ya think you're doing?"

"We were hoping to speak to you – we were told to wait in your office," I said. I reached out and ran my fingers along a few of the books. "I was just admiring your collection. It's terrific."

His expression softened. "I don't know who told you to come in here, but . . ." he looked at his watch. "I can spare five minutes. What's up?" He walked round behind his desk and sat down, gesturing for me to sit opposite him. Gabriel took one of the plastic chairs from the corner and placed it beside me. We introduced ourselves.

"I was thinking of taking your course on orchids," I said, "and I wondered if you think reading this will be of help to me?" I held up the library book.

He nodded and relaxed back in his leather chair once he saw his own creation.

"The April course?"

I nodded.

"My book's very useful but perhaps a little technical for a beginner. You are a beginner, right?"

"I am, yes."

He picked up one of his elegant pens, took a sheet of paper from his drawer and began to write.

"These are the names of some books that might get you started," he said, handing me the page.

I took it from him. "Thank you."

"That's no problem. Would you like me to sign that for you?" He indicated the book I'd brought.

"I'm sorry," I said, feeling a little uncomfortable, "it's a library book . . . It's hard to get in the shops."

There was an awkward silence until Gabriel said, "I have it on order".

"Can I just ask you one other thing?" I sensed he would tell us to leave very soon. "A friend of ours, Paddy Hogan, he was painting plants from the gardens when he died. We thought they were really good. Did you know?"

"Sure, he asked me for advice from time to time. In fact, I put him in touch with a publisher in the US and I believe there was quite a bit of interest in his work."

"That was kind of you," I said, hoping I didn't sound too taken aback.

"He was a talented guy. I was happy to be able to help him." He tilted his head to one side. "Haven't we met before?"

I feigned pleasure at being recognised. "We met at one of your lectures."

"Ah yes, I remember. And you asked me about Paddy Hogan then, too. Didn't you say you found him?" He looked a little suspicious then. "You didn't say he was your friend."

"More Gabriel's friend really."

He looked from Gabriel to me and back again.

"Well, if that's all, it was nice to meet you both."

"Thanks for your time," I said.

"So what did you think of him?" I asked on our way to the car park.

"He certainly seems to know his stuff," was his response. "You were impressed by him, I think?"

"What do you mean?"

"I'm just saying, you smiled a lot."

He wasn't looking at me while he spoke but I was watching him and the half-smothered grin playing on his lips.

"I was trying to get information," I said, attempting to sound businesslike.

"Of course you were, but you didn't get any."

"I don't think he had any to give." Should I go on or end the conversation there? "And I have to say I was surprised that he'd helped Paddy – I didn't think he was the type to help anyone." I could feel heat in my face – was I blushing?

"Okay then," Gabriel said, sounding even more amused.

I didn't think there was any point in going on with the discussion. "Will I fix you a bit of lunch?"

He laughed out loud then, aware of my diversion. "That'd be nice . . . it'll keep you out of trouble for a while."

As it turned out though, trouble came to find us, in the shape of Detective Inspector Rebecca Maguire.

Chapter Twenty-Four

We had finished our lunch and Gabriel had gone out to the hall to put his coat on when the doorbell went. He answered it.

"I suppose you're Gabriel," I heard Maguire say.

I heard her stride into the hall, though she hadn't been invited, and the sound of another pair of feet, an officer with her.

"Sorry, who are you?" Gabriel said, though I was sure he knew quite well who she was. She introduced herself.

"And is Beatrice here?"

"In the kitchen."

As her clomping came closer I had that feeling of being guilty of something. I looked around the kitchen in case there was anything there I wouldn't want her to see. Then I laughed at myself for acting like a criminal. It was strange how she managed to have that effect. She paused in the doorway, settling her green eyes on me before proceeding. She was in full uniform which made her more intimidating.

"Detective, nice to see you. Can I make you and your officer a cup of tea?" I gestured for her and the young officer behind her to sit down. She nodded and pulled out a chair which creaked slightly when she sat on it. She put her cap face down on the table, revealing her tight, blond bun at the back of her head.

"I think you know why I'm here."

I turned my back and filled the kettle.

Gabriel, who was also now seated at the table, said "What can we do for you, inspector?"

"We've had complaints." She nodded toward her officer, whom she had failed to introduce.

He reached into his pocket and took out a notebook. He looked so young to me that I thought he could be a schoolboy playing dress-up.

"National Botanic Gardens," he said.

I wondered why she bothered getting him to do that when she obviously knew where the complaints came from – a touch of the theatrics, I thought.

"Yes, more than one person has been in touch with us." She paused as though expecting us to confess immediately. "You've been harassing people."

I poured the water in.

"That's nonsense," Gabriel said.

"You've been accosting various members of staff and trying to quiz them about Paddy Hogan."

I placed the pot on a mat and left it to draw.

"Not quizzed," I said. "We just asked a couple of questions." I laid out cups and saucers, milk and sugar.

"Is that right? Questions? What are you doing going around asking people questions?"

"It's a free country." I said the words and realised as soon as they were out that they made me sound petulant and unreasonable.

"Then, I'm told, you were snooping around the Teagasc College." Her voice had risen.

"Who told you that? Was it the professor?" I asked.

"Why? Have you been annoying him too?"

I admitted to myself that I would have been disappointed if she'd said yes. I didn't think the professor was the sort of man to make a complaint like that. I poured out the tea. She took a cup without thanks.

"You've been upsetting people." She drank it black, which appalled me.

I sat down and took a cup for myself.

"You keep saying 'people'. It would be helpful to know who's been complaining about us and what they've been saying," Gabriel said.

"I'm telling you what they're saying – they're saying you, Ms Barrington, are a bloody nuisance and you," she pointed a finger at Gabriel, "aren't much better."

Could it be George Delaney, I wondered, or Bob Richmond?

"Whoever it is must have some friends, though, up in the Park, to get a reaction like this," Gabriel said. He was referring to Garda Headquarters in the Phoenix Park and his words made her flinch.

"You should know better than that, Mr Ingram," she said, squinting her eyes at him.

My instinct was to say no more now, to let her lecture us a bit before she left. But then I thought about Paddy Hogan and his mother and Ava. They deserved the truth and if annoying Maguire was going to get to it, then I would just have to annoy her.

"Paddy Hogan didn't jump. I know it, Gabriel knows

it and so do you but you're not doing enough about it. You have time to come here and berate us yet you haven't time to tell the Hogans what's going on in this investigation, if anything!"

"You know nothing!" she growled, standing up and making the chair scrape along the floor. She picked up her cap, put it on and directed herself to Gabriel.

"I'm very surprised at you." She sounded like a school headmistress then and I was impressed by her range.

"We're only trying to help the Hogans," he said quietly.

"Well, you're not helping – you're making things worse for them. And the last thing I need is two bloody interfering fools making my job harder and wasting my time."

Neither of us spoke.

"Honestly, how do you think you're helping?" She glared at us then turned and walked into the hall and the young officer followed.

We both walked out behind them. I couldn't interpret the look on Gabriel's face.

She turned back as she opened the door, pointed at him and said, "Watch yourself". Then she left.

"Well?" I asked him once the vibrations from the too firmly closed door had ceased.

"She's very good," he said.

"Really? I think she's terrible. She's already made up her mind about Paddy. She obviously thinks he killed himself." I was incredulous at his attitude.

We went back into the kitchen and he sat down once more at the table. I began putting the tea things into the dishwasher.

"That looks like a bit of a problem all right but you

know how these lads work. They keep up the facade for as long as they need to. For all she knows, you could have pushed him."

"Ah, come on, you're just making excuses because she's one of your own. And she's not a *lad*, by the way."

He tutted at me. "You know what I mean. You were at the gardens when Paddy died. If you're in her position you don't rule anybody out until you've found the only person to rule in."

"Well, she doesn't have to be so hostile."

"Granted. But there might be a bit of that on both sides, Bea."

I conceded he was probably right about that, but I didn't trust her and I didn't like her and I said so.

"We don't have to like her. We just have to let her do her job and maybe help her out discreetly if we can."

His practicality and calmness irritated me and I tried not to let it show but I did throw the cutlery into the basket in the dishwasher with too loud a clatter.

"I'll have to work on my discretion so."

"I felt a bit sorry for her to be honest," he said. "She wasn't wearing her uniform for no reason – probably had a visit from HQ or something or got called in there for a grilling. They're probably on top of her to get this case cleared up."

I didn't answer. Of course she had a tough job but I thought pitying her was going too far.

"And somebody in the gardens must have friends in the right place to get a reaction like that from a detective inspector," he said. "No, I definitely feel for her."

"You must be joking. She's as tough as old boots. And

I don't think she's on top of this at all, Gabriel. I don't think she cares what happened to Paddy Hogan."

I closed the dishwasher with a thud and sat down at the table.

"Who do you think complained about us?" I asked.

He scratched his chin. "Doesn't matter, does it? Our card is marked now."

Ava came into my head then and I wondered if she'd had any news from Maguire.

"I'm going to ring Ava – let's see if the gardaí have done anything for her."

I took my phone into the living room.

Ava answered after three rings.

"Have you time to talk?" I asked.

"Just a minute."

In the background, I could hear the sound of a door closing, footsteps and then another door. I supposed she had gone into the kitchen at the back of the house, putting distance between herself and her mother.

"Go ahead."

"We've had a visit from the guards – me and Gabriel, I mean. Remember you met him earlier?"

"Yes. And?"

I told her about the encounter with Maguire. When I'd finished she said something I didn't quite catch. She sounded far away, as though her mind was drifting, and then she was back again.

"What does it mean though, Beatrice? Does it mean the guards are going to do something about Paddy's death now?" Her voice rose a little with a flicker of hope.

I wanted to warn her against it. It felt like a dangerous

thing – too often followed by disappointment. And I worried that neither she nor her mother could deal with disappointment right now.

"I don't know, Ava. I'm not sure. But we won't be giving up – there's a couple of other questions we need to ask."

I remembered something then from my conversation with Kaya Nkosi that had somehow slipped my mind.

"Kaya told me Paddy was fighting with someone a few days before he died. He didn't mention that to you, did he?"

"No. Who?"

"We don't know but we'll try to find out. Did I tell you Gabriel is a retired detective?"

"And he's helping us?" There was that hope again.

"He's trying. Can I ask have you heard anything from Maguire or the guards recently?"

"Not a word – I sent an email asking to speak to her and just got one of those 'your email has been received' messages. I felt like I was talking to the wall." She sighed. "Or a robot. Maybe she's a robot."

"If it's any consolation, Gabriel thinks she's good at her job. So I suppose we have to let her do it."

"If you say so."

She thanked me and rang off.

I felt like a hypocrite – I didn't really believe what I'd just said.

I went back to Gabriel in the kitchen. He had his coat on.

"I've a few things to do – I'll talk to you later," he said.

Chapter Twenty-Five

Wednesday, March 15th

On the way to Lansdowne Road for the result of the Marina Fernandez case, I thought again of Paddy Hogan's illustrations. They were so precise, so perfect. He must have spent many hours working on each one. I had a picture of him in my head, perched on a stool in the Orchid House, visitors walking around him, sketching out every detail of whichever plant he was focused on right then. His life seemed entirely absorbed in his love of plants and of the gardens. He lived in his childhood home with his mother and his sister. That small area in Glasnevin was effectively his world. People said he was kind. Why would anyone murder a man like that?

I set up my stenograph in the Labour Court hearing room at ten minutes to ten. The committee members had not yet arrived. Their low voices could be heard, though, on the other side of the door that opened at the top of the room close to their desk.

Marina Fernandez sat, as before, at one side of the long table with Joe Waldron and Caroline Brophy. Her union rep wasn't present and I wondered if that was a good or a bad sign. Marina had her hands clasped before her on the table as though in prayer. Her hair was freshly washed and shining. Her make-up had been carefully applied and it seemed to me that she was a woman ready to meet her fate and probably glad to have got to the point where a decision would be made, whatever it was. Dr Adrian Dunboyne was there too, sitting across from her with his legal team. Neither of the parties were looking at each other.

The door opened at ten past ten and the three committee members entered, nodded to those present and sat down.

The chairwoman coughed and straightened in her chair, Joe Waldron adjusted his tie and Reginald Taylor brushed invisible lint from the lapel of his suit jacket.

I held my fingers over the stenograph keys.

"We've reached our decision," Miriam Lynch said.

She looked at both barristers and down at her page then.

"We find the allegation of unfair dismissal against Chapels Nursing Home Ltd to have been proven."

Marina let out a small cry, and quickly put a hand over her mouth.

Reginald Taylor looked at his junior.

The chairwoman addressed the room again.

"We believe that in its investigation of the events surrounding the thefts at Chapels Nursing Home, management did not follow robust principles of fair play. Negative behaviour and attitudes toward Ms Fernandez tainted that investigation and, possibly, prevented the apprehension of the person or persons responsible for the thefts."

She paused and turned over the sheet she was reading from. I hoped she'd slow down a little.

"In terms of the internal investigation process itself,

fair procedures were not followed and Ms Fernandez was not given an opportunity to defend herself except in writing. We believe that the procedures followed were contrary to good practice and denied Ms Fernandez the right to fair process and justice. The explanation for not involving the gardaí was not sufficient to assuage our fears that the nursing home was seeking to cover up events there."

She took a breath and I worked as quickly as I could to catch up, my fingers aching already because of the speed.

"Finally, given the serious issues arising from evidence here, including nurse to resident ratios, we've decided to write to the Health Information and Quality Authority and suggest Chapels Nursing Home be inspected without delay to assess conditions at the home, its staff ratios and its recordkeeping."

There was a small gasp from someone on the nursing home's team.

"Given all that has happened and the fact Ms Fernandez has found new employment, we are not recommending that the nursing home offer to reemploy her. We are recommending an award of €17,500 to be paid by the nursing home to Ms Fernandez."

Dr Dunboyne glared at Reginald Taylor and muttered to himself. The committee stood up then and left the room. There was a moment of silence followed by chatter on all sides. Marina Fernandez stood and hugged her barrister and then Caroline Brophy. The solicitor was beaming. She saw me looking down and crossed the room to talk to me.

"That was a great result," she said. "And the referral to HIQA – that was amazing."

"Congratulations," I said. I had to admit that I was relieved for Marina Fernandez and felt, on balance, that justice had been done.

"I'll have this to you as soon as I can," I told her and then turned away to pack up my stenograph. It wouldn't take me long to finish the transcript and send it to both sides. I'd do that before going home and then, I supposed, I'd have to start looking for other work. I rested my hands on my lap for a minute first. They looked puffy and were throbbing very slightly.

At home again, I thought about what I'd said to Ava – that I would try to find out who it was Kaya Nkosi had heard Paddy fighting with a few days before he died. I was disappointed in myself that I hadn't remembered sooner what Kaya had told me. Perhaps I should seek her out and ask her to tell me again, in case there was anything else important I'd forgotten. I found her number on my phone and tried to call her but couldn't get through.

She had heard the argument where? In the courtyard outside the coffee shop, wasn't it? Who else could have heard that or witnessed it? Bob Richmond might have if the coffee shop was quiet at the time . . . Kaya hadn't said anyone else was present in the courtyard when she walked through the arch and, besides, it was unlikely they'd have been arguing in front of other people. I'd have to start with Bob.

I sent a text to Gabriel.

Are you busy?

Nothing I can't change.

I called him then and told him I thought we ought to ask Bob about whether he'd heard the argument.

"You're not worried about going to the Bots after our visitor yesterday?" he asked.

"Visitor" was one way of describing Maguire – "bully" was another, I thought.

"A bit but . . . we don't have to stay in the gardens long."

"Right then, I'll meet you in the car park at two."

I hesitated. "I was going to park on Mobhi Drive. I thought it might be better just to slip in the front gate and around to the coffee shop. And if we leave in a hurry we won't need to get out of the car park."

He agreed, though I think he thought I might be overreacting. I got dressed and readied myself to leave. I put on my camel wool coat and wrapped a scarf around my neck but realised when I stepped outside that I didn't really need it. The day had improved. There was a light breeze and the sun appeared intermittently between clouds. As I got into my car, I took the scarf off and dropped it on the passenger seat and my heart lifted just a small bit, in the way it does when the first daffodils are visible pushing up through the dark soil in my neighbour's garden.

I found a parking space easily enough on St Mobhi Drive on the river side of the road ten minutes ahead of our meeting time. Ordinarily, I would have got out and wandered round the gardens before meeting Gabriel, but my wariness prevented me. I decided to stay in the car instead and wait. I hadn't realised I was looking at Constance's house until her hall door opened and someone stepped outside. Who was that familiar shape, leaning in now to receive the light kiss Constance was offering to his cheek? He turned then and strode down the drive and my heart thumped so hard I thought it might burst through my ribs – it was Gabriel. I slid down in my seat, hoping he wouldn't look back up the road and notice me. He didn't. He just walked on in his usual way. Did his step look a little lighter? I stayed in the car until he had rounded the corner onto Botanic Gardens Road and then I stayed a bit longer.

When my pulse settled I got out and made my way to the gardens. I didn't know what to think. Had he called in to ask her more questions? Was her peck on the cheek just a polite gesture? Or had he been there longer, had he been there when I phoned him? He was leaning against a granite pillar at the entrance gates, his hands in the pockets of his navy donkey jacket, his gaze directed into the gardens. I felt a ridiculous surge of jealousy at the thought of him with Constance. Was he with Constance? No, that couldn't be right, could it? As soon as I said hello, he'd explain everything and let me in on the information he had gleaned. I was sure of it.

He turned then and saw me. "There you are," he said.
"Am I late?"
"Not at all. Lovely afternoon, isn't it? Will we go in?"
He walked through the gate and to the left, passing the security desk and waving as he did at the man behind the glass screen. He clearly wasn't as anxious as I was about being seen in the gardens.

I followed, waiting for him to tell me about his meeting with Constance.

We walked through the arched gap in the stone wall that enclosed the coffee shop's courtyard. There were a few customers sitting outside, enjoying the sheltered sunshine that made the space comfortable so early in the year. He opened the glass door into the coffee shop and, as he did, we heard a woman's voice, raised in exasperation.

"Just forget it, for fuck sake!" She said, over her shoulder in the direction of Bob Richmond. She brushed past me on her way to the exit, her elbow accidentally finding my arm. "Sorry," she said before she disappeared.

Bob gave a sigh of resignation and caught Gabriel's eye.

"I don't think I'll ever understand women," he said.

Gabriel laughed. "That's where you're going wrong, Bob. You're not supposed to understand them."

I wanted to give him a sharp finger in the ribs and ask him how he could be so chummy with Bob when he knew what he'd done to Celine Deegan, but I didn't. I took a seat in the corner and waited for him to do what needed to be done to persuade Bob to talk to us for a few minutes.

They chatted as they walked down to the table, Bob carrying the tray with tea and a plate of biscuits.

Bob looked forlornly in the direction of the door. "That was Alice my partner . . . or ex-partner, I think," he sighed. "Why do relationships have to be so complicated?"

"I'm afraid you'd need a Solomon to answer that question," I said though in my head I was thinking 'It might help if you stayed away from amateur porn'. "May I ask *you* something, Bob?"

He looked at me, lifting his chin like a boxer in defensive pose.

"What?"

"A few days before Paddy died someone overheard him having an argument in the courtyard outside. Do you remember that by any chance?" I added, "Ava Hogan asked us to find out."

"Ava asked?" He seemed sceptical and shook his head. "I don't remember any argument. That's not to say it didn't happen but . . . even if it did, I don't think I could have heard it from in here." He glanced over in the direction of the exit.

"It's a pretty heavy door," Gabriel said. "Actually, can we try something?"

"Okay – what?"

"Go back to the counter and let me know if you hear anything."

Bob did as he was asked and Gabriel went outside to the courtyard, closing the door firmly behind him. I listened too and tried to make out his voice but couldn't.

Gabriel reappeared and Bob came back to our table.

"Well?" Gabriel asked.

"Not a thing," Bob said. "I'm sorry."

"Me neither," I said. So that was that. It was frustrating.

"There definitely was an argument – Kaya Nkosi heard it," I blurted out.

"I didn't say there wasn't – I just didn't hear it. I'm sure Kaya told you the truth. She was the type."

"Was?"

"Yes. She's gone now."

"Gone? Gone where?" She hadn't mentioned she was going away when she'd called to the house.

He shrugged. "I heard she was offered a job – don't know where."

"When did this happen?"

He turned to go. "Last week. George Delaney mentioned

it – he was complaining that she didn't work her notice and they were short-staffed because of it."

"Just one other thing," Gabriel said. "You didn't have a row with Paddy yourself by any chance?"

"No." He said it firmly, showing his annoyance at the question by staring hard at Gabriel. "What would I have to fight with Paddy about anyway?"

I argued with myself about whether I should bring it up. Was it the right time to tell him what we were aware of? I glanced at Gabriel who knew what I was thinking and nodded his support.

"Could you have been fighting about Celine Deegan?" I asked.

Bob's face changed colour from embarrassed red to pale to red again. "That's over. How did you . . .? Kaya, was it? *Bitch!*"

"You argued with Kaya, didn't you? I saw you in the Teak House. Maybe you argued with Paddy Hogan, too."

I thought I heard a low growl from his throat.

"Are you being blackmailed about it, Bob?" I asked, recalling the one-sided phone conversation I'd overheard.

"*Blackmailed?* What the fuck?"

He looked from me to Gabriel and back again.

"Fuck off out of my coffee shop, the both of you, and don't ever come back," he said.

He turned away and walked back behind his counter.

"We'll finish our tea first," Gabriel said after him and then in a lower voice, "Has a right temper on him." He was being his logical self, sifting for information that could be of use like a prospector panning for gold, instead of worrying about the threat Bob had made.

"He certainly has, and I'd say he's strong enough to push someone over that railing." I could almost picture him then, struggling with Paddy Hogan in the Palm House high above those deadly flagstones. I reached for a biscuit.

"What's wrong with your hand?" Gabriel asked.

"Nothing." I put my hand in my lap where he couldn't see it.

He looked doubtful but changed the subject. "I wonder why Kaya Nkosi left. Constance told me she was an excellent gardener."

"Did she? When?"

"Last time we spoke."

Was he deliberately evading my question? He finished a biscuit and took a slurp of tea. I waited for him to tell me he'd seen her earlier. He didn't.

"Did Constance say anything else I should know?" I tried not to sound irritated.

"Not really."

I topped up my tea from the pot that sat between us. I was determined to finish it all before leaving and it was easy to be determined with Gabriel there, even if I was finding him a little annoying right now. I wanted to tell him I saw him coming out of Constance's. I wanted to ask him what he was doing there. But it was too late. He would know I'd held back because I'd drawn my own conclusions. And what did it matter if he was interested in her or if they were having a relationship? He and I were friends, that's all. I didn't own him. I gulped my tea.

"Don't look now . . ." he said, which of course I did, just in time to catch the eye of Maguire coming in the door with one of her uniformed juniors trotting after her. She approached our table.

"Ms Barrington and Mr Ingram, nice to see you again." The tone in her voice said the opposite. "What has you here today?"

"Just enjoying the fine weather, detective. It's a lovely afternoon for a stroll," I said.

"Well, you needn't be annoying people while you're strolling, do you hear me?"

"We hadn't planned on it," Gabriel answered.

There was no point in saying that we already had. I imagined Bob would take care of that once he had a chance. Or perhaps he wouldn't – he wouldn't want to have to explain the Celine Deegan episode to gardaí.

"What has *you* in the gardens today?" I asked.

She arched an eyebrow at me. "Surely you don't expect an answer to that, do you, Ms Barrington? Or are you still confusing me with Matt McCann?"

"Definitely not – you're no Matt McCann."

"We were just leaving actually." Gabriel stood up.

The detective moved out of the way to let us both out. I followed him reluctantly.

"We'll be in touch," she said.

As we left I saw that she was approaching Bob and that her junior was taking out his notebook.

"I wonder what she's doing here. Do you think she's found out about Celine Deegan or the blackmail?"

He didn't answer but when we'd passed through the courtyard and were heading back to the entrance gate he stopped and turned to me.

"Tell me something, Bea, do you always have to do that?"

"Do what?"

"Do you always have to be antagonistic with her?"

I felt like the air was being sucked out of my lungs.

"You don't have to be on the attack all the time, you know," he continued. "She's only doing her job."

Why was he speaking to me like this?

"She was antagonising me, not the other way around!" I was exasperated that he couldn't see that. "It's always the same with you, Gabriel, isn't it? The *lads* are always right."

He shook his head. "For God's sake!"

"I thought you were on my side," I said.

"Your side? Did you say 'side'? What are you, twelve?" He was incensed. "Can you not put yourself in someone else's shoes for once?"

"What do you mean – I do that all the time!"

"There's no talking to you when you're like this, Bea." He turned his back then and walked away.

I was frozen to the spot. What had just happened? What had I done that was so terrible? Nothing, as far as I could see. I'd defended myself against Maguire, that was all. Why did I feel on the outside all of a sudden? On the outside looking in at him and the *lads* and at him and Constance. And why did it damn well hurt so much?

I made my way to the shelter next to the entrance gates and sat down. I had a headache and a tight sensation at the base of my throat that was, when I was younger, a precursor to tears. I longed to be at home on the sofa looking out at the sea. But I couldn't leave, not until I was sure that Gabriel had driven away.

I was sitting there a couple of minutes when George Delaney appeared and walked over to the flower bed opposite the shelter. He knelt down on a mat and began weeding between what looked like tulip plants, though they had barely come through the soil.

I got up and went over to him.

"We won't see these till April – it's been too cold," he said as I approached. He turned over a trowelful of soil.

"I hear you've lost a gardener," I said.

He shifted his weight back onto his calves and stood up.

"You mean Kaya? Yeah. I was sorry to see her go. She didn't even say goodbye, just emailed HR to say she was resigning. Never mind that she left us in the lurch." He scratched his chin for a moment with the tip of his trowel as though he found it hard to believe. "I didn't think she was the kind to go off like that without saying goodbye."

Thinking of Bob Richmond, I asked, "You don't think something happened to her or she was frightened away, do you?"

"Frightened? Of what?"

I shrugged. "Before she left, did she ever mention anything to you about hearing Paddy Hogan having a row with someone?"

He groaned at the question. "No, Beatrice, she didn't."

He turned then, knelt back down on the mat and resumed his work, stabbing the earth with the trowel. I left him at it and walked back to St Mobhi Drive to get my car.

Chapter Twenty-Six

I had waited a full fifteen minutes before leaving the Botanic Gardens, sure that Gabriel would be gone by then. But when I turned the corner onto St Mobhi Drive I could see him next to my car, leaning against the driver door, his arms folded across his chest. He'd decided to wait for me then? He wasn't looking in my direction and I was tempted to go back and spend a little time in the coffee shop across from the gardens but I knew that would be petty. If he had something more to say, I should let him say it.

As I got closer I saw Constance Anderson walking down her driveway. She was not wearing a coat, just a pink blouse and black trousers, and she was smiling and waving across the road at Gabriel. I thought she must have seen him from her window. She crossed the footpath and then stepped out onto the road. At the same moment a dark car appeared at the edge of my vision and seemed to speed up. It was over in a second – Constance was stepping forward then falling back as the car almost clipped her and kept on going. She let out a shout of dismay and Gabriel and I both ran toward her. She was sprawled on the footpath.

"Constance!" Gabriel called.

She sat up slowly, looking dazed and pale.

"He came out of nowhere," she said.

"The speed of him – bloody dangerous fecker!" He hunkered down beside her. "Don't move for a second – are you all right, anything broken?"

She put her hands down to feel her calves and ankles through the fabric of her trousers.

"I'm okay. I'm fine. Help me up."

We both helped her to her feet.

"You didn't see the reg, did you?" Gabriel asked me.

"No." There had barely been time to note the dark navy, the saloon shape. Had I seen the driver? Only a shadow at the wheel – a man, I thought.

"Look at your wrist," I said to Constance. It was red and already beginning to swell. She must have put her right hand down instinctively to soften her fall. "That's not broken, is it?"

She moved her hand in a circle, clockwise and counter-clockwise.

"No, it's just sore." She wiped the dust from the back of her trousers with her left hand.

Gabriel took out his phone. "I'm going to call the guards."

"*No!*" She spoke so sharply that we were both startled and, seeing our reaction, she softened her tone. "There's no point in calling the guards . . . There's nothing they can do and I don't want a fuss."

"I really think . . ."

"No, Gabriel. I just want to get inside and sit down."

He put his phone away reluctantly. She turned around but in doing so lost her balance and lurched sideways. Gabriel caught her by her left elbow.

I supported her on the right side and between us we guided her up to the house. The door was ajar and Gabriel pushed it open. We helped her inside and through a door to the left into a chintzy living room.

"Here we are," he said, and we eased her down onto the couch. It was pale pink and overstuffed, with lace doilies on each arm and a lace antimacassar across its back. Constance sank back into it and swung her legs up, kicking off the black court shoes she'd been wearing. She had small feet and toes of uneven lengths, which were visible through black nylon pop socks.

I sat down on an armchair which was also protected with little bits of lace.

"I'll get you a drop of brandy," Gabriel said. He walked across the room to a table near the window that held a silver tray with glasses and bottles. He opened one and poured out an amber liquid. I couldn't help but notice that he'd had no trouble finding it.

She took the glass from him and sipped. "Have one yourself, why don't you?" she said. "And Beatrice?"

"No, thank you," I said at precisely the same time as he said, "Bea doesn't drink."

She looked at me with what I thought was pity. Then she began to shiver violently. I took my coat off and put it over her.

"Take another drop," Gabriel coaxed. She drank again, a long, emptying gulp this time, put the glass on a little table next to the couch, and pulled my coat up to her chin.

"Did you see the driver?" Gabriel asked, coming back with a small brandy in his hand and sitting on the other armchair.

She closed her eyes as if picturing the moment the car appeared then opened them again. "No."

"He wasn't a neighbour or anything, was he? I mean, did you recognise the car?" I asked.

"No."

I wasn't sure I believed her.

"Driving like that – he ought to be arrested," Gabriel said.

Constance closed her eyes and then opened them slowly a couple of times as though they were weighed down with something invisible. I thought the brandy had probably taken effect too quickly.

"I'm scared, Gabriel," she said, in a small voice.

"You must have got a dreadful fright," he said.

But I knew that wasn't what she'd meant.

"What is it you're scared of, Constance?" I asked quietly, leaning forward in my seat.

"Do you believe in divine retribution?" she said.

"Retribution for what, though?" I could see Gabriel out of the corner of my eye, seated now on the other armchair, a look of concern on his face.

"But do you believe it's possible?" She spoke with intensity now. "Even if you get involved in something without meaning to?"

"What is it you're involved in?" I asked.

She put her hand to her lips as though she was trying to prevent herself from saying too much. "It doesn't matter."

"Why would a god be interested in our little lives anyway?" I said.

Gabriel gave me one of his 'not now' looks.

"I think God sees everything we do, Beatrice, and he judges us," she said. "He looks into our hearts too though, I hope, and sees what is really there before he seeks his retribution."

"What do you mean though, Constance? What retribution?" Gabriel asked.

She didn't answer. I felt frustrated by her riddles and wanted to cut through the nonsense.

"Did you have something to do with Paddy Hogan's death?" I asked.

She let out a long breath. "Don't be silly."

"Do you know something about it then?"

She looked at me and then at Gabriel. "I don't know a thing about it except what we both saw, Beatrice, that day in the Palm House." She shuddered. "I'm too tired for this. I think I'll go up to bed."

"Are you sure we shouldn't call a doctor?" Gabriel said.

She got up off the couch slowly. "No doctor, no guards, Gabriel. I just need a rest. Will you see yourselves out?"

"Do you need help getting up to bed?" I asked.

"I'll manage."

We left, pulling the door closed behind us as Constance made her way slowly upstairs.

"What do you make of all that?" I asked.

"I don't know. That was very reckless driving."

"And the retribution thing . . ."

"Could have been the brandy and the shock."

It didn't seem that way to me. I thought there was real fear there and I wanted to argue with him but didn't feel like getting on his wrong side for a second time in the one day.

"I wish I'd had a chance to get the reg from that car," he said. He looked up and down the road. "Pity there's no CCTV around here."

We crossed to my car and stood beside it.

"I think it was deliberate," I said.

"What makes you say that?"

"I'm sure that car pulled out when Constance appeared. I think someone is trying to frighten her."

"They'd have to be waiting for a chance then, watching her house," he said. "That seems like a lot of effort just to scare her."

"You don't suppose it could be that young man we saw her with? The one in the black leather jacket?"

"But why? They looked like friends, didn't they?"

"I don't know. Couldn't we . . .?" I wanted to say we should check out the young man ourselves or at least ask a few questions.

"We wouldn't want to jump the gun there," he said.

His reluctance puzzled me, but I said no more. I began to open the driver's door but he put a hand on it to stop me.

"About earlier," he said, hesitating, "I'm sorry I was short with you."

"Forget about it," I said.

I wanted to say something funny then that would lighten things between us. I realised suddenly how much I wanted to see him smile. But I couldn't think of anything to say.

"Will I talk to you later?" was all I could manage.

"I've a few things to do – I'll call you after."

I got into the car and pulled away slowly, checking in my rear-view mirror to see if he went back to Constance's house, but he got into his own car, indicated out and drove up behind me. When we got to the junction with St Mobhi Road, I turned left and he turned right for Stoneybatter, beeping a goodbye as he went. He was going home then. I felt a certain amount of relief but not enough. It rankled that he hadn't told me he'd been in Constance's before I met him at the gardens. It wasn't like him, was it, to be so secretive? And then he had been so quick to anger. That wasn't like him either. There must have been other things on his mind, things that he didn't want to share with me. Driving down the coast toward home I told myself again that I had no right to complain now – he was entitled to his privacy, to his own life and I had to stop feeling that I had some claim to it.

I was almost home when my phone rang.

Chapter Twenty-Seven

I pulled over to the side of the road just past the Clontarf train station to take the call.

"Is that Beatrice?" a woman asked when I answered.

"It is, yes."

"It's Eileen Cassidy here, from Hazelgrove Lodge."

"How are you, Eileen?" I hadn't been expecting to hear from her so soon after our visit.

"You mentioned I could give you a call if I was up in Dublin . . ."

"I did. Where are you?"

"Beaumont, Beaumont Hospital. Peter's getting a bit of a job done."

"Is he okay?"

"He'll be fine. He's only in for the day. The nurse said to come back for him at six. What I wanted to ask was, since I'm here can we meet up?"

"Absolutely. Will I come up to the hospital?"

"Ah no, it's out of this place I want to get. Couldn't we go for a walk in the Botanic Gardens? I've never been there before and I'd love to see it."

I was conscious of the time, almost four, and the gardens closed at five. I was reluctant too to go back there so soon but I didn't want to disappoint her. "All right, we'll need to be quick though. Closes at five. Do you want me to collect you or give you directions?"

"Sure can't I put it into the Google maps?" she said.

"Of course. I'll see you there so. There's a car park round the side." There was no point in trying to explain to her why I'd prefer not to park there. And we'd be quick.

"Great, thanks, Beatrice."

She hung up and I swung the car around back in the direction I'd come from. I wondered briefly whether I should ring Gabriel to let him know. He might like to see Eileen again. But I decided against it – he didn't tell me everything and I didn't need to tell him everything.

I parked on St Mobhi Drive and walked over to the gardens and around to the car park. Eileen Cassidy's green Range Rover was just coming through the barrier. She saw me and beeped her horn as she parked. Before I could reach her she had already hopped down from the high-up driving seat and crossed over to me in brisk steps. She was wearing the same brown pleated skirt I remembered from the first time we met with a quilted green jacket and laced brown shoes.

"How are yeh?" she said. And she put her arms around me in a hug.

Though I'm not the hugging type I felt comforted by it.

"I'm . . . fine. How's Peter?"

"He was nervous going in, but grand, he'll be grand."

She didn't elaborate on what the procedure was that he needed and I didn't ask.

We walked through the Teak House and its colourful pelargoniums.

"Aren't they only glorious?" she said.

We went down to the left then round the back of the herbarium and library building past the connecting gateway into Glasnevin Cemetery. I pointed out its round tower in the distance and told her about the Easter Rising memorial and the cemetery museum.

"Peter would love to visit that," she said.

"How are things otherwise? In yourself, I mean?" I asked.

"I'm not so bad now. After you left, Peter was . . . I'm not sure what Gabriel said to him but he was different – more open, I think. The other day he even reminded me of a little song Daisy used to sing and when I started to cry he didn't get cross or walk away. He put his arm around me."

"I'm glad, Eileen."

We walked the perimeter of the gardens, skirting the cemetery walls, past the entrance to the vegetable garden, past the alders, maples, ash and lime trees down to the river.

We were walking along the riverbank behind the Curvilinear House when we met George Delaney pushing a wheelbarrow. We stood to one side to let him get by.

"Thanks," he said gruffly at us, only barely looking up.

When he had gone Eileen squeezed my arm. "He's the one," she said.

"The one what?"

"Remember I told you? About the fella creeping around during the night, paying a little visit to one of the women." She chuckled.

"Him? That's George Delaney. He's married with two children."

"Well, his wife wasn't with him."

"You still don't remember which of the women he visited?" I was thinking of that night in Tolka House when I'd seen George sitting with Constance Anderson.

She pursed her lips and shook her head. "It'll come back to me," she said.

We walked on and she enthused about the gardens.

"You'd never imagine a place like this could be so peaceful in a big city," she said. "When Peter's better I'll persuade him to come here with me. We're both getting too old to be always wrapped up in the B&B."

"You can both stay with me if you like," I said, surprising myself.

"Thanks. Though it'll be a while yet before he can walk again."

"Oh?" That sounded serious.

"Did I not say? He's having his veins done." She ran her hand along her shinbone and I took it to mean Peter had varicose veins.

I winced. "That'll be sore."

"It will but it'll be worth it. They've been giving him a lot trouble the last while."

We went up the steps leading from a path near the river to a path that curved back toward the main gate. I glanced in the direction of the Teagasc buildings and saw white lights on tall poles, a microphone on a stick and the professor speaking into a camera. I had thought the filming was finished but perhaps they'd needed some extra shots. Someone shouted cut and I thought the professor looked up in my direction though I may have imagined it.

"That's Professor James Christakos," I told Eileen. "They're making a documentary about his work."

"Oh yes – he was part of the group that came down with lover boy," Eileen said.

We stood at the top of the steps and watched the bustle below as though we were glimpsing life on a Hollywood set.

"Enough?" I asked after a while.

"Yes. Wait till I tell Peter!"

We walked on past the director's house and the main entrance gate and paused at the door to the visitor centre. I noticed, for the first time, a poster stuck to the glass. The professor's face looked out at me from it and round its edge was the distinctive *Natural World* band of blue.

Join us for a celebration of our upcoming documentary, *Christakos: Botanist and Plant Hunter*, at the National Botanic Gardens, Sunday, March 19th, 7.30pm.

I remembered then that the receptionist had mentioned some sort of celebration.

"It's only a wrap party really – you oughta come."

I turned round and the professor was standing behind me. I couldn't hide my surprise. "Hello," I said.

"Sorry, didn't mean to sneak up on ya."

He smiled to his molars and I couldn't help smiling back.

"I'm sure you remember Eileen Cassidy," I said.

They shook hands.

"Nice to meet you again, professor," she said.

He blinked a few times, obviously struggling to remember where they'd met.

"Eileen owns a B&B near the Burren," I prompted, to ease his discomfort.

"Sure she does – forgive me, Eileen – of course I recognise you."

"No bother," she said.

"Are you ladies free on Sunday night? You'd both be very welcome."

Eileen shook her head. "Not me. I'm going down home this evening with my husband but I'm sure Beatrice here . . ."

"What d'ya you think, Beatrice?" He gave me a warm smile.

"I should be able to make it," I found myself saying.

"See you there then." He opened the door of the visitor centre and went inside.

"Aren't you a dark one all the same!" Eileen said.

"I don't know what you mean." I could feel myself blushing and thought I must look ridiculous.

"He's very charming and a fine bit of beef," she said.

I couldn't help laughing. Then I checked the time.

"This place is closing shortly but would you like to go somewhere else for a sandwich?"

"I won't, thanks," she said. "It's time I was going back up to himself. They might let him out a bit early."

We went back to the car park and her Range Rover.

"You're not driving home tonight, are you, Eileen?"

"No. We're staying in a guesthouse near the hospital. We'll go down in the morning."

"Call me, won't you, if you need anything?"

She said she would and then pulled out of the car park and drove away. I followed her up the lane, though there was no footpath, out onto Botanic Gardens Road and back to my car.

As I drove home I thought of George Delaney. I could almost picture him skulking along the dark corridor in Hazelgrove Lodge, reaching the door, knocking gently, slipping inside. But who was it he was visiting?

Chapter Twenty-Eight

Thursday, March 16th

I'd intended sleeping late. I was inordinately tired and put it down to the anti-inflammatories I'd been prescribed for my hands. I had thought my body might welcome the opportunity of extra rest, might leave me cocooned in sleep. But, of course, that's not how these things work. Instead of a restful night I'd been tortured with dreams of vines that were growing and creeping behind me as I ran and ran through the Botanic Gardens and there were cameras following me and music laced with such awful tension and anxiety that John Williams himself could have written the soundtrack.

When I awoke I was relieved to find myself safe in my own bed. I checked the time – seven-thirty – and dragged myself slowly upright. I might have stayed like that for a while if my mobile phone ringing from downstairs had not forced me to quickly grab a dressing gown and run down. It had stopped by the time I reached it, but I could see it was Eileen Cassidy. I called back.

"Everything okay?" I asked.

"Sorry, Beatrice, I forgot it was so early. We were organising ourselves to go home."

"I was awake. How's Peter?"

"Sore but happy to be done," she said. "I wanted to say goodbye and thanks for yesterday."

"Not at all!"

"And didn't I remember something about that woman!"

I took her to mean the woman who was with George Delaney. I suddenly felt wide awake.

"Yes?" I said, hoping I didn't sound too eager.

"It came to me this morning when I went to breakfast. The woman here is lovely, very chatty."

"And?"

"It brought back a chat I had with the gardener's *amore* at breakfast the night after I'd seen him. I still can't remember her name, but I do remember she told me she was invited down by her brother."

"Brother?" Ava Hogan? It must have been Ava. "Ah, I think I might know who it is. My curiosity is satisfied! Thanks, Eileen."

"No bother."

"Safe journey," I said and rang off feeling a little dazed . . . and what? Uneasy? Doubtful? Why did it make me uneasy thinking that Ava might be the one George had visited that night? He was married, of course, but that wasn't it. He wouldn't be the first married man to have a fling on a trip away. But with *Ava*? It felt, it definitely felt to me like an imbalance of power. There was no escaping that she was – what was it her mother had said? "Vulnerable". Had he taken advantage of her, manipulated her in some way? Or was I doing a disservice to Ava thinking that? Wasn't she as capable as anyone else of wanting and of having a clandestine relationship? My thoughts were spinning. No wonder he'd been trying to stop me from asking questions. It was probably he who'd complained to gardaí. He was afraid his affair would come out. But was that all he was afraid of? Was that all he had to hide?

I'd have to talk to Ava and not on the phone. I waited until ten o'clock then sent her a text asking if she had time to meet for a coffee at the Tolka House. She said she could see me at half eleven.

"Do you have news for me?" she asked.

"No . . . just a couple of questions you might be able to help me with."

The Tolka House pub was almost empty when I arrived and had that greasy smell that can linger in a building that serves carvery meals every day.

Ava was already there, sitting on an armchair at a table for two just inside the door. I ordered tea from the bar and sat opposite her.

Though we were next to a window the room was dim and it took me a few moments to adjust my eyes. She looked tired and pale and there was a trace of egg yolk on her chin, left over from her breakfast. There was no drink before her.

"Do you want something?" I asked.

"I've ordered," she said and as she spoke the barman arrived and put a hot port before her.

"I think I'm getting a cold," she said, cupping the glass.

The barman returned with my tea and I paid for both drinks.

"How's your mother?" I asked, stirring the pot and pouring myself a cup.

"That's not what you wanted to ask me, is it?" she said abruptly and then less sharply, "I haven't got long."

I took a sip from my cup. "I need to know, that is, I've heard . . . is it true that you and George Delaney were . . . an item?"

If she looked pale before I spoke, she looked even paler now.

"Where did you hear that? He swore he'd never tell!" She looked as though she might lash out at me or else burst into tears.

I was taken aback by the intensity of her reaction. "Not from anyone in Dublin," I said.

"Not from Dublin?" she gasped. "I suppose that means you know all about Liverpool too?"

She did start crying then and muttering to herself, though I couldn't make out what she was saying. I found a pack of tissues in my handbag and gave them to her. She pulled two out of the plastic wrapping and began to mop her face.

"Did you know the nurse, is that it? She told me she was from Dublin." She took another tissue and held it to her nose. "I warned George that Dublin's too small for secrets but he said it would be okay."

"I'm sorry, Ava. I don't know anything about Liverpool. I only knew about your . . . relationship with George because the landlady in that B&B in the Burren saw him go into your room."

"Oh." She stopped crying and blew her nose. "Oh," she said again, as it dawned on her that she'd told me more than I'd needed to know.

"I won't tell a soul," I said, in my mind excluding Gabriel from that pledge.

"And you won't say anything to George, will you? Because I promised him I wouldn't tell anyone."

There might come a time when I would have to say something to George, I thought, but by then perhaps she'd understand why.

"Not if you don't want me to," I said.

She picked up her drink then, its steam dissipated, and took a gulp. "I don't want you to misunderstand things, Beatrice. I don't want you thinking we were . . . It was just a bit of fun between me and George, that was all, and we didn't mean to do any harm."

I thought she might cry again but she finished her drink.

"He was kind about it. He brought me over to Liverpool and he paid for everything. And we promised each other we'd tell no-one after and just get on with our lives."

I wondered if George had persuaded her that it was best not to tell anyone. Had he made her feel she had something to be ashamed of? I thought of her afterwards going back to her childhood bedroom on St Teresa's Road. How lonely she must have felt.

"Did your mother know?"

"Are you joking? No. I told her I was going to Wexford for the weekend to visit a cousin."

"And Paddy, is there anyway Paddy could have found out?"

"Ah no," she said, shaking her head. "Ah no."

I didn't say 'What if he did know?' though that was what I was thinking. What would he have done if he knew?

Ava looked at her watch. "I have to go now. I promised Mammy I'd be there when the public health nurse comes to dress her arm – she has an ulcer."

I winced.

"It doesn't hurt her. It just gets a bit smelly sometimes." She stood up, took her yellow raincoat from the back of her chair and put it on.

"You won't tell Mammy, will you?" she said, looking for a moment as trusting and solemn as a child.

"No, of course not."

"All right then." She turned away, put her hood up and walked out the door.

I finished my tea and left shortly afterwards. When I was back in my car I phoned Gabriel and told him.

"I wasn't expecting that," he said. "If it was anyone with George I would have thought Kaya Nkosi or else one of the gardeners from Kew."

"Never mind that. What if Paddy found out about it? He might have confronted George."

"It's certainly possible."

"And what if they argued, up there on the walkway in the Palm House and George pushed him over?" I could almost picture it. I thought again of George's hands in gloves and those heavy steel-toed boots. Could he have run down and out through the Cactus House and then back around once he heard Constance screaming?

"I've been thinking about that fall, Bea," he said. "We know he didn't fall but I don't think it was an accidental shove either. That railing was too high." He paused for a moment. "Do you think George would be capable of that?"

I thought about the question. "I've no doubt he'd be physically capable and I suppose he had a lot to protect . . . but has he got it in him?"

"We all have it in us somewhere, Bea."

I remembered the look on George's face when he confronted me that day in the Alpine Yard. There was a temper there and strength. And what would happen if his secret came out? What if Paddy had threatened to complain about him or tell his family?

"What do we do now?" I asked.

"We'll have to go back to Maguire."

I groaned. "Could we not . . .?" I wanted to say question George ourselves.

"You know we can't, Bea." He was resolute.

"Okay. Tomorrow." I wanted time to figure out the right things to say to Maguire. I wanted to be able to convince her finally that Paddy hadn't killed himself.

"Tomorrow then," he said and rang off.

I drove home.

Chapter Twenty-Nine

Friday, March 17th

I was stirring beaten egg into melted butter when my phone rang. The toast had popped and I'd chopped a little green parsley to add for the day that was in it. I was tempted to let the call go but when I glanced at the phone I saw it was Ava so I turned the heat off under the pot and answered it.

She didn't even say hello. "I couldn't sleep last night. I've been thinking about everything." She spoke rapidly. "What if you're right? What if Paddy found out about me and George? What if they had a fight?"

"Slow down, Ava. We don't know that happened."

"I know, Beatrice, but we can find out. We can *ask*, can't we? Nothing's made any sense since Paddy died but this does – this makes sense." Her voice was tense and higher than normal, like her throat was constricting. "I want to ask him. I want to look him in the face and ask him."

I could hear the sound of her feet and thought she must have been pacing up and down the hall.

"I'm going to see him right now and ask him straight out."

"*Hold on, hold on!* What if you're right and he did have something to do with Paddy's death? Just say he pushed him

260

– what will he do to you if you confront him?" I tried to talk her out of it. "It's St Patrick's Day – he probably won't even be at work. He'll be at the parade with his family."

"He won't. I know he won't. He told me he hates parades and always tells his wife he has to work."

Oh God. We went on talking in circles for a few minutes. I emphasised the danger she was putting herself in if she was right. I told her that if he had lost his temper with Paddy he could lose it with her too.

"I don't care, Beatrice. I want to know what happened. I want to know."

Her determination frightened me. I had a vision of her then alone with George. I had seen the flash of his anger. I could imagine him turning on her. I couldn't let that happen.

"If you must see him then I'm coming with you." What else could I do?

"This is between me and him, Beatrice."

"It was but you've involved me now. If you're going to talk to him, you have to let me come along."

She was quiet for a moment. "All right then," she said.

We arranged where to meet and she rang off.

I thought about calling Gabriel. I really did. He would disapprove of the idea I was sure. He would argue with me just as I had argued with Ava and then he would offer to come with us to lend his quiet strength. And what would be the consequences of that? I had promised Ava I wouldn't tell anyone else about her relationship with George. She would know then that I'd broken that promise and I would lose her trust. And, anyway, Gabriel was adamant about not annoying Maguire again. He'd probably want to tell her everything right away. Best to leave him out of it, I decided. I could be there for Ava and surely George wouldn't try to hurt both of us?

It was raining horizontally at the Botanic Gardens and I was glad of that. It meant when I got out of my car in the car park I could hide under my black umbrella, holding it at an angle close to my head so that a person would have to make an effort to see my face. I admitted to myself that I didn't want to be seen.

When Ava arrived she didn't have an umbrella but was wearing the same yellow raincoat she'd worn to Tolka House, like something a fisherman might own. Her hood was up and her hands were dug into her pockets. She hadn't come far but the jeans she was wearing, tucked into ankle boots, were streaked with rain and the tan make-up on her face was striped as though she'd been crying. I led her toward the small shelter to the right of the entrance gate and gave her a tissue to mop her face.

"This weather," she said.

We agreed that she should make enquiries about where George might be. I waited in the shelter while she walked over to the visitor centre. When she returned she said the receptionist had told her to try the gardeners' office or else the greenhouses.

"Will we try the office first?" I asked.

"I know where it is," she said. "My father used to bring me and Paddy there when we were kids."

We walked, both under the umbrella now, in the direction of the office. There were few visitors around though there was a small group ahead of us who quickened their pace and ducked into the Orchid House.

As we approached the office building I began to feel anxious about encountering George. Was it right to be imposing myself into an argument between ex-lovers? Though, no, it was more than that.

As we neared the green wooden door, I wondered whether I had better hang back a bit. He might get angry when he saw me and then she'd get nothing out of him. On the other hand, I wanted to be nearby to protect her – in case he lashed out.

The door was not locked. She turned the brass doorknob and pushed the door open. I closed my umbrella and we stepped into the hall. All was quiet. I could see the door to the kitchen was wide open. Not a sound. There was no one inside.

I gestured toward the room on the left where I'd found Paddy Hogan's computer. The door was ajar. Ava pushed it and it swung inwards.

"*Dear God!*" She took a step back, putting her hand over her mouth to suppress a scream. I moved around her and could see George side-on, sitting at a desk in the centre of the room leaning to the left, his head lolling, eyes closed. I dropped my dripping umbrella, pulled my phone out of my bag and called for an ambulance. Then I crossed the room. His right hand was covering the left side of his chest and the spaces between his fingers were red, the stain spreading down his overalls. There were red sprays on the desk in front of him.

"*Get somebody!*" I shouted to her, but she remained frozen in the doorway. "*Go on!*"

She moved then, running out the door, silent at first, then shouting "*Help! Help!*"

I put my hand on his shoulder and called to him. "*George! George!*" He slumped a little more. The air was filled with the metallic smell of blood. I placed two fingers on his throat where I thought a pulse should be. There was nothing. His chest was still. He wasn't breathing. What was I supposed to do? Try to resuscitate him? Stop the blood? I grabbed some tissues from my bag and placed them over his hand and pressed on them. The blood wasn't really pumping out now. It was only seeping like a stain across dry blotting paper. My actions, I knew, were useless. George was beyond help. His left hand was holding something. What was that? It looked like the corner of a page, bloodstained. What were those words on it? The blood was spreading into the tissues – they were sodden with it.

There were noises then, voices, people running. They were in the room. I moved my hand away and took a step to one side. My shoe struck something. I looked down. It was a knife, long and thin and bloody, but still glinting at its edge.

Someone took my arm and led me out to the hall. I slumped against the wall and a chair was produced. A paramedic came and though I knew she was talking I couldn't understand her words. I could only hear the beat of my own heart in my ears. She prised from me the wad of scarlet tissues I was still clutching. I looked down at my shaking hand and there were red stains in the folds of my fingers, in the creases of my palm. My breath came in short gasps.

"Slowly, slowly," the medic said. She gave me a glass of water.

I sipped it and gradually steadied myself. I looked around. Three paramedics were retreating from the computer room and a guard was standing there with a roll of tape to cordon off the doorway.

"My handbag is in there." I tried to stand but I couldn't make my legs work.

"Don't worry," the paramedic said.

She walked over to the garda, said something and he fetched my bag, which I had dropped near George's desk.

She gave it to me and I searched inside it for my phone. Where had I put it? My fingers felt around for the familiar shape and there it was, in the corner. I must have thrown it back into the bag after making the emergency call though I couldn't remember doing that.

I dialled Gabriel's number.

"I'm at the gardens. Can you come?" was all I could manage.

"On my way." He didn't ask me why.

I sat still, the phone in my lap, and waited for him, holding my right hand slightly away from my body as if I had cut it or as if I were a beggar looking for alms. Around me, gardaí were moving people on, clearing the area. I couldn't see Ava.

"Where's Ava?" I asked the paramedic.

"Who?"

"The woman I was with."

She shook her head. "You were on your own, love."

"No, I wasn't. She went to get help."

She patted my arm like someone trying to soothe a delusional invalid. "She could be outside. There's lots of people outside."

Ava must not have wanted to come back in. I didn't

blame her. Who would want to revisit that scene if they could avoid it? I wished we hadn't come at all. I wished someone else had found George. I wished I could banish the sight of him from my memory. At the same time there was another part of my brain trying to remember every detail – how the room looked, the rain jacket on the back of his chair, his head to one side, the blade on the floor.

Gabriel arrived.

"Did you see Ava outside?" I asked him.

"What?" He leaned down to hear me.

"She's a bit confused. It'll be the shock. Might be best if we took her in for a check-up," the paramedic said.

"No, thanks," I said firmly.

"I'll look after her," Gabriel said.

The young woman took my pulse.

"If you're sure," she said, more to Gabriel than to me.

He nodded and she left us.

A garda approached then, a middle-aged man with the lean, worn face of someone who ran five miles every morning before breakfast.

"'Twas you found him, I hear," he said. "Name?"

I gave him my name and address.

"What happened exactly?"

I gave him as detailed a description as I could manage and tried to tell him everything in the right order though I was confused. At what point had I phoned emergency services and how long was it before other people arrived?

He wrote in his notebook and when he had finished looked down at my bloodied hand.

I closed it into a fist, opened it again.

"I tried to . . . with tissues," I said.

He nodded his understanding. "This woman you say you were with, Ava Hogan – where is she now?"

"I don't know. She ran to get help."

"She probably spoke to one of the lads outside," Gabriel said.

The guard nodded again but kept his eyes on me. I felt I was being appraised.

"I think I should get her home now," Gabriel said. "You'll know where she is if you need to talk to her."

"We will," the garda said and put his notebook back into his pocket.

I made a sort of growling noise in the back of my throat as he walked away.

"Only doing his job, Bea," Gabriel said quietly.

I stood up and wobbled a little and Gabriel put his hand to my elbow. We walked slowly out of the building. The rain had stopped but the trees were still dripping with it and two garda cars parked nearby were getting splashed. I wondered how they had got there.

"Did they come in through the car park and drive up that way, do you think?" I asked Gabriel, aware as I spoke that my question was bizarre and pointless.

"Are you okay, Bea?"

I shook my head to try to clear it. "Yes," I said. I looked around at the officers and the people. "No sign of Ava."

"She's probably gone home," Gabriel said.

"I suppose so. What time is it?"

He looked at his watch. "Twenty past twelve."

"Oh." Only a couple hours since we set out to talk to George. It felt like days, it felt like a long bad dream. Another long, bad dream.

"Where did you park?" Gabriel asked.

"In the car park."

"Do you want to give me your keys?"

"But where's your car?"

"I was off on a walk when you phoned so I took a taxi."

I found my keys, handed them to him and when we reached the car I sat gratefully into the passenger seat. The radio came to life when he turned the ignition.

I had left it tuned to Lyric FM and the Intermezzo from *Cavalleria Rusticana* was playing. I closed my eyes, letting the strings sweep over me, bringing a modicum of calmness with them.

Then the news began.

"*And the headlines – a second man has been found dead at the National Botanic Gardens in Dublin –*"

Gabriel clicked off the radio.

"Let me hear it," I said.

When he switched it back on the crime correspondent was speaking. "*The pathologist is awaited and the scene has been cordoned off for forensic examination. People here at the gardens have said they are shocked at the death and describe the deceased as a well-liked member of staff. One gardener told me he couldn't imagine why anyone would want to harm him.*"

"*And what are the gardaí saying, Ray?*"

"*At this stage, gardaí are appealing for witnesses. They've said they're applying all the resources of a murder investigation to the case. Sources tell me the victim was stabbed once in the chest with a sharp implement.*"

I wanted to tell the radio that they couldn't have done it with a blunt implement but I stayed quiet.

"A weapon has been recovered from the scene and taken to the Garda forensic science laboratory in the Phoenix Park."

"And the victim, what do we know about him?"

"I can say that he is a man in his late 30s who worked at the gardens but, at this stage, given his family hasn't yet been informed, gardaí are not formally naming him."

"And any connection with the death last month of gardener Paddy Hogan?"

"Gardaí are saying they're not ruling out a connection, though sources have told me that Mr Hogan's death was most likely a tragic accident."

"All right, thank you, Ray. Next, British Prime Minister Theresa May tells the House of Commons she will shortly invoke Article 50, triggering a two-year process to leave the European Union."

Gabriel turned the radio down to a low hum.

"Did you hear that? Paddy Hogan's death was a tragic accident? I bet that reporter's been talking to Maguire," I said.

"She didn't strike me as the type to speak to the media."

"Well, he's getting it from somewhere." I considered challenging him further on his defence of the detective inspector but didn't have the energy.

I closed my eyes and tried to shut down the images floating up.

"I need to wash my hands," I said.

Chapter Thirty

At home, Gabriel made me strong tea while I scrubbed my hands at the kitchen sink. I noticed then that there were specks of blood on my clothes so I went upstairs and changed. I bundled up what I had been wearing, carried them down and put them in the washing machine.

"What are you doing?" Gabriel asked when he saw me.

"If I don't wash them now the stains will never come out." I put in the detergent, closed the machine door and reached for the dial.

He put his hand over mine to stop me setting the wash programme.

"The lads might want those . . ." he said.

My stomach lurched and I put my hand to my mouth, thinking I might vomit.

"Here, let me." He found a plastic bag, opened it and emptied my clothes from the machine into it. He tied a knot in the top and put the bag in the press under the sink.

"We'll just leave them there," he said.

"Jesus. Why would they want them, though, Gabriel?"

"Don't worry. It's just in case they need them. You

don't want to have washed them."

I couldn't imagine what use my bloodstained clothes could possibly be. Then I thought perhaps they might need to eliminate fibres from the scene that I might have left behind me. That made some sense to me.

"Let's take our tea inside," Gabriel said.

He carried our cups into the living room and I followed him.

We sat on the couch. I looked around.

"Where did I leave it?" I said aloud.

"What?"

"My bag."

He got up and came back from the hall with the nude shoulder bag I'd been carrying. It too was splattered with red, on its strap and down the side.

"They'll hardly need that as well?" I said.

He gave me an apologetic smile and got a small carrier bag from the kitchen. He held it open for me and I tipped in the contents of the handbag, which he then took away. I could hear the rustle of plastic and assumed he was putting the handbag into the plastic bag with my stained clothes.

I found my phone in the carrier bag and took it out. Gabriel returned.

"Who are you calling?"

"I want to know where Ava went." I pressed her number and let her phone ring until it rang out, then I sent a text.

Where are you, Ava? Are you all right?

I put it down on the coffee table, screen up so that I could see immediately if there was a response. I drank the now lukewarm tea and closed my eyes. I saw again the scene in the gardeners' office and could hear the speeding beat of my own heart in my ears and feel sweat on my palms. I breathed in and out deliberately through my nose, then held the air still for a few seconds in my lungs, until I managed to slow myself down.

When I opened my eyes I was lying down, there was a blanket over me and Gabriel was gone. I lay there confused about what had brought me to that position then remembered George Delaney was dead. I longed to be back in the dreamless sleep I'd just left where I knew nothing and nobody knew me. That desire felt like an old friend I'd first met when Laurence died and who had revisited me a few times since then. I wouldn't allow myself to indulge it. I resisted the yearning to close my eyes again.

Outside, a watery dusk had settled over the bay and when I sat up I could see a row of cars queuing beyond my gate, all pointed toward Sutton. It was after six. I supposed they might be families coming home from the city-centre festival. I reached for my phone, touching the screen to awaken it, but there was nothing from Ava. I should stand up, I told myself, but I felt heavy, almost glued to the couch and I stayed where I was until the murky sky turned black and the traffic dwindled. My phone rang then. It was Gabriel.

"What would you like?"

"Sorry?"

"The takeaway, do you know what you want?"

"Oh – nothing." I was aware of a nauseous feeling and, though I knew I couldn't be right, I thought I could smell blood.

"You can't have nothing."

"Anything, then."

I could hear him sighing.

"Right, I'll be back soon."

When he hung up I thought it was a most peculiar conversation even by our standards. Had he asked me about food before I fell asleep? Had I blanked out the exchange in some sort of shocked reaction to what I'd seen in the gardeners' office? But when I went into the kitchen I saw that he had left a note written on a brown-paper bag beside the kettle. He'd assumed that when I woke up the first thing I'd look for would be tea.

I have to go out. Will bring some food on the way back. Gabriel.

I put the kettle on, made tea and took out some plates. I found myself shivering as I placed the knives on the table, picturing again the scene in the office, the glint of metal, the stench of blood. Would I have time for a shower?

I was about to go upstairs when I heard Gabriel at the door. He came in with a steaming paper bag. He had gone for a safe though not a very healthy option – fish and chips. I wanted to remind him that they wouldn't be good for his heart but I knew there was no point. And it would have sounded unkind after the effort he had made to get me home and now to feed me.

I divided up the food and poured from the pot of tea I'd made. We sat in silence for a while. I picked at the chips and prised a few flakes of fresh cod from its batter. The food tasted of nothing.

I pushed my plate away. "What a mess."

"It is."

I swallowed some tea, letting it dissolve away a thin coating of fat on my tongue and the roof of my mouth.

He gave me another one of his steady looks like he was assessing my tolerance level.

"You may need to prepare yourself, Bea."

"I know." I could only imagine what Maguire would say when she was told who found the body. She'd probably march back in through my front door and insist on an explanation and a barring order from the gardens.

I watched as Gabriel chased the last fragments of crispy batter around his plate with a fork before opting to pick them up with his fingers.

"The main thing is she'll be wanting to get as much out of you as she can to help her investigation. You have to remember that."

I began to feel a little less lost when he said that. I could be of some help. Like every other good detective, Maguire would assess the dependability of witnesses and would hardly be able to find me wanting, even if she didn't like me.

"It will all be fine," he said, when I hadn't spoken for a few minutes.

"I know. It's just, I was thinking about how I'd thought George had something to do with Paddy Hogan's death. I thought it was a personal thing, a one-off. Now I don't know what to think."

"Are you going to tell me how you ended up there?" he asked quietly and without any judgment but I still felt defensive.

"I had no choice, Gabriel. I couldn't talk Ava out of going and I couldn't let her go alone."

He didn't argue with me but began to clear the table and was scraping leftovers into the bin when my phone rang in the living room. He fetched it.

"Will I answer it?" he asked.

I shook my head and took it from him, instantly recognising the number of Ballymun Garda Station.

"Ms Barrington?" It was a woman's voice.

"Speaking."

"My name is Garda Francine Gibson."

"Hello, Francine. We've met before." I remembered her from when she worked with Matt McCann and from the Botanic Gardens after Paddy died.

She didn't acknowledge either of those meetings.

"I've been asked by Detective Inspector Rebecca Maguire to arrange an appointment with you here in Ballymun Station."

An appointment, as though I was going to the dentist.

"All right, would next Thursday suit?" I wasn't sure why I'd said that, except that some part of me wanted to delay the experience for as long as possible.

"Might tomorrow morning be convenient?" she countered, still pretending for the sake of civility that I had a choice.

"That's fine. What time?" I could see now there was no point in suggesting a time. I would be required to go whenever Maguire wanted me.

"Ten-thirty?"

"Right, see you then."

"You know where we are?"

"Yes."

"Good." She hung up.

"That was quick," Gabriel said and I thought he looked worried.

"Quicker than the last time anyhow. Should I take a solicitor?"

He considered the question for a bit longer than I thought he might, then shook his head.

"There'll be no need – and it'd make you look like you'd something to hide. You'll only be . . ."

"Helping them with their enquiries?" I finished his sentence.

How many times had I heard that on the news? And how many times had it ended badly for the helper? I shook myself then. I was letting my imagination get the better of me. Maguire was a professional. She would do her job and get to the truth of what happened. Of course she would.

"I'm going to make more tea. Will you have some?" I was aware that there was a plea in my voice.

"Let me do it, Bea. I'll bring it in to you."

His tone was so kind that I thought I might cry.

I went into the living room and closed the curtains, shutting out the evening traffic and the lights of the city and the bay. I felt heavy and sad and foolish.

"I really thought I knew what had happened to Paddy," I said. "But now this . . . What's going on, Gabriel?"

"I don't know, Bea."

I thought of Bob Richmond then and his sleazy appetites and I wondered if he could have been involved in George's death. He could have killed Paddy over Celine, couldn't he? And then if George had found out about her somehow and confronted him, he might have killed him too. Or what if Ava had been to see George before she met me? She had been so sure he had questions to answer . . . And she had been so agitated when we spoke on the phone. Could she have killed him and then set me up? I shook my head to rid myself of that idea. It was ridiculous. She wasn't capable of such a thing.

I thought about the scene in the office again, going over the details in my head. There was paper in his hand, torn paper, wasn't there, with words on it? But what had it said? I couldn't remember.

"George was holding part of a letter. I think it meant something."

"Did it? What?"

"I don't know."

He put his arm around me and I rested my head on his shoulder and let the weight of everything sink into him. We sat like that together for a long while in silence until he got up and went home.

Chapter Thirty-One

Saturday, March 18th

I was nervous about going to Ballymun Garda Station, so much so that Gabriel said he would come along and I didn't try to argue with him. He collected me in his car and parked not far from the building. I brought the bag containing my stained clothing with me in case they wanted it. By ten-thirty we were both sitting in the public waiting area on those hard, plastic chairs when Maguire came in the main door with two officers.

"I'll be with you in five," she said as she passed us at speed, while the officers flanking her both talked at the same time.

I contemplated what it must be like to have her job – pressurised, I assumed, very busy, result-driven and political too no doubt. For a second I had the smallest feeling of pity and admiration for her. Then she reappeared.

She beckoned to me. "You should go and get yourself a coffee or something – we'll be a while," she said to Gabriel.

He stayed where he was.

I stood and followed her back through the door that led to the interview rooms and the cells, taking the bag of clothes with me.

"I'll be back to you when I get a chance," she said to a garda who approached her with a bundle of files.

She led me into an interview room where another officer, a young man, was already seated at a table. She sat down beside him and indicated that I should sit on the opposite side of the table.

I handed her the bag of clothes, took my coat off and sat down, draping my coat across my lap.

"What you were wearing?" she asked, holding up the bag.

I nodded.

"I'll get them back to you as soon as I can." She dropped the bag on the floor and turned to the officer. "Is that working, Gerard?"

"'Tis," he nodded.

"We're going to record this, Ms Barrington."

So not just a written statement this time. And I noticed Gerard was ready to take notes. My heart fluttered inside me like a panicked bird.

"Before we begin, would you mind just rolling up your sleeves and showing me your forearms."

I waited for her to explain but she didn't so I pushed up the sleeves of the jumper I was wearing as far as I could and stretched my arms out in front of me.

She looked at them but didn't touch.

"And over," she said.

I turned my palms up.

She nodded.

"Can you look toward the door for a moment?"

I turned my head toward the door.

"And back."

She signalled right and I looked toward the wall. Its

paint, I noticed, was bubbled in a couple of places. A shoddy job. I could feel her eyes on my face.

"Okay, thank you. You can roll your sleeves down now."

I was glad to – the room was cool and the fine hairs on my forearms had begun to stand up.

She clicked a button on the recorder.

"I need you to start from the beginning, Ms Barrington. Tell me what time you arrived at the Botanic Gardens."

I told her everything I could recall. How I'd found out about Ava and George's relationship. How Ava wanted to ask him about her brother's death and how I was afraid to let her go alone.

She spoke only to encourage more information. I told her what I saw when the door opened and what I did. I included as much detail as possible – how I ended up with blood on my hands and everything I saw from where I was standing when I looked down at the desk. As I spoke the images became more real to me as though I was looking at them again through the lens of a camera.

"And there was a knife on the ground."

"A knife?"

I began to shake then and the tremor entered my vocal chords but I continued.

"It was on the ground and when I stepped sideways I felt it under my foot. There was blood on it."

"Yes. Forensics would have picked that up. And you stepped on it, you say. Shoes in that bag?"

"Yes."

"Good. We'll need your fingerprints too, for elimination purposes. Did you touch anything?"

I tried to picture what I'd touched.

"The table maybe and the back of the chair. George obviously."

She nodded, put her hand to the back of her neck and scratched it. "Tell me about Ava Hogan. Where did she go after she ran for help?"

"I don't know. She just disappeared. I've phoned her but I can't get an answer."

"And we don't have a statement from her, do we, Gerard?" she asked the young officer. He shook his head. "And you say they had some sort of a relationship?"

"They did, yes. But it was over as far as I know."

"Did his wife know?"

She gave me a sly sort of look and I didn't like it.

"I wouldn't know that. Ask Ava."

I thought I could almost read her thoughts – revenge of the jilted lover or maybe the cheated wife? But then where did Paddy Hogan fit in?

"Do you think there's a connection with Paddy's death?" I asked.

She sighed and I knew she had no intention of answering me. "I don't have any other questions at this stage. Do you have anything you want to add?"

"I think I've told you everything . . ."

"Obviously, if anything else occurs to you give us a call. And if we have any questions we'll be back to you." She turned to the officer beside her. "Gerard, will you arrange for fingerprints?"

She stood up.

"We'll be in touch, Ms Barrington."

"Okay."

She left the room in a hurry and I felt relieved that she

obviously had bigger things to worry about. What I'd feared could be a confrontational encounter turned out to be calm enough, tame even. She hadn't badgered or lectured me at all, which I had to admit amazed me.

Gerard stood up. "Can you follow me, please?"

He led me into another room where my fingerprints were taken. It was a strange experience, and I felt as though I was offering up a part of myself for scrutiny. I thought of all those old films I'd seen with the bad guy having his prints done before he was locked away, his fingers smudged with black. Reality was far less dramatic and there wasn't even any ink. Instead there was a digital recorder, essentially a sheet of glass onto which I pressed my fingers.

When it was finished, Gerard let me back out into the waiting area where Gabriel was chatting to a man I took to be a plainclothes detective.

"I'll be back to you," the man said, walking away.

"Who was that?" I asked as we left the station.

"Robert, used to work with him in Pearse Street. He's helping Maguire out."

"Useful?"

"We'll see. How did it go?"

We sat into the car and he started the engine.

"Okay, I think. They recorded me, and that was a bit intimidating, but otherwise it was straightforward."

Once there was a lull in traffic Gabriel did a U-turn so that we could drive back to Clontarf.

"And you told her everything?"

"Every last detail. There was one odd thing though that she didn't explain." I told him about being asked to roll up my sleeves and to show both sides of my face.

"I'd say she was looking for marks – scratches maybe. They might have found something under George's fingernails, skin fragments or the like."

I shuddered, imagining him reaching out, trying to fight off his attacker.

"Actually, don't drive me home, please, Gabriel. I need to speak to Ava."

He nodded and drove straight through the junction at Griffith Avenue and down St Mobhi Road.

"How did she react, to your statement, I mean?"

"Very calmly. She was calm the whole time."

"You look surprised." He glanced at me, then back at the road and signalled to turn right into St Mobhi Drive.

"I had myself built up for, I don't know, something a bit more confrontational."

"Well, it's over now anyway. Where am I leaving you?"

"St Teresa's Road – but anywhere around here will do."

He left me at the gates of the Botanic Gardens. There were people going in and out as though everything was normal. There were no gardaí, no security tape. It was as though nothing had happened.

"I might drop in there for a bit of a walk and a look around. Give me a shout when you're done," he said.

I wanted to tell him that he didn't have to wait for me, that I didn't need minding, but I thought he was probably worried and wanted to be sure I was safe. I said I'd find him later and he pulled the car into the car park at the side of the gardens.

I spent the few minutes it took for me to walk around to Ava's house trying to decide what to say to her. I wanted to know why she had disappeared after we found George and left me to deal with everything. It didn't seem fair. But then didn't I already know why she'd fled? She must have been terrified seeing him there stabbed and bleeding only weeks after her brother had died. And didn't everyone know, including me, how vulnerable she was?

Still, I was taken aback when I knocked at the door and Mrs Hogan answered. I'd been under the impression that she rarely left her chair in the living room. Standing up, she looked taller than I'd imagined but there was a curve at the top of her spine that made her navy cardigan hang strangely from her shoulders.

"Is Ava in?"

She looked me up and down. "What do you want?"

"I need to talk to her for a few minutes."

"She won't talk to you. She isn't talking to anyone." She opened the door, though, and stood to one side to let me in. "She has me worried sick."

I waited for her to close the hall door then followed her into the dim front room. It was cooler there than before. There was only a low fire in the grate and no coal in the bucket. Ava was tucked into the corner of the couch, which was under the window. There was a blanket over her. She looked diminished, like a toy puppet that had its strings broken.

"Hello, Ava." I sat at the other end of the couch.

She didn't acknowledge my presence or turn to look at me.

"Do you see?" her mother said, settling herself into her armchair.

"How are you, Ava?" I asked.

There was no response.

"She's been like that since she came home yesterday. She came running in here and all she said was 'He's dead'. She hasn't said another word since. I didn't even know who she was talking about until I saw it on the news last night."

"Did you call a doctor?" I was concerned that she was suffering from shock.

Rita looked at me with what I thought was resentment for making the suggestion. "I don't think she'd want me to," she said.

I wondered whether paying for a medic might be the issue.

"I think it would be a mistake not to," I said as firmly as I could. "I have money with me if you're short of cash."

"We don't need your money." She sounded insulted. Then she looked at Ava and sighed as though her daughter was putting her to too much trouble. "If you think she needs a doctor you can phone. The number is in the address book on the hall table."

I left the room and found the phone on an old-fashioned, spindly-legged hall table. Beside the grey 1990s handset was a leather-covered address book of indeterminate age with flimsy pages, filled with handwritten numbers. The doctor's surgery was easy to spot, in capital letters recorded under "D". There were in fact three doctors in the practice.

I dialled the number.

"Can you hold the line, please?" a voice said, not waiting for my reply before switching on the music. I flicked through the pages of an address book as I waited and a tinny version of "Greensleeves" played in my ear for minutes. I wondered how dangerous shock could be if that was what was wrong with Ava.

"How can I help you?"

I explained about Ava's problem and asked if a doctor could visit as soon as possible.

"Do you mind which doctor it is?"

"No."

"In that case, someone will be with you in an hour."

"Thanks." I hung up quietly and went back to Ava and her mother.

I didn't sit down.

"He'll be out in an hour. Would you like me to wait?" I didn't think Mrs Hogan would want that.

"I'm sure you have more important things to do," she said.

"Right. Ava, please get in touch if you need anything." I noticed the empty coal bucket again then and put my hand on the handle. "I'll just fill this up for you before I go."

Mrs Hogan nodded. "It's out the back."

I went through the kitchen and turned the key in the back door, which brought me outside to a small yard. On the left there was an old-fashioned coal bunker made of blocks with a sheet of thin wood for a lid and an opening the size of one block at its base. Against the wall a hand-shovel leaned, its plate dense with coal dust. I shovelled coal into the bucket, carried it back inside and locked the back door after me.

In the front room Mrs Hogan muttered her thanks.

I felt pity for her then, reliant on Ava for simple tasks, unable to fetch her own coal. I picked up the tongs to put some on the fire.

"I'll do that!" she said, taking the implement from my hand.

The wave of sympathy I'd felt ebbed away.

"I'll call later to see how Ava is. What's the landline number?"

She told me and I stored it in my phone. I took a pen and a piece of paper out of my bag and wrote my number on it.

"I'll leave this by the phone in case you need me."

She made to stand.

"Don't get up. I'll see myself out," I said.

She relaxed back into her chair and nodded a goodbye. I closed the living-room door and was about to open the hall door when something came in through the letterbox. I bent and picked it up off the hall mat. It was a postcard with a picture on the front of trees and grasses in the foreground and a clock tower and buildings seen from a distance through a haze. In small print at the bottom the words "**University of California, Berkeley**" were written. I knew I shouldn't, but I turned it over. It was addressed to Ava from Kaya Nkosi.

Hi, Ava, Sorry I didn't get to say goodbye before I left but I got an offer of a post here that I couldn't refuse. California is an amazing place and there's so much sunshine. I'll be in touch, Kaya.

So that was where she'd gone. No wonder she'd had no qualms about leaving the Botanic Gardens. Berkeley was prestigious. She'd been lucky to get a post there, and talented too of course. I put the card on the hall table and left.

Outside I thought about Mrs Hogan and how she'd cope without Ava to fetch and carry for her. She would need help of some kind. Leaning against the wall of the house, I found the number of the local health clinic, called it and spoke to a public health nurse there, telling her that Ava was unwell and unable to help her mother. She said she knew Rita Hogan and visited her once a week but would call by later to check on her and see if there was anything more she could do.

Chapter Thirty-Two

I phoned Gabriel and he suggested coffee in the garden's coffee shop but I declined.

"Have you forgotten we're barred?" I asked.

"I'm sure Bob's forgotten," he said.

"All the same, I'll meet you out front," I said firmly. I didn't tell him that the sight of those wrought-iron entrance gates made my stomach flip over and my legs weak.

He came around the corner from the car park and pulled up, half on the footpath, outside the gates.

I jumped into the passenger seat and he drove away.

"What did Ava say?" he asked.

"Nothing. Absolutely nothing. She hasn't spoken since she came back except to tell her mother someone was dead."

"She must have got some shock."

We were passing Constance Anderson's house and I thought he glanced for a moment in its direction before looking back at the road.

"Mrs Hogan hadn't even got a doctor for her. I phoned for one but she didn't want me to wait till he arrived. I'll ring tomorrow and see how she's doing."

"And how are you doing?" He glanced over at me. He didn't miss much. "Would it be any harm for *you* to see a doctor?"

I shrugged. "I'll be all right – it's not the first time I've seen a dead body."

"This one was very nasty though, Bea. And I know you're strong but you're not made of stone."

"Am I not?" I had a longing to reach over and cover his left hand, which was on the gear stick, with mine. I pushed down the sensation. He went down the gears to slow the car coming up to the traffic lights at Griffith Avenue and St Mobhi Road and braked to a gentle stop.

"Bea?"

I sighed. "I'll give it a couple of days and if I'm not myself then, I'll see the doctor. Will that do?"

"It's going to have to, isn't it?"

The lights changed and he drove on and turned on his Johnny Cash music, flicking through each recording until he found "Guess Things Happen That Way". He hummed along to it absentmindedly. I told him about the postcard from Kaya Nkosi.

"She must have been delighted to get a post like that," he said. "It'd be a very hard thing to refuse."

"I suppose so. What young person wouldn't want the American experience for a few years, anyway?" I wondered what path my life might have taken if I'd got a plane to New York in 1982 instead of a ferry to Holyhead. "Will we get a bit of lunch?"

He checked his watch. "Twenty past one. Okay, where?"

I suggested the Yacht on Clontarf Road and he parked

in the pub car park. Inside, there was a mixed crowd with young professionals from East Point business park, retired couples eating half-dinners, one or two older men alone and drinking pints of stout with their meals, and women in small groups talking over each other. We queued up at the carvery, paid for our salmon lunches, collected glasses of water, and managed to get a table for two at the window. I unloaded my tray, put it on a nearby empty table, took off my coat and sat.

"I have to tell you, Gabriel, I'm impressed that you're keeping to the healthy stuff," I said, discounting the fish and chips he'd bought for me on Friday night.

"Most of the time," he said.

I looked at the view as I ate. Beyond the traffic and narrow band of shorn grass and low coastal wall, there was a full tide. And the sea, stirred by a strong breeze, was intermittently sending white foam over the wall. On the other side of the inlet, the stony embankment below the East Point business park was almost topped. Cloud, like upside-down grey drumlins, hung low over it all.

"Do you not get enough of that view from your own house?" Gabriel asked after a while.

"Not quite this view," I said, smiling at him.

He looked at me in the old way he used to for a moment and then looked away.

"I was thinking, Gabriel, what do Paddy Hogan and George Delaney have in common?"

He scooped up a flake of pink salmon and ate it. "The Bots, I suppose. They both worked there, they're both gardeners. They were both killed in their workplace . . ."

"Yes. But what does that mean? Does it matter? And

can we assume they were both killed by the same person?"

I picked at what was left of my food – the thin end of a buttery salmon darn, a few carrots and a couple of spoonfuls of potato gratin. If Gabriel had asked me right at that moment what they tasted like I wouldn't have been able to tell him.

"No, we can't, definitely can't. The deaths were very different. Paddy's could have been accidental, easily confused with a suicide. But George's death – there's no mistaking the savagery in that, the deliberate intention."

"Just say it was the same person for a minute – what was motivating him or her? What had Paddy and George in common that would be worth killing them for?"

Gabriel forked up the last of his potato and ate it. "What about Bob?"

"Go on."

"We know Paddy intervened with him about Celine . . . what if George found out about her too and wasn't content with Bob behaving himself? What if he was blackmailing Bob?"

I put my knife and fork together on the plate and moved it to one side.

"Maybe. Or what about Constance and her friend in the leather jacket . . . could they have something to do with this?" I warmed to that possibility. "She *was* in the Orchid House next to the Palm House on the morning Paddy died."

"Why though, Bea? I'm not seeing why they'd do it."

"What if she knew about George's relationship with Ava and was blackmailing him and it went wrong and she killed him?"

"And Paddy?"

I couldn't think why she might have wanted to kill Paddy. Still I wondered about that figure running through the Cactus House and about the deep discussion I'd seen Constance and George in the night I met Ava in the Tolka House.

"I can't help feeling Constance is hiding something," I said.

I thought I saw a flicker of something on Gabriel's face then, just for a moment. What was that? Irritation? Was he trying to protect her? No. I was imagining it.

"Here's another possibility," he said. "What if Paddy did find out about George and Ava and there was a row and an accidental push?"

"Then why did George end up dead?"

He looked at me steadily and spoke carefully. "Think about it – what if Ava believed that's what happened and she found George and killed him herself, and, I don't know . . . cleaned herself up at home and then returned to meet you?"

I thought of that phone call we'd had – how distressed and wound up she was. Could she have?

"I think that would require a level of deviousness I'm sure Ava's not capable of. And besides, I saw her face when we discovered him. You can't fake that shock, Gabriel." I drank some water, which tasted of lime. "There's something we're missing here, something big. Isn't there?"

"We don't know why either of them died," he said. "That's our fundamental problem."

I put my hand to my temple and rubbed it. "What time is it?"

"Ten past."

"Right, I'm just going to the ladies' before we leave – I won't be a minute."

On the way back from the ladies' someone sitting at a table nearby drew my attention. It was her dark hair that was familiar first, the way it swung when she moved her head. As I came closer I recognised the face – it was Marina Fernandez from the fitness-to-practise hearing. Seeing her was jarring, as though she was out of place here in Clontarf, on the wrong side of the River Liffey, though I knew that was absurd. Her elbows were resting on the table and she was talking with animation, gesturing with her hands to her male companion. It was then I noticed it, catching the light at her wrist, a bracelet heavy with charms. I paused at a pillar close by, where the pub's menu was displayed, and pretended to be reading it. Could it be? Surely not. Every high street in Europe had a shop that sold bracelets like that. What was it they were called? Pandora? I tried to remember what the barrister, Reginald Taylor, had said at the hearing when he described the bracelet that had been stolen from the nursing home. Then one charm caught my eye – a ruby heart on a silver loop. Hadn't he described something like that? Hadn't he said it was bespoke, a unique charm made especially for its owner? There couldn't be a second one, could there? That would be too great a coincidence. I slipped my phone out of my bag, took a quick photo of her as discreetly as I could and I walked out.

When we got to the car I told Gabriel what I'd seen.

"I was so sure the nursing home was wrong," I said. "I was convinced they'd made it up but now . . ."

How clever she must have been to besmirch the men and women she worked with. She'd managed to undermine each of them using their own weaknesses. And she'd convinced everyone on the committee as well as her own legal team. I had been convinced too, completely. How could my judgment have been so wrong? I took my phone out, selected the photos I'd taken of her and sent them on to her solicitor, Caroline Brophy.

I see your client has a new bracelet, I said. Then I found the mobile number that had been supplied to me by Dr Adrian Dunboyne's team. This time I wrote: **Not sure if this is of any use to you now.** Perhaps they might consider an appeal to the High Court. Neither of the numbers responded.

"It's all about presentation, isn't it?" I said to Gabriel.

"What is?"

"Everything."

Chapter Thirty-Three

Sunday, March 19th

I called Ava's house at ten. The phone rang four times and I was about to hang up when it was answered.

"Yes?" It was Rita Hogan.

"Hello, Mrs Hogan, it's Beatrice. I'm just wondering how Ava is?"

"Oh, it's you. She's a bit better but she's sleeping now."

It was obvious that she didn't want me to talk to Ava and she wasn't interested in letting me know too much detail about her daughter's well-being, but I persisted.

"What did the doctor say?"

"He said it was shock. He gave her a few pills. She'll be fine in a few days, he said."

I wondered how he could be sure of that. Would he not have suggested counselling or something for her? I supposed he might have but Mrs Hogan wouldn't want me to know that private detail.

"That's good news. When she wakes up, could you let her know I called?"

"All right." She hung up abruptly.

I had wanted to explain it was Ava who was keen to

visit George, and I only went to support her, that it wasn't my fault her daughter had seen what she saw. But then I berated myself – this was an old woman who had lost her son and now her daughter wasn't well. She didn't need to hear my justifications. And who was I to them anyway? Nobody.

What I needed was something to divert my attention away from Paddy Hogan and George Delaney. I should concentrate on finding some work. There were many days to fill before the commercial case I was due to cover near the end of the month. And there was no point in worrying about my hands. They would recover, I felt sure.

I made a fresh cup of tea and picked up my laptop to check emails before remembering, as soon as I had the screen open, that not only was it a Sunday, it was a bank holiday weekend and no one would be working. The city centre would be filled with people – families and visitors from other countries all there to enjoy the annual St Patrick's festival. It held no attraction for me. I thought a brisk walk along the seafront would be a better option until I looked out and saw that it was raining heavily. I considered calling Gabriel to see how he would be filling his day, but I decided not to. What if he was spending it with Constance? I didn't want to hear that. I was listless and uneasy and I wanted to understand all that had happened. I wanted to know why Paddy and George had died. And there was only one place where I might find answers.

The rain was falling heavily as I drove toward the Botanic Gardens. And though I could have driven into the gardens' car park, I opted to pull up on St Mobhi Drive. What was it I was thinking? That I might see if Gabriel was visiting Constance? I told myself that wasn't it at all.

It was just that I needed to be able to work myself up to walking in those gates. The windows inside my car had fogged and I was cold. I turned on the heating and by the time I had parked in a space across the road from Constance's house the glass was clear again.

Now that I'd arrived, though, I didn't know what to do. I had an urge to just walk up to Constance Anderson's door and ask her what she was hiding and tell her to leave Gabriel alone as well. And then I would march round to the gardens' coffee shop and berate Bob Richmond until he told me the truth. But what was the truth? Would I recognise it if I saw it anyway? Considering my judgment about Marina Fernandez I could hardly trust myself to assess the difference between truth and lies.

I sat for a few minutes just thinking about everything, about Paddy and George, about the gardens going on as though nothing had happened. What was it Seamus Lennon had said? *"The gardens were here before them and they'll still be here when they're long gone."* Something like that.

My phone rang then. It was Gabriel.

"Where are you?"

"I was going to go for a walk in the gardens." I hoped I didn't sound like he'd caught me out though I felt he had.

"In the rain? Don't do that, Bea. Just wait, wait until I get there."

I didn't answer.

"Bea? Do you hear me?"

"Yes, all right." I hung up.

I would wait but not in the car. I needed to clear my head. Having forgotten my umbrella, I walked quickly round the corner to the coffee shop opposite the gardens' gates. I could wait for Gabriel there. It was quieter than the last time I was in it. And on the inside of the door there was a poster like the one at the visitor centre, inviting people to the celebration for the professor's documentary. So it was still going ahead despite George's murder. It seemed distasteful to me. I ordered a pot of tea.

"If you want to take a seat I'll bring it down to you," the waitress said.

I paid and got a table by the window, leaving my coat on against a chill that had invaded my bones. I felt hopeless and entirely confused and out of ideas. The waitress brought my tea. I milked it and held the cup in both hands for warmth. The rain slowed and then stopped and people passed by outside the window, letting down their umbrellas, shaking them out, crossing the road and going into the gardens. There were people coming out too, couples, families, friends and then a man on his own who looked familiar.

He stood still near the edge of the footpath and spoke into his phone. Who was that? I squinted. Was it Bob Richmond? Yes. He talked for a minute or two, put his phone in his pocket and moved to the edge of the footpath. He paused there to let three cars go by then he crossed the road and walked straight toward the coffee shop and the window I was peering through. He looked angry. Had he seen me watching him? I didn't stop watching though. If he wanted to confront me, he could. I had plenty of questions for him.

But as he reached the glass he turned to the left and then I saw it. On his right cheek there was a long, pink, raised scratch, a fresh scratch. Wasn't Maguire looking for someone with a mark like that? I jumped up, abandoning my tea, and followed him.

Chapter Thirty-Four

I saw Bob ahead of me turning right into St Mobhi Drive as I left the coffee shop. I walked as quickly as I could to try to catch up with him. I wanted to stop him and ask him where that scratch had come from. I wanted to say that I knew he'd fought with George before he'd killed him. But by the time I got around the corner he was getting into a car and pulling away. There was nothing I could do but stand there and watch.

Almost immediately, Gabriel arrived and parked in the vacated space. He waved to me and I crossed to the passenger side, opened the door and sat in. I was still breathless.

"There's something you need to know about Constance," he said firmly.

"No, wait," I said, and I waved my hand for him to stop while I caught my breath. I didn't need to know now. Whatever he had with Constance was none of my business. "I don't care about Constance – it was Bob – I saw him just now. He has a long scratch down his face." I ran my finger down my cheek and let him consider that. "I think he killed Paddy because he knew about Celine Deegan and

OnlyFans." He nodded as I spoke. "And somehow – I don't know how yet – George found out Bob had done it and challenged him, or maybe tried blackmailing him, and Bob killed him too." I caught my breath and continued. "Maybe he even planned to kill Kaya Nkosi because she knew about Celine but she left before he had the chance."

"Was that him I saw in the car that pulled out?" he asked.

"Yes." I told him where I'd seen Bob and that I'd wanted to confront him.

"I'm glad you didn't catch him. He might have hurt you."

"On the street in daylight? He's not that stupid."

"We'll have to go to Maguire with his," Gabriel said and for once I agreed.

"Let's go now, then, before he has a chance to disappear or something."

"Why would he? He doesn't know you suspect him. Better wait until Maguire is ready to pick him up."

I wondered when that might be. "He may be at that event tonight – the celebration for the documentary."

"We can tell her that," he said.

I hadn't intended going but now had second thoughts. "I think I'll go myself," I said. "I did get an invite . . . and wouldn't it be satisfying to see Bob picked up?"

He raised his eyebrows at me. "Who invited you?"

"The professor."

"Oh."

Was that disappointment in his voice? Good.

He didn't speak for a few minutes just stared out the window. Then he asked tentatively "I think I ought to go with you – you don't know what might happen with George."

"Okay."

"Right." He nodded but still didn't look at me. "Now I want to tell you about Constance . . ."

I was about to protest again when he stopped speaking and nodded in the direction of an approaching car, a navy saloon.

"Is that the car we saw trying to knock down Constance?" I said.

He nodded. "Think so."

The car pulled up and parked across the bottom of her driveway. The driver, dressed in dark jeans and a black leather jacket, got out. It was the young man I'd seen before.

"That's the man I've been telling you about, Gabriel, that I saw with Constance on the day Paddy Hogan died."

Gabriel surreptitiously took out his phone and took a couple of photographs. The man walked up the path to the house and knocked on the door. Constance let him in. Gabriel texted the photos to someone.

"Who are you sending those to?"

"Maguire." He looked worried and kept checking his phone for a response. There was none. After waiting a few minutes he put his hand on the door.

"I think I should go in," he said, getting out.

"Not on your own."

I followed him and we walked up to the hall door.

Gabriel pressed the buzzer. There was no answer at first, and he pressed again. Then we heard two sets of footsteps coming down the stairs. When Constance opened the door to us her visitor was standing in the hall beside her.

"Hello!" Her voice was an octave above her normal tone. "Come in."

We stepped inside.

"You haven't met my nephew. This is Brendan."

The man smiled at us and waved with his right hand, while his left rested in the pocket of his leather jacket. I couldn't help wondering what he had in that pocket.

"This is Gabriel Ingram, a retired garda, and Beatrice Barrington – you're a stenographer aren't you, Beatrice?"

I admitted to that and waited to hear what it was Brendan did. She didn't say.

"I'd better be going, Auntie Connie," Brendan said. "I'll see you again."

There was something about the way he said it that made it sound like a threat. He leaned down and kissed her on the cheek.

"Goodbye," she said.

When the door had closed behind him, she turned and walked straight into the kitchen.

"*Tea?*" she called over her shoulder.

We followed her and sat at her kitchen table while she made a pot. None of us spoke. It was obvious she was nervous and when she put the china cups and saucers down, they made a tinkling sound from the tremor in her hand. She sat heavily into her chair.

"Well now, you're unexpected visitors," she said a little sourly.

I looked at Gabriel. I was confused. I'd had the impression she was frightened of Brendan and would have been glad that we'd called.

"Is there anything I can do for you, Constance?" Gabriel said.

"I don't know what you mean."

"I think you do."

"Is that man really your nephew?" I asked.

"As a matter of fact, he is . . . and it's no business of yours anyway." She picked up her cup and took a drink. "Do you believe in God, Beatrice?"

"You asked me that before."

"Did I? Well, I believe *He* sees all and protects those who deserve protection."

"Constance," Gabriel said gently, "he also sends people to help you when you need help. You have to recognise that."

She opened her mouth and I thought she was about to tell us something but then the noise started, a pounding on the hall door, pounding and then shouting.

I couldn't make out what was being said at first and then I heard one word: "*Gardaí!*"

"Oh God!" Constance said, her hand to her mouth. "Did you bring them?"

"You'd better answer it or they'll burst the lock," Gabriel said.

She stood up and got to the door before they could break it in. There was the sound of rushing feet on the stairs and the unmistakable voice of Detective Inspector Rebecca Maguire.

"Go in there and sit down," she said to Constance, who came back into the kitchen and slumped into her chair.

Maguire came in.

"He made me do it," Constance said. "He said he'd break my legs if I didn't."

"Really?" Maguire didn't sound like she believed that. "We've seen your bank accounts, Ms Anderson."

Constance looked like she might faint.

I got a glass of water and put it in her hand. Then I walked to the open kitchen door and looked out. There were uniformed gardaí going down the stairs, leafy green plants in their arms.

"Close that door, Beatrice," Maguire said.

I closed the door and sat.

"Those weren't orchids," I couldn't help saying to Gabriel.

"Please be quiet," Maguire said.

Constance gave a deep, resigned sigh. "I'm sorry," she said.

Gabriel gave her what I thought was a look of sympathy. "Best if you say nothing for the moment, Constance. Wait till you have a solicitor."

"Best if you two head on now, I think," Maguire said.

We did what we were told, and she followed us out to the hall as the last of the cannabis plants were being taken downstairs.

"Thanks for the photos, Gabriel," she said. "We'll have him now." She spoke as though they both knew who they were talking about.

Gabriel saw my confusion. "Constance's nephew, Brendan Anderson . . . The lads have been after him for a while. I've been keeping an eye out."

"Oh!" So he'd been helping Maguire. Why hadn't he told me? What else did I not know?

"We'll take statements from you later," Maguire said.

"Wait a sec . . ." I stopped at the door, remembering only then about Bob Richmond. I told her about the scratch on his face and my theory about why he might have killed Paddy and George.

She looked back toward the kitchen. "I have my hands full at the moment."

"I think I overheard Bob being blackmailed, probably by George," I said, hoping to make my argument seem more convincing.

"Thanks. We'll have a chat with him later."

"He'll likely be at the gardens this evening for the promotion of that documentary," Gabriel said.

"We'll see," she said.

We left and sat back into his car. A weak sun was making the roof slates and the footpaths glisten. We watched gardaí load up a double-parked van. At either end of the road there were Garda cars preventing access and uniformed officers were diverting traffic. The navy saloon had been loaded onto the back of a truck and two other Garda cars were parked in people's driveways either side of Constance's house. I thought of George Delaney sitting in the corner of the Tolka House with her, their heads bent together, deep in conversation.

"Do you think George knew anything about this?" I asked.

"I don't know."

"If he did, could I be wrong about Bob? Could Constance have had something to do with his death?"

He shook his head. "That was Friday morning, wasn't it? I was sitting here just like this on Friday morning."

"But she could have sent her nephew."

"I'm not sure she does much sending in that relationship."

"I wish you'd told me you were doing surveillance." I was thinking of all the other things I'd been worried about.

"I couldn't, Bea, not until the lads were sure who we were dealing with."

Constance came out of her house then, walking between two gardaí. She was handcuffed and the sight of it made me catch my breath. They manoeuvred her into the back seat of a garda car and pulled away.

"It looked like a big operation with all those plants," I said.

"That was her problem really, too many of them. There was too much heat in the house. I noticed it the first time we were in there. It was too warm in the kitchen, do you remember, but her stove wasn't on."

"I wondered why the frost on her roof melted so quickly."

"She was touchy too, wasn't she, that time you went upstairs?" he said.

I'd forgotten that. "She was. I thought maybe she didn't want me seeing that Burren photo. So how did you get roped into it?"

"I bumped into one of the lads from the drugs squad operating out of Ballymun about a week ago – you saw me talking to him up in the station – and it turned out they were keeping an eye on her."

"You'd never imagine it around here though, would you?" I said.

"It's everywhere, Bea."

"But she was so . . ." I was going to say 'respectable' and couldn't think of an alternative. I waited a few seconds before I asked, "Were you ever upstairs yourself then?"

"What?" He gave me one of his looks of exasperation. I didn't answer.

When the Garda cars had moved and access was clear again I told Gabriel I'd see him later in the gardens for the professor's party.

"And hopefully for Bob's arrest," I said, getting out of the car.

Chapter Thirty-Five

The visitor centre at the Botanic Gardens was humming with the conversation of wine-sipping, well-dressed guests. The reception area had been transformed for the promotion of the *Natural World* documentary. Tall thin tables with white tethered-down tablecloths were strategically placed around the area. People were resting their wineglasses on them or leaving their napkins after eating. There were nibbles being proffered on wooden platters by uniformed waiters. Pull-up banners had been placed around the room, carrying the image of Professor James Christakos, not in his usual three-piece suit but in a khaki safari jacket buckled at the waist. He was smiling and gazing out and his right hand was touching the petals of a white orchid. The whole thing was framed with the *Natural World* blue stripe and had the famous logo in the bottom left corner. Across the top were the words: *Christakos: Botanist and Plant Hunter*.

"What d'ya think, Beatrice?" the professor said. He was standing next to me, admiring his own poster.

"It's extraordinary," was all I could manage.

"Too much?" He looked at me then with those brown eyes and I felt sure he genuinely cared what I thought.

"It's very upbeat. I imagine it'll do well in the American market."

"You Irish," he said, touching my arm before spotting someone across the room and raising his glass. "Bertie! You made it," he said and then, "Let's talk later, Beatrice," before he walked away.

I scanned the room and along with staff from the gardens, I recognised faces from public life – politicians, a couple of ministers, some minor celebrities, a knot of literati and some prominent business people. The event was quite a draw but where was Bob?

"Will I get you a drink?" It was Gabriel at my shoulder.

"Where did you spring from?"

We walked together to a table covered in glasses with various drinks inside. I chose a sparkling water and so did he.

"I want to be sharp tonight," he said.

"Is Maguire here yet?"

"No, but don't worry she will be."

There was a cough then and someone tapped a microphone. The room quieted. I recognised the man at the mike as Mason Bryant, the documentary director.

"*Welcome, everyone!*" he said. "And thank you for coming along to our little gathering." There was a tinkle of laughter.

"Tonight, we're celebrating the completion of our exciting and excellent documentary – *Christakos: Botanist and Plant Hunter*."

Applause followed until he put his hand up to silence it.

"And there are so many to thank . . . starting with the man who gave us permission to film around here – the director of the Botanic Gardens – Henry, where are you?"

A man standing in the corner nodded modestly.

"Great guy," Bryant said. He took a deep breath. "I've also gotta thank . . ." He went on to name-check a list of people who had worked on the documentary and a list of financial supporters. "Of course to get this to the widest possible audience we're gonna need more support so if any of you are feeling generous . . ." He glanced around the room then waved a hand in dismissal. "Let's talk about that later. Now let me tell you about our star." He raised a glass in the direction of the professor and began describing the professor's "great achievements", "astounding abilities" and "natural talent in front of a camera". "And we mustn't forget his crowning achievement – the discovery of *Orchidaceae Platanthera christakii.*"

Light applause spread through the room like a breeze across a field of flowers.

"And tonight we'll be showing you footage specially put together to give a flavour of the finished product." Light applause again. "Bear in mind, though, it's been prepared in a hurry by the boys." He signalled to three men who were standing together at the edge of the room.

"*Give us five!*" one of them shouted, the splayed fingers of his left hand held up for display.

Then the three walked to the lecture theatre door and disappeared inside.

The professor approached the mike then and pushed in beside Bryant.

"I just want to say thank you too, to all the wonderful

people who have made this possible." He gazed around the room. "And thank you to everyone I've had the pleasure to work with here, in the National Botanic Gardens Ireland." He paused for the applause to subside. "My time here, as you know, was due to come to an end in May, at the end of the semester. Unfortunately, for personal, family reasons I need to return home to the US sooner than planned."

I scanned the faces of the gathered staff. There were looks of dismay and astonishment.

"This will, in fact, be my last night in Dublin and in Ireland," he said. "So all I want to say is," he took a piece of paper from his pocket, "*go rev meal a moth agut.*"

More applause followed and a burst of pleased laughter at his attempt to say thank-you in Irish. He bowed deeply.

At that precise moment I noticed Bob for the first time. He was talking to one of the waiters. I elbowed Gabriel and nodded in Bob's direction.

"There he is," I said.

We began to make our way across the room and as we did Bob turned around, a phone to his ear, and walked toward the exit. We followed as he went out the door into the darkness of the gardens. The air was cool and misty-damp around us and Bob's footsteps could be heard ahead as well as his voice.

"Where are you?" he said.

He walked past the Alpine Yard and followed the path left toward the entrance gate between the gardens and Glasnevin Cemetery. There was a sound of a siren in the distance, a Garda car or perhaps an ambulance.

Bob stopped walking then and Gabriel and I stopped too. He was out of sight, behind the herbarium building and close to the cemetery gate.

"Why did you come?" his words drifted toward us.

"I had to." It was a woman's voice. She was with him now in person.

"I told you I'll get the money when I can." He sounded sorrowful, heartbroken almost. Was this his blackmailer?

"I know you will and . . . and you can see Lorrie whenever you want to." The woman began to cry. "He misses you."

"Jesus Christ, Alice, you have to stop doing this to me."

I glanced at Gabriel and he looked as uncomfortable as I felt. Alice – wasn't that the woman we'd seen arguing with him in the coffee shop. What were we doing listening to this?

"And I'm sorry about your face, Bob," she was saying. "I shouldn't have lashed out at you like that."

"I know you are," he answered.

We turned and walked back toward visitor centre.

"So that was how Bob got scratched," Gabriel said when we were close to the building.

I nodded and felt my face go crimson. "And he wasn't being blackmailed. Alice was trying to get maintenance from him."

I'd been so pleased with myself and now I felt like a fool.

"Oh God! I suppose Maguire is still on her way."

We walked back into the reception in time to see the guests filtering into the lecture theatre. At the back of the group Maguire was standing.

"Will you talk to her? I really need time to think," I said, acutely aware of my own cowardice.

"Detective Inspector . . ." I heard Gabriel say as I slipped into the theatre.

312

Inside, people were chatting and settling themselves in their seats. The professor and Mason Bryant were sitting in the centre at the front. I made my way to the back and took up a place at the end of a row. A large screen had been unfurled at the wall of the theatre and it began to flicker as the lights were lowered and the room became quiet.

Music began, something orchestral and grand, and the screen was filled with the image of an orchid. It was as though we had an insect's view close up and in overwhelming detail, then the strings picked up and the camera moved higher and higher on the vertical and the orchid got smaller and smaller until it disappeared and we were looking from the stratosphere down at a green island, a chain of islands surrounded by blue. A narrator's velvet voice began then.

"On the beautiful Azores island of Sao Jorge nature through the majesty of genetic adaptation gave a gift to the world. This is the story of how that gift was discovered and of the man who made that discovery."

There were gasps, the screen went blank and then there was applause.

Was that it? Mason Bryant stood up and signalled for the crowd to be quiet.

"Well, what d'ya think?"

There was more sycophantic applause.

I got up and made my way to the exit.

Outside I was horrified to see Maguire still standing in the reception area, talking to Gabriel. If I slipped out quietly, would they notice? But just then Gabriel looked up and saw me and I reluctantly joined them.

"Hello, Ms Barrington," Maguire said, and I thought I

caught a hint of a smirk on her face. "It's just as well I didn't bring the cavalry with me, isn't it?"

I was afraid to speak.

"A simple apology will do," she said.

I wanted to explain my train of thought – how I'd reached the mistaken conclusion that I'd come to, how logical, though incorrect, I'd been. I wanted to justify myself but what was the point?

"Sorry," I said to her.

"That's all right," she said.

I turned to Gabriel. "I'm going to go now." I felt suddenly exhausted.

"I won't be long after you," he said, and turned back to talk to Maguire as I walked away. I had a sinking feeling in the pit of my stomach, a combination of failure and longing, though I wasn't sure what the longing was for. Not still for Gabriel surely? I made my way toward the car park. The mist had cleared but the air was still cool and damp, making me shiver.

I was close to the Teak House when I felt it – something gnawing at the back of my mind. Words I'd just heard had triggered a memory or was it a question? I didn't know. I looked back in the direction I'd come and stood and listened to the night sounds of the gardens, the chatter from the visitor centre, the rustling of leaves and somewhere a song thrush.

A low moon appeared from behind a cloud, almost full, illuminating the flower beds and the trees and great glasshouses. It shone on the visitor centre and on the director's house, silvering the windows, and it reflected on the windows of the gardeners' office where George Delaney had been killed. I began to walk toward it in a daze, as though something was drawing me there. And as I walked I felt myself back in the gardens on the day George died. What was it I thought I might find? I didn't know but I kept going. If I had listened carefully, concentrated, I might have heard footsteps at a distance behind me, but I didn't. I felt like I was moving in a dream and knew only there was something in the gardeners' office I needed to see.

Chapter Thirty-Six

When I got to the door of the gardeners' office, I hesitated. Garda tape was still in place at the door. I slipped my hand beneath the tape and tried the doorknob. It was unlocked. Did I care that I could be contaminating a scene the gardaí might not have finished with? At that moment I didn't.

I pushed open the door, ducked under the tape and went inside. The hallway was almost in darkness but the door to the front office, where George Delaney had died, stood open and the moon shone in through the window, illuminating the desk where he'd been seated. More Garda tape crossed from one side of the doorframe to the other and again I went under it and stepped inside. I stood on the spot close to where his body had been, almost in the centre of the room and I took in the dried blood-spatters and the marks made on the desk and the walls and floor by forensics.

Then I closed my eyes and called up my memory of how it had been. I could picture the way George was slumped, the spread of blood on his clothes . . . and what? He had a torn piece of paper in his hand, and there were words on it. What were they? I willed myself to see them again. What were they? What? And then there they were . . . three words, almost – **"nil genetic divergence"**. What did they mean? No genetic difference? Was that it? His killer must have ripped the page from him leaving only the fragment in his grip.

And then what else? Something under my foot, a glint of silver on the floor. No, it was probably steel. And it was familiar, wasn't it? Where had I seen it before? *Think, think.* It wasn't really a knife at all. I could picture it now.

It was a letter opener.

And I'd seen it in the professor's office. I caught my breath with that realisation and opened my eyes.

In the moonlight I could see him then, standing there.

"It was you, wasn't it?" I was shaking with cold and fear and anger.

He was in the doorway, pressing against the Garda tape, filling up the doorframe.

"What is it you think you know, Beatrice?" he drawled.

There would be no way to get by him while he stayed there.

"You're a fraud, professor."

"Harsh words."

"The orchid you discovered wasn't new at all, was it? Paddy found that out. That's why he never finished his drawing of it. What did he do? Send it off for a DNA test?"

He didn't answer me, just kept looking.

"Your *christakii* was the same as something else he'd drawn, wasn't it? Which one?"

He shrugged.

"How did you get away with that? Did you pay off the Portuguese journal that published your discovery?"

"Everyone has a price, Beatrice. And who was I hurting?"

"Until Paddy found out. Is that why you killed him?"

"Oh gawd, here we go!" He shrugged again in the way a teenager might who'd been caught smoking by the school principal. "He came and asked me about the differences between my discovery and another one. You wouldn't know it – grows in the Burren. I was just trying to *explain* to him that he didn't need to worry about it. I said he just needed to do his job and I'd do mine and then . . . he fell."

I looked toward the window. Would I have time to get to it? Could I open it if I did?

"And George? What happened with George?"

"Poor George. He called me, said he'd found a letter in Paddy's post that he was worried about. You're right, Paddy had sent off samples to a lab without telling me and they'd written to him with the results. So I came right over to try to explain to George."

"But you didn't intend to explain to him. You brought the letter opener – it was yours, wasn't it, from your desk?" I needed time to think.

"I only wanted to scare him . . . but sometimes you just can't get through to people."

I could see now that the window was a sash style. There was a good chance it was painted shut and even if it wasn't it would be heavy to lift. It would take too long.

The professor let out a sigh. "It's a terrible shame you had to get involved, Beatrice," he said. "I was flying out tomorrow morning, you know. There would have been no need for all this."

No one would be looking for me. They thought I'd gone home. And the gardeners' office was so far from the visitor centre that if I shouted no one would hear.

"They don't know you're here, do they?" he said as though he'd read my mind.

I began moving backward. If I could draw him into the room, if I could put a few desks between us I might be able to get around him and out the door. He tore away the Garda tape and stepped in. I edged to my right. He looked at me and then at his two hands as though sizing up if they alone would be sufficient to do what needed to be done. I looked around at the desks. Was there anything I could pick up and throw at him? A computer? Too heavy to travel any distance. A keyboard? So light it would bounce off him.

He came further into the room. I picked up a chair and held it out in front of me, its four legs pointing toward him like a circus lion-tamer's stool. He stepped forward and grabbed one of the legs. At the same time I pushed the chair toward him and let go. I tried to run around him. The chair clattered to the floor. I was almost at the door and then I felt his fingers on my upper arm, squeezing. He wrenched me backward and slammed me against the wall. My head hit brick.

"Stupid woman!"

His two hands were on my throat then, squeezing. The room was swimming. My eyes were watering. I was struggling to breathe and then, and then, there was a spot of white light growing larger and I thought it must be the moon getting closer and closer to the earth. I passed out.

"Bea! Bea!"

I gasped for breath and opened my eyes. It was Gabriel bending over me.

"He, he . . ." My throat burned when I tried to speak.

I put my hand to where the professor's fingers had been and coughed.

"Don't worry – Maguire has him," he said.

I was lying on my back. I could feel the cold ground through my clothes. Indoors? Outdoors? I couldn't remember how I got there or where I was. I tried to move my head to see my surroundings.

"Best not to move. You're in the gardeners' office," he said.

He was kneeling beside me and he brushed a hair gently from my forehead.

"He could have killed you." There was a barely perceptible crack in his voice and I wanted to say that he must be cold because he wasn't wearing his jacket. Then I realised it was under my head. I put a hand up and touched it – and touched a spot on my scalp that was sore. When I took my hand away there was blood on my fingers.

"There's an ambulance coming," he said.

I thought of the ambulances I'd seen going to and from the gardens in the last few weeks, for Paddy Hogan and for George Delaney. I supposed the twin lime trees inside the gates were used to seeing medics now.

"I'm tired," I said. I fought to keep my eyes open but it was as though the lids were weighed down. I could feel Gabriel taking my hand, squeezing it.

"You're going to be fine," he said.

There were noises then coming from behind him, voices, lights, people. I let myself drift away.

When I opened my eyes again there were starched white sheets up to my chin and a drip attached to my left arm.

Gabriel was sleeping in a chair at the right of my bed. My throat was sore and dry and my head seemed to be pulsating. I reached for a glass of water on the locker beside me and Gabriel opened his eyes.

"There you are," he said, and with a sleepy smile picked up the glass and held it to my lips.

I swallowed and flinched as the fluid ran down my throat like ice over a burn.

"What time is it?"

He checked his watch. "Just after four. The night nurse left me something in case you woke up – something for the pain." He offered two yellow capsules in a little plastic cup.

"In a minute," I said. My voice was strange to my ears, as though my future self, old and feeble, and far away, had spoken. "Tell me first."

"Do you want to . . .?"

I nodded and he helped me sit up in the bed and propped me up with pillows before taking his seat again. He knew what I wanted to hear.

"After you left, I stayed for a while and spoke to Maguire about the investigation and other things." He waved his hand to signify those things weren't important right now. "Then I went out to the car park. I was about to leave when I noticed your car and realised you hadn't gone home. I knew there had to be something wrong." He looked at me as though judging whether I understood him.

I nodded encouragingly and then winced at the movement.

"So I went back and told Maguire and she said she'd help me look for you."

I wanted to ask him how sceptical she was but I didn't have the energy to spare – sitting up was costing me enough.

"We had a quick look around the visitor centre and then I went over toward the Palm House and she went down past the director's house. That was when she noticed the door to the gardeners' office was open and went to have a look." He stopped to take a breath.

I remembered the light I'd seen before I blacked out. It must have been Maguire's torch at the window.

"She saw movement inside and called your name and the professor came rushing out and tried to push past her. She managed to grab him and shouted to me and I came and helped her get the cuffs on him."

I would have liked to have seen that.

"I went in and you were lying there not moving." He swallowed. "He would have killed you if we hadn't come."

I nodded and felt again the professor's hands on my throat, pressing on my larynx, squeezing the life from me, the sheer terror, the helplessness. Tears came burning down my cheeks. I gulped to try to control them but they were unstoppable. Then Gabriel was sitting on the edge of the bed and his arms were around me and he held me, murmuring my name, for a long time.

Chapter Thirty-Seven

Thursday, March 23rd

Maguire actually smiled at Gabriel and me when we were shown into her office in Ballymun Garda Station shortly after we'd given our statements. She hadn't been present for those – she'd had too much paperwork to do, we were told. But the officer who'd taken our statements had said the Detective Inspector wanted to talk to us and now here we were sitting across the desk from her, a desk that was tidy though covered in files, and she was smiling. I found that unnerving. She spoke to us almost as if we were her confidantes.

"I can't tell you how good it is to have the Park off my back over this," she said. "There's a lot of people high up politically with a big interest in what goes on in the Botanic Gardens."

"Congratulations," Gabriel said. "Two murders in the one day. That'll keep them off your back for quite a while."

She beamed. "I know – it makes everything easier." She picked up a pencil and twirled it in her fingers. "I thought I should fill you in on some of the details. I think I owe you that."

Gabriel and I exchanged glances and I tried hard not to

show my astonishment. I thought of all the things she'd said to me over the last month about not telling me anything and not being like Matt McCann.

"Would you like tea?" she asked.

Before we could decline she got up, opened the door and shouted down the corridor. A young garda came scurrying.

"Cig?" he said. It was short for "*cigire*" – the Irish for 'inspector' – and it was the first time I'd heard her called that. It seemed to me to be a term of respect.

"Two teas here, please – no, make it three."

She sat down opposite us again and slapped the desk with the palms of both her hands.

"You must have questions."

The garda returned with the teas, not in styrofoam cups, but in relatively clean mugs and with fresh milk.

"Do you need sugar?" he asked.

Gabriel requested two and the garda pulled sachets out of his pocket along with a spoon and put them on the table.

"Close the door on your way out, will you, Mulligan?" Maguire said.

When he'd left she turned back to us.

"I'm only going to tell you this the once and you needn't repeat it to anyone else, okay?"

We both nodded.

"Professor James Christakos is saying nothing at the moment. He's got a very fancy solicitor, one of the Blennerhassets." She looked at Gabriel when she said that.

"You'll have your work cut out," he said in a commiserating tone.

"The good news is we've been able to charge him with

assault on you for starters, which is enough to hold him in custody. And we'll be getting directions from the DPP shortly. Your statement and the things he said to you will give us great leverage in that." She nodded at me.

"Not to mention you catching him in the act," I said.

"He killed Paddy Hogan and George Delaney. He would have killed you too, Beatrice, if he'd had the chance. We want to get him for everything."

Gabriel nodded, tore open the sachets of sugar and tipped them into his mug.

"And all on account of an orchid," she said. "And his reputation, of course, his standing in botany."

"And the money," Gabriel said. "He stood to make quite a bit if the film was a success."

I suppose he'd envisaged tours and TV chat shows and more films or maybe a series.

"We have others to talk to, too," Maguire said. "We believe another gardener, who worked here at the time of Paddy Hogan's death, may have been suspicious of the professor's discovery."

"Do you mean Kaya Nkosi?" I asked.

"Yes. We think Christakos got her a post in California so she'd stop asking questions."

"Did you find anything on Paddy Hogan's computer?" Gabriel asked.

Maguire flushed a little. "You know how it is in Cyber Crime," she said. "And it wasn't top priority so we only got a file back from them after we'd arrested Christakos."

Gabriel nodded and I bit my tongue. I suddenly felt the injustice of how Paddy Hogan's case had been handled and I wanted to say so. I wanted to tell her that if she'd done a better job of finding his killer, George Delaney would still be alive. But what would that achieve now? And, besides, she was an intelligent woman – she didn't need me to spell it out for her.

Gabriel stirred his tea, took a drink and stirred again.

"Have you spoken to the Hogans and George Delaney's family?" I asked.

"Yes. We've been to see them."

I wondered how Ava took it. Had she made a recovery now that the man who killed her brother and her lover was in custody? For a second the gardeners' office was in my head again – the blood on the desk and the walls, and George Delaney's clothes and then later in the darkness, the professor's breath close to my face, smelling of champagne.

Maguire was speaking again but I couldn't hear her. I had to focus hard on her words to make sense of them, to rid myself of the images in my head.

"Sorry. I missed that," I said.

"I said we've been in touch with the Portuguese about the professor's orchid. They're in the process of ensuring it's removed from the international register."

That was something, I supposed, some comfort to Ava that her brother would be vindicated. Poor Paddy, lying face down on those slabs, those useless vines in his fingers. My breath began to speed up.

"Bea, are you okay?" Gabriel asked.

"Yes."

Maguire gave me a hard look. "You'll need to talk to someone, Beatrice," she said. "This isn't something you're going to be able to just shake off."

I nodded. The hospital had already enrolled me for

counselling before I was discharged. There was a knock on the door then it opened.

"Cig, you're needed in the incident room," an officer said.

"I'll be with you in a minute." Then turning her attention back to us, she said, "I think that's probably everything."

"I haven't had a chance to say," I said, "I mean, if it hadn't been for you. You saved my life. So thank you."

She smiled. "You're entirely welcome."

We stood and she shook our hands.

"You two . . . you make a good team," she said.

We went for lunch to the Yacht again and after queuing at the carvery found a table for two. Gabriel smiled at me as he unloaded his tray and sat down.

"You look better," he said.

"Do I?" I'd chosen a blouse to wear with a high collar almost to my chin. I thought it made me look Victorian but it hid the finger-shaped bruises that remained on my neck, purple at their centres fading into yellow at the edges.

I felt relieved that it was over and glad for the Hogan family that they got to the truth of Paddy's death.

I'd given Ava one last call when we left the station and wished her and her mother the best. I'd been glad to hear her voice and to be told she was no longer in bed.

"Thanks for everything, Beatrice," she'd said. "You never gave up on finding the truth about Paddy."

I wanted to say that it was more to do with my stubbornness than anything else.

"How are you keeping?" I said instead.

"I'm okay, thanks. I've been seeing someone that the doctor recommended."

I said I was glad to hear it and that we ought to go for coffee soon.

"I'll give you a call," she said as she rang off.

But I didn't expect to hear from her again. I knew everything that had happened. I knew about her and George and the abortion. I knew the detail and location of every point of pain she carried. Seeing me would be too much of a reminder for her. For my part, I felt only sympathy for her and sympathy is of little use to anyone.

I ate slowly and watched Gabriel enjoying his food. He looked contented with himself and somehow more handsome because of that. I wondered if this was how he felt when he'd been a detective and a case had been completed with the culprit in custody. I thought of the last time we were in the Yacht and the misapprehension I'd been under about who was responsible for all that had happened.

He swallowed a mouthful of fresh cod in batter. He looked up and smiled again.

"Once in a while it's no harm," he said.

"And you deserve it."

He put his cutlery down on the edge of his plate then though he hadn't finished eating. "There was something else I wanted to talk to you about, Bea."

I knew that meant he was serious. I stopped eating too and met his gaze.

"I'm still a relatively fit man . . ."

"You are." He'd retired early and was in his late fifties, and in better shape now than his age allowed.

"I have to be honest, Bea, I enjoyed these last couple of weeks with you and the bit of work I did there for the drugs squad."

"I could see that." I sipped at my glass of tap water that I'd picked up with my meal and waited.

"And you're not working full-time anymore really, are you?"

"I suppose I'm not." I took another sip. I couldn't remember the last time I'd been in continuous employment.

"I was thinking, like Maguire said, we're a good team – when we work together, I mean."

What was he trying to say? "We are but I'm not following you, Gabriel."

"Would you think about it maybe? The two of us?"

"The two of us?" My heart began thumping hard then and loud enough to disturb the other diners. I thought it must be visible to Gabriel, pushing against the wall of my chest, moving my blouse.

"I need to be doing something with myself, Bea. I need to be better occupied. It keeps me fit, you know, and makes it less difficult to go easy on the pints."

"Right," I said uncertainly.

"We could set up our own agency sort of thing, like a consultancy."

"Oh, right." I looked down at my plate so that he couldn't see my eyes. I nodded and hoped he would stop talking so that I could say I needed to visit the ladies', so that I could have a chance to locate my sense of dignity.

"I've been looking into it. It's not too difficult to get a licence and there's a little office available. Do you know the Capel Buildings?"

I nodded again. I'd passed it on the Luas many times on my way to the courts. He'd already looked for an office – he really meant to do this.

"It's only small, so the rent isn't too bad, and it's in a good spot."

It was a perfect spot, I thought, with good access and there were so many offices in the building that people could enter without feeling vulnerable to exposure. But was that what I wanted? I thought of my hands and how sore they'd been during the Fernandez hearing. What would they be like on a longer case?

"I'll think about it, Gabriel."

He picked up his cutlery again and speared a bit of batter. "I can't ask for more than that," he said.

I wanted to say that he could have and he would have got it. But I didn't.

THE END

ACKNOWLEDGMENTS

I'm very grateful for the support and encouragement of everyone at Poolbeg Press especially Paula Campbell and Gaye Shortland. Both women manage to combine kindness with firm direction when required which I think are admirable traits in publishing.

I would like to thank Brendan Sayers of the National Botanic Gardens of Ireland for his guidance. And I'm quite sure the staff at the gardens are not at all like the villainous characters in this fictional work.

I'd also like to thank John McKenna for his policing tips.

As always, I'm grateful to my sisters and brothers for their support and confidence in me. I want to thank my children who are always optimistic and positive about my writing. Thanks also to my husband Paul who built the writing room in which I work and who always says I can do it even when I don't believe it myself.

Made in the USA
Las Vegas, NV
16 June 2022